KT-380-371

Other Life-Changing Fiction™ by Karen Kingsbury

Stand-Alone Titles
Fifteen Minutes
The Chance
The Bridge
Oceans Apart
Between Sundays
When Joy Came to Stay
On Every Side
Divine
Like Dandelion Dust
Where Yesterday Lives
Shades of Blue
Unlocked

Angels Walking Series
Angels Walking
Chasing Sunsets
Brush of Wings

The Baxters–Redemption Series
Redemption
Remember
Return
Rejoice
Reunion

The Baxters–Firstborn Series
Fame
Forgiven
Found
Family
Forever

The Baxters–Sunrise Series
Sunrise
Summer
Someday
Sunset

The Baxters–Above the Line Series
Above the Line: Take One
Above the Line: Take Two
Above the Line: Take Three
Above the Line: Take Four

The Baxters–Bailey Flanigan Series
Leaving
Learning
Longing
Loving

Baxter Family Collection
The Baxters
A Baxter Family Christmas
Love Story
In This Moment
To the Moon and Back
When We Were Young
Two Weeks
Coming Home

9/11 Series
One Tuesday Morning
Beyond Tuesday Morning
Remember Tuesday Morning

Lost Love Military Series
Even Now
Ever After

Red Glove Series
Gideon's Gift
Maggie's Miracle
Sarah's Song
Hannah's Hope

e-Short Stories
The Beginning
I Can Only Imagine
Elizabeth Baxter's 10 Secrets to a Happy Marriage
Once Upon a Campus

Forever Faithful Series
Waiting for Morning
Moment of Weakness
Halfway to Forever

Women of Faith Fiction Series
A Time to Dance
A Time to Embrace

Cody Gunner Series
A Thousand Tomorrows
Just Beyond the Clouds
This Side of Heaven

Life-Changing Bible Story Collections
Family of Jesus
Friends of Jesus

Children's Titles
Let Me Hold You Longer
Let's Go on a Mommy Date
We Believe in Christmas
Let's Have a Daddy Day
The Princess and the Three Knights
The Brave Young Knight
Far Flutterby
Go Ahead and Dream with Quarterback Alex Smith
Whatever You Grow Up to Be
Always Daddy's Princess

Miracle Collections
A Treasury of Christmas Miracles
A Treasury of Miracles for Women
A Treasury of Miracles for Teens
A Treasury of Miracles for Friends
A Treasury of Adoption Miracles
Miracles—a Devotional

Gift Books
Forever Young: Ten Gifts of Faith for the Graduate
Forever My Little Boy
Forever My Little Girl
Stay Close Little Girl
Be Safe Little Boy

www.KarenKingsbury.com

KAREN
KINGSBURY

SOMEONE LIKE YOU

A Novel

ATRIA BOOKS
New York London Toronto Sydney New Delhi

ATRIA BOOKS
An Imprint of Simon & Schuster, Inc.
1230 Avenue of the Americas
New York, NY 10020

This book is a work of fiction. Any references to historical events, real people, or real places are used fictitiously. Other names, characters, places, and events are products of the author's imagination, and any resemblance to actual events or places or persons, living or dead, is entirely coincidental.

First Atria Books hardcover edition May 2020

ATRIA BOOKS and colophon are trademarks of Simon & Schuster, Inc.

For information about special discounts for bulk purchases, please contact Simon & Schuster Special Sales at 1-866-506-1949 or business@simonandschuster.com.

The Simon & Schuster Speakers Bureau can bring authors to your live event. For more information or to book an event, contact the Simon & Schuster Speakers Bureau at 1-866-248-3049 or visit our website at www.simonspeakers.com.

Manufactured in the United States of America

1 3 5 7 9 10 8 6 4 2

Library of Congress Cataloging-in-Publication Data has been applied for.

ISBN 978-1-9821-0431-3
ISBN 978-1-9821-0433-7 (ebook)

Dedicated to my husband, Donald, and our beautiful family. The journey of life is breathtaking surrounded by each of you. And every minute together is time borrowed from eternity. I love you more than words. And to God, Almighty, who has—for now—blessed me with these.

1

Like a tumor in her chest, for twenty-two years Brooke Baxter West had carried the lie.

Every morning she woke to the reality of it. She lived and loved around it and tried not to think about the way it pressed against her heart and soul and how it sometimes took her breath. But the bombshell that was her very life had never felt more ominous, never consumed her the way it did today.

Here in Amon G. Carter Stadium at her daughter Maddie's graduation from Texas Christian University.

Brooke slid a little closer to her husband, Peter. He was on her side, at least that. She put her arm around their younger daughter, Hayley. Brooke's dad and stepmom were here, too—John and Elaine Baxter. Also Maddie's longtime boyfriend, Connor Flanigan.

All six of them sat in the stands together, thrilled that the day had finally come. Brooke glanced at Connor, at the anticipation in his expression and the way his eyes locked onto the place midfield where Maddie sat with her class. The boy had loved Maddie for years. He'd already talked to Peter. The engagement was coming. Probably as soon as they returned to Bloomington. Maybe even at the party the extended family was throwing for Maddie.

A party happening tomorrow night.

She drew a deep breath and leaned into Peter's shoulder. Graduates were still streaming into the stadium, still filling the seats while a marching band played from the bleachers across the field. The ceremony wouldn't begin for another ten minutes at least. "Can you believe it?" Brooke turned to her husband. "When did she grow up?" Brooke found their daughter amidst the sea of students on the field. Tan high heels and a white sundress beneath her navy gown.

"One day at a time." Peter shaded his eyes and looked at the field. "Every morning moved her closer to this day. Diapers and pigtails, homework and prom dates. All of it went way too fast." Peter took Brooke's hand and sat a little straighter. His smile barely lifted the corners of his mouth. "I'm proud of her. All she's accomplished."

He was right. Better to think about Maddie's success than Brooke's own weighty lie. Maddie had started her college career as a dancer. Back then all she talked about was Broadway and the New York City Ballet. But midway through her sophomore year she found a different passion.

Working with animals.

On breaks from school, Maddie had volunteered at the Humane Society and spent twenty hours a week at a local veterinarian's office. Last summer she interned at the Indianapolis Zoo in the animal husbandry division and now she was waiting for a call from her supervisor about a more long-term position.

"I like the stripes." Brooke's dad grinned at her from two seats down. "She's easy to spot."

"That she is." Brooke smiled down at their daughter, her cap decked in black-and-white zebra stripes. "She should hear about the position by the end of the week."

Hayley nodded. "Maddie is a zoo worker. I know it . . . I already talked to Jesus."

Of course she had. Brooke patted Hayley's hand. "You're such a good sister, Hayley."

She smiled. "I try."

For a long moment Brooke studied her other daughter. Hayley was only a few years younger than Maddie, a pretty blonde with special needs because of a near-drowning accident when she was only three. Hayley had a job at the local market with a group of friends who shared her limitations. She also had a boyfriend. But still Brooke wondered.

Was Hayley's accident a punishment from God? His way of repaying Brooke for the lie that at the time of Hayley's accident was still taking root? Brooke dismissed the thought, the way she always did. The idea was ridiculous. Of course God hadn't punished Brooke and Peter by allowing harm to come to Hayley.

Right?

Brooke drew a quick breath. She and Peter should've said something by now. It was that simple. They had planned to tell Maddie before she started kindergarten and again the day after her tenth birthday. But there never seemed to be a right moment. Time passed and the summer before high school became the perfect time to sit her down and tell her the news.

But again the talk never happened.

Now Maddie was graduating from college and still she didn't know the truth. Brooke pressed her free hand to her stomach. She and Peter were doctors. They ran a pediatric clinic near downtown Bloomington. She better than most people knew the toll stress could take on a person.

Carrying a lie like this one could cause an actual tumor. Science had proven that.

The stadium was filling up. Brooke met Peter's eyes again. He wasn't thinking about the lie. Not today, in the midst of such a highlight. The falsehood wasn't on his mind at all, at least it didn't seem like it. Peter's expression grew softer. "I blink and I can see us again, holding her for the first time that day at the hospital."

"Mmmm." Brooke nodded. Labor with Maddie had taken twenty hours. But holding her that first time made her forget every minute of it. She angled her face, her eyes still locked on his. "Forever in my heart."

Brooke stared off. No matter what came out of her mouth, times like this—milestones and major moments—she could barely think about anything but the lie. These moments were totally different for Peter. He seemed to focus on anything but the truth. And Brooke never wanted to ruin the mood. But how could she talk about the truth with Maddie if she couldn't first discuss it with Peter?

Every now and then they would both be on the same page. Brushing their teeth, getting ready for bed, and the topic would come up. When were they going to tell her? How were they going to break the news? Together they would agree on the following weekend or the next Christmas break.

But when those times came, the last thing they wanted was to ruin Maddie's happiness.

Brooke let the years roll back. It was on a day like this that the whole thing had started. Brooke's brother Luke had been about to graduate from Indiana University and Brooke was sitting with Peter and her family when Chad Daniels, a fellow doctor and friend, approached them.

"Can we talk?" Chad had been Peter's friend since medical school. He and his father ran a fertility clinic in town. That day Chad had looked serious. So Brooke and Peter excused themselves from the group and moved with Chad a few rows back to an empty section in the stadium. When it was just the three of them, Chad pressed on. "My father has a colleague who has gained ownership of three frozen embryos. Siblings. He thought . . . you might be interested."

Back then, Brooke and Peter had been trying for years to have a baby. Their families would've been shocked to know they couldn't get pregnant. With their busy careers everyone just assumed Brooke and Peter weren't ready for babies yet. Their struggle with having a child was something they hadn't told anyone except Chad and his father.

And so they had met a few times with Chad in the weeks leading up to Luke's graduation. The plan was to take the least invasive steps at first, and if they still had no baby, to move toward in vitro fertilization. But there was a problem. Peter's numbers made even that a remote possibility.

Brooke could still remember the way her heart had skipped a beat when Chad began the quiet conversation that day. Frozen embryos? Neither of them had considered such a thing. Peter spoke first. "You mean, taking someone else's frozen embryos and . . ."

"Implant them in Brooke." Chad had never seemed more serious. "It's only been done a handful of times, but with a relatively high success rate."

That day, in the most surreal conversation Brooke could remember before or since, Chad explained that a couple in Portland, Oregon, had successfully delivered a baby through IVF. But the birth was complicated, so the couple decided they were finished having children. But there was a problem.

Three frozen embryos remained.

Tiny little souls on ice, ones that the couple wouldn't dream of having washed down a medical office sink. "As you know, embryos are very small children." Chad had looked intently at them. "That's what I believe, anyway." He paused. "My dad told me to see if you were interested. Before he found another couple."

"Has the Portland couple signed a release form?" Peter leaned over his knees and stared at Chad. "Is there even paperwork for this kind of thing?"

Chad nodded. "It's new, but yes. The Portland couple has officially terminated their rights to the embryos and signed them over to a doctor in Oregon. That was five years ago. The babies have been in a deep freeze canister since then."

"And they're still viable?" Peter had looked doubtful. "Embryos on ice that long?"

"All research suggests they are." Chad had shrugged. "A few weeks ago that doctor met my dad at a conference. He'd sort of forgotten about the three embryos until he and my dad talked. He found out my father and I work with infertility." Chad took a breath. "He signed over the embryos to our clinic so we could find a willing couple."

"How would that work with us?" Peter shook his head. "The babies already belong to your clinic."

"It's temporary. We would sign rights to you and

Brooke . . . if you're interested." Chad took a breath. "It's a transfer of property, technically. You would sign paperwork at implantation." His expression had darkened. "There is one thing. The Portland couple wants complete secrecy surrounding this."

Understandably the pair had known how rare embryo adoption was and that the media might turn the situation into a circus. "You two would have permission to tell your child or children, of course. And any close family members. But otherwise you'd have to keep the details to yourself. Any baby you might have from the embryos would not have permission to find his or her biological parents, and the biological parents have committed to never look for any children that might come from this."

Secrecy had seemed like a small concession at the time. Peter and Brooke promised to talk about the possibility and get back to Chad. But in the end there was nothing to talk about. If Brooke took the appropriate hormones, and if she allowed Chad's father—Dr. Daniels—to surgically implant the three embryos, she could be pregnant in a matter of months.

Which was exactly what happened.

Dr. Daniels implanted all three frozen embryos into Brooke's uterus and before Brooke and Peter had time to explain the situation to their families, she was expecting. Not three babies, but one. One precious child.

After that, with everyone they knew congratulating Brooke and Peter on the pregnancy, it had seemed awkward to talk about how the baby got there. No one had ever heard of embryo adoption. Why worry their families? And in an attempt to honor the other couple's wishes, Brooke and Peter made a decision. Better to keep the details to themselves. That way they wouldn't be in danger of violating the contract.

Besides, it was easy to believe the baby really was Brooke's. The child had grown inside her, after all. When the tiny infant kicked, Brooke felt her little feet, and week by week she watched her belly grow. What could be more real than that?

When they found out the baby was a girl, they chose the most obvious name.

Madison. Gift of God. Which was the only way to describe how Brooke had gone from infertility to motherhood so quickly.

They were always going to tell Maddie, really they were. But most days it was easier to go along with the lie, pretend Maddie was their own flesh and blood. Maddie looked like them, after all. And Brooke even had the stretch marks to prove it.

Two years later, Hayley was a surprise. A natural pregnancy. Dr. Daniels told them that sometimes after an embryo adoption, a woman's body is able to get pregnant. For Brooke and Peter their second baby was simply a miracle. Another gift from God.

But somehow Brooke and Peter fell away from God. Too busy, too academic. They had the children they wanted so God fell by the wayside. Not until after Hayley fell into the swimming pool at a birthday party did Brooke and Peter run back to the faith they'd started with.

And even then they didn't tell Maddie the truth.

The memories faded as the familiar refrains of "Pomp and Circumstance" filled the stadium. Brooke stared at Maddie again. She would tell Connor yes if he asked her tomorrow. So Maddie was about to get married. Which meant she would likely have babies of her own one day. And then she would *have* to know the truth.

Please don't hate me, baby girl. God, please help her not to hate me.

Now these twenty-two years later, Brooke had no idea how she and Peter would break the news to Maddie. How could she tell her daughter, the one she gave birth to, that she had biological parents in Oregon? That she wasn't a part of the Baxter family or the West family, like she'd always thought.

And that everything she's ever believed about her life was not the truth, but a lie.

A terrible, cancerous, all-consuming lie.

2

Wind and water sprayed Dawson Gage's face as he leaned into his Jet Ski and tore across Portland's frigid Columbia River that sunny May afternoon. Dawson locked in on the back of the female rider a few yards in front of him, focused on the way she flew over the water. He couldn't catch her no matter how hard he tried. Not here on the river. Not in life. Not since high school. Whatever he did, he could never quite catch her.

London Quinn.

The machine was louder than her laughter, but Dawson could hear it all the same, the music and harmony of it. Her long brown hair whipped across her pretty face and every half minute she glanced back at him. Those amber eyes all lit up with the ride and the cold water, with her love for life and whatever this was the two of them shared.

Whatever it had always been.

She made a sweeping arc, and as she headed toward the other shore Dawson caught a glimpse of her smile. In the time it took him to wipe the spray from his face, he could see the younger London again. Second day of their senior class trip the week after high school graduation. They had flown from Portland to Los Angeles to spend a day at Disneyland. The park's annual Grad Night.

And there, sometime before midnight in an hour-long

line for Space Mountain, as they weaved their way through the dimly lit futuristic tunnels toward the ride, Dawson had done something he hadn't planned on doing. He had taken her hand. Without saying a word, he eased his fingers between hers, and she did the same. They stood there that night, side by side, inching along, so no one saw their hands, not even their friends in line with them.

Then, before they climbed into the roller coaster, she leaned close and whispered, "Don't fall in love with me, Dawson Gage." Her sparkling eyes held his for a long moment. "Promise."

Dawson chuckled, but he could still feel the way his heart had pounded in his chest. "Don't worry, London." He had grinned. He'd been an eighteen-year-old kid and saving face took precedent over honesty. "I'm not looking to fall in love with you."

That was ten years ago. It was the only time he ever lied to her.

The memory lifted with the next spray of river water. Dawson waited till she looked back at him again, and he made a circle motion over his head. He didn't have to yell. She knew what that meant. Back to the pier. He had an investor dinner that night with his father and a few executives from the firm. Time to bring it in.

Dawson's house sat on the Vancouver side of the Columbia River, making him a Washington State resident, even though he worked in Portland. In the last five years, Gage Development had singlehandedly transformed the waterfront on both sides of the river. Properties had been remodeled and replaced, high-end tenants clamored for space, and prices were at an all-time high.

And Dawson had been a major part of all of that.

They docked the Jet Skis and peeled off their wet suits. She slid her bare arm free and cast him a look. "How long have you lived here?"

She was playing with him, after all she'd been here when he bought the place. He rolled his eyes and stifled a laugh. "I know . . . I know."

"Three years, you say?" Her arm brushed against his as she stepped free of the wet suit. She adjusted her bikini, her attention still on him.

Dawson shifted his gaze to the house. "Three years. Yeah, yeah. And in all that time I only beat you across that river twice." He shook his head and turned his back to her. London danced for a living and she was easily the most beautiful girl he'd ever seen. Long ago he'd learned not to stare. A chill ran over his body. Bare chest and flimsy shorts were no match for a Northwest afternoon.

Even when the sky was clear.

"It's freezing." His clothes were a few yards up the dock. But before he could make a move toward them, he felt her hand on his shoulder.

"Dawson." Her fingers were silk on his skin.

A quick glance over his shoulder. "Don't worry . . . I'll beat you next time."

"No, not that." She came around to the front of him. "Look at you." She raised her eyebrows. "CrossFit should make you their poster boy. Your six-pack's an eight-pack."

"Funny." His quiet laugh filled the space. He could feel her eyes on him as he pointed to her sweats folded nearby. "Get dressed, crazy girl. Cold's getting to your head."

"Okay." She did a low whistle. "Remind me again why we're just friends?"

Only you can answer that one, he thought. But he kept that to himself as he pulled his sweatshirt on and stepped into his jeans. Better to pretend he hadn't heard her, because she wasn't serious. She was currently dating another guy. Dawson couldn't remember his name. There was a different one every month or so.

London was dressed now, and the two of them walked up the dock, onto Dawson's back deck. The place had been a fixer-upper, something thrown in on one of his father's deals. His dad gave it to him as soon as they signed papers on the deal. "It'll take a year of work and half your salary," his father had told him. "But it has a ton of potential."

Now London hesitated before they stepped inside. "I still can't believe what you did with the place." She smiled. "It's the house everyone wants. You know that."

"Thanks." He walked her out front to her Honda and they hugged a little longer than necessary. The way they always did. "See you tonight?"

"Yeah." Her eyes softened. "I wouldn't miss it. Grad Night Anniversary."

"Every May fifteenth." A breeze whispered through the trees that lined River Drive. "See you, London."

When she was gone he turned and stared at the house, at the expansive porch and rich white columns, and for a moment he remembered what it looked like the first time he had brought London here. The roof had been caved in on one side and deep cracks cut across the old tiled entry. The kitchen cabinets were black with mold, the walls had gaping holes, and every bit of the green shag carpet smelled like wet dog.

London had stepped over a rip in the vinyl and peered

around a dark corner. "I wonder what happened to the dog?" She looked at him. "Assuming there was a dog."

"He's not here. It's been empty six months." Of course London would ask about a dog. As long as he'd known her she had loved animals. That day he and London had headed toward the back of the house. The door fell off with a single touch.

Oh, but the view on the other side of that busted-down door.

"Are you kidding?" London had gasped. "This is gorgeous."

"I'll transform the place." He had picked up the back door and leaned it against the house. "And get a couple Jet Skis."

"One for you and one for me!" She had taken hold of his arm, eyes wide. "I can't wait!"

Dawson rebuilt the place from the foundation up.

Never mind that they were only friends, Dawson couldn't picture anyone else riding beside him down the Columbia River. Back then he still assumed she'd wake up one morning, dump the guy of the month and give her heart to Dawson. It was just a matter of time, he had told himself. One day she'd see what his dad and her parents and everyone else who knew them had always seen.

Dawson and London belonged together.

Every year since that senior trip to Disneyland, they had celebrated their Grad Night Anniversary. And tonight, like every year on this date, Dawson would ask God to change her mind. Because if she was ever going to see him as more than a friend, it would be on a night like this. When they would celebrate everything about their relationship.

And maybe—just maybe—she might agree it was time to celebrate something more.

Dinner ran till eight o'clock. Gage Development was acquiring a hundred yards of riverfront on the Portland side in an area previously home to drug dealers and gang members. The spot wasn't quite cleaned up, but it was about to be. Over rib eye at Ruth's Chris Steak House, Dawson and his dad nailed down details for the purchase of the land and the plans to renovate it.

On the way back to their cars, his dad took a deep breath. "That was all you tonight." He stopped and faced Dawson. "I want to expand in the next few years. You're ready, Son. You could run a division by yourself."

The challenge shot adrenaline through Dawson's veins. "What about you?"

"Depends." His dad started walking again and Dawson kept up. A thousand stars blanketed the crisp, cool sky overhead. His father smiled. "I want to be near my grandkids."

Dawson crossed his arms. "I need a wife before I can give you grandbabies, Dad."

"Exactly." His father laughed. "I'm just saying when you do find that girl, and when the little ones come along, I'll sell everything to be where you are."

His words touched Dawson to the core. "I'm glad." He gave his father a long look. "You're all I've got."

"Same." His dad winked at him. "Have fun with London tonight."

For a long moment, Dawson stopped and faced his father once more. "She's not interested. You know that."

His dad shrugged. "I see the way she looks at you." He didn't break eye contact. "I mean, come on, Dawson.

What's not to like? Of course she's interested." A few more steps and they reached their cars. "She needs time. That's all."

If only it were that easy. "Okay." Dawson knew better than to push the subject. "Good meeting tonight."

"Like I said, all you." His dad didn't leave a meeting or workday without hugging Dawson, and tonight was no exception. "I love you, Son."

"Love you, too." Dawson climbed into his Chevy truck and called London before leaving his spot. "On my way."

"I'm already here." Her voice was soft against the sound of the wind on the river. "Out on the dock."

Dawson smiled. "See you in ten."

His dad turned right out of the parking lot. He lived in a condo a mile down the river, the place he bought after Dawson moved out. Dawson's mother had died when he was seven. His dad never remarried. He dated a few times for a year or two, but always he would share the verdict with Dawson. *She's not your mom*.

No one ever would be.

Dawson's father—David Alan Gage—had been a college football quarterback with a gun for an arm. But his arm was only half as strong as his business sense so he walked away from the game and became a developer. Now he was one of the most successful players in the Northwest land game.

His dad met the love of his life at the closing of his first real estate purchase. Lila had been born in Colombia and moved to the United States when she was a child. Six years at Harvard and she became a skilled real estate attorney with a love for the outdoors and a beauty that took his father's breath. She had a laugh Dawson remembered to this day.

A week after they met, Dawson's parents hiked Mount Hood and by the time they reached the summit they were officially an item. Six months later they married and became one of Portland's power couples. Active in business and church and a number of charities.

For a while it seemed everything Dawson's parents touched turned to gold. Whatever they wanted they got, including him—the baby they had prayed for. Their future was wide open, practically guaranteed.

Right up until the cancer diagnosis.

Two months later Dawson's mother was gone and overnight his dad changed. Development wins were nothing to the time his dad spent with Dawson. Someone else could close the company's multimillion-dollar deals. David Gage would be at Dawson's Little League games. Period.

After Dawson graduated from college six years ago, his dad brought him into the business. Since work was something the two of them did together, his dad was having fun again. He could hardly wait for Dawson to marry and have children.

Which was why his relationship with London Quinn was so complicated.

If only she would change her mind about him. Then the pieces of their lives would fall into place the way they had with his parents. Instead London hadn't thought differently about him since that night at Disneyland—they were friends. Nothing more.

A friendship that kept Dawson from being interested in any other girl.

He turned in to his driveway and parked just past her car. Minutes later he stepped through his back doorway with an oversize faux mink blanket, a thermos of hot chocolate and two mugs. London sat in one of two low-slung chairs at the end of the dock.

She looked over her shoulder as he walked up. "Good. You brought a blanket." She was in jeans and a white sweatshirt, not warm enough for the chilly night.

He took the seat beside her, wrapped the blanket around their backs, and filled their mugs. Their shoulders touched as he leaned back in his chair and gazed at the reflection of lights on the water. A long sigh came from deep inside him. "I've looked forward to this all day."

"Me, too." She turned to him. "I'm glad we take time . . . to remember."

Dawson wanted tonight to be about more than that, but he only nodded. "Yeah."

For a while they sipped their cocoa and stared at the river. Finally, London turned to him. "I'm a match. I wanted to wait till tonight to tell you."

"For your mom?" Dawson slid to the edge of his chair and a splash of hot chocolate spilled on his jeans. "That's incredible!"

London leaned back. "We'll do the transplant in a month."

Dawson was as close to London's mother as he had been to his own, but since January, Louise Quinn had been battling kidney disease. Her doctors blamed excessive use of over-the-counter pain medication she'd taken all her life for migraine headaches. A few weeks ago she had gone on dialysis and her doctor explained to the family how desperately Louise Quinn needed a new kidney.

Without a transplant she wouldn't live another year.

Dawson let the news sink in. "I've been praying every day about this. That you'd be a match."

"I mean . . ." Her smile faded a bit. "I was a match from the time I was born. Right?" She thought for a bit. "And if I would've had the sister I always wanted, odds are we'd both be matches. As long as we shared the same blood type." She shrugged. "Prayer didn't have much to do with it, Dawson."

There it was.

He turned toward the water again. The real reason he and London never found their way past friendship. Dawson's faith held her at bay, made her uncomfortable even in moments like this. When something wonderful had just happened.

"Prayer has everything to do with it." He took a slow breath and turned to her. "Is she happy?"

"I guess." A faraway look clouded London's beautiful eyes. "She's worried about me. That something will happen in the transplant."

"It won't." Dawson had researched the procedure extensively. "You'll be fine. And so will she." Peace washed over him and he set his mug on the dock. "You aren't nervous, right?"

"Not at all." London held her hot drink close. "I just want it to work." She shook her head. "I couldn't bear . . ." Her eyes found his again. "I'll never know how you survived this long without your mom."

"I have my dad." He reached for her fingers, the way he had years ago at Disneyland. "And you . . . and your mom."

London didn't pull away. They held hands this way often, complicating things and simplifying them all at the same time. He kept the conversation anchored in reality. "How's Chuck?"

She laughed. "Charles." Without letting go of his fingers, she elbowed his ribs. "His name is Charles."

"Whatever." Dawson was back on comfortable ground. "You gonna marry this one?"

"Probably not." She tilted her head back and looked at the sky for a long moment. "He doesn't make me laugh."

Of course he didn't. Dawson turned to her. He ran his thumb over the top of her hand. "I make you laugh." He didn't feel like joking anymore. "So why, London? Why are you with him?" This was the moment he'd been waiting for. He needed to be clear.

"Don't, Dawson." She stood and moved to the edge of the dock. "You know how I feel."

He rose to his feet and eased her into his arms. For a while they stayed like that, caught up in the embrace. As if their bodies knew more than their hearts ever would. Usually he would cut up at a time like this. Practice a dance move or kiss her hand. Anything so she wouldn't have a reason to tell him what she'd told him so many times before. That she didn't love him like that.

That he wasn't the one.

But not tonight. He didn't feel like being funny, and he wanted an answer. "Tell me why." He put his hand alongside her face. "That's all, London. Why not us?"

"The answer's the same." She put her hand over his and lowered it from her face. "I'm too wild. I drink with the girls and stay over at my boyfriend's apartment. You come home and read the Bible."

Her words hurt. "It's a bestseller, you know. You might actually like the Bible." He tried to find his lighter voice, but it was too late. He raked his hand through his hair. "You make me sound like a monk."

"No." Her voice rose a notch. "Your beliefs . . . they're just . . . they're not mine." A long sigh came from her. "You know what I mean. I love you, Dawson, but I'm not right for you." Sadness welled in her eyes. She shook her head. "I never will be. You deserve better. Someone like me . . . but with your faith and goodness."

"I don't want someone *like* you." He ached at the thought. "I want you, London. You're all I want." He wondered if he should pull her close again, kiss her in a way that took her breath and changed her mind. But already the moment was gone. She took a step back and returned to her seat. After a minute or so, she patted his chair and waited till he sat down again.

Minutes passed while the water lapped against the dock. Finally she took a quick breath. "I didn't tell you about the Humane Society."

"No." If this was all she was going to give him, he would take it. But only because he had no choice.

She launched into a story about her volunteer work walking rescue dogs and how earlier today during a break from her mother's coffee shop—London Coffee—in downtown Portland she had taken five dogs for a walk on Twenty-third Street.

"Bad idea." She seemed to force a laugh. Like things weren't quite back to normal. She faced him. "Before I knew it the dogs were running in different directions, twisting their leashes around my legs and—"

Dawson wasn't listening. Sure, he nodded and smiled and tried to pretend the awkward conversation from earlier hadn't happened. But he didn't take her hand this time. Half an hour passed and they talked about her mother's transplant and how long London would be in the hospital, and when she could get back to dancing for the Portland Ballet. Then they walked together to her car.

"I'm sorry." She searched his eyes. "About earlier."

He felt a grin creep up his face. "Your loss." He couldn't let her see how bad her rejection hurt. Not if he was going to keep her friendship. "One day you'll settle down. And just maybe, I'll still be here."

She kissed him on the cheek and Dawson savored the connection, the way her amber eyes held his. Then he watched her drive away and he had to admit the truth.

The opportunity to change London Quinn's mind had passed.

Maybe forever.

And there wasn't a single thing he could do about it.

She stared at the stars outside her window. Maybe she and Connor needed a break. Maybe they were too serious, too connected, too often. This past semester they had talked on FaceTime nearly every day. It was a lot, and once in a while she had told Connor so. They'd go a few weeks with less conversation and then the calls would pick up again.

Maddie blinked. A break from Connor? What was she thinking? She loved Connor. He was probably the one she would love forever. The incident earlier must've been just the busyness of school. She relaxed her head against the seat rest.

Yes, that had to be it.

Now that she was headed home, everything between her and Connor would fall back into place. He'd pick her up on special summer mornings and they'd watch the sunrise over Monroe Lake. They'd play tennis after dinner and drive to Indianapolis for their favorite concerts. Every couple had their ups and downs, right? This summer the thrill was bound to return.

Just like when they first fell in love.

Maddie closed her eyes and smiled. She and Connor didn't need a break. And now, the plane wasn't only taking her home. It was taking her to her future. Tomorrow's graduation party with her entire family, the job at the zoo, and her relationship with Connor Flanigan. Peace came over her and she did something she should've done earlier.

Maddie took hold of Connor's hand. Even in his sleep he gave her fingers a gentle squeeze, and Maddie smiled. What happened at the restaurant earlier was just a random off moment, she was sure. All was right with the world.

She rested her head on his shoulder and fell asleep.

• • •

THE GRADUATION PARTY was at her aunt Ashley and uncle Landon's house. The place where they always met for special get-togethers. Once a long time ago, before Maddie's grandma Elizabeth had passed away, this was where her grandparents had lived. The house they had moved their family to when Maddie's mother was in middle school.

The Baxter house, they called it. The home had big gathering spaces and sweeping porches along the front and back. It sat on ten acres that ran to a creek far behind the house. Today there were round tables set up just off the back porch and a food table with dishes everyone had brought for the occasion. Because that's how Baxter parties were. All the Baxter siblings were there with their spouses and kids. Even uncle Dayne and Aunt Katy, who had houses in both Bloomington and Los Angeles.

This was the family reunion they hadn't had in far too long and Maddie planned to love every minute.

She sat at one of the tables and surveyed her family. Her parents and Hayley sat with Aunt Kari and Uncle Ryan and their kids. All of them were laughing. At the closest table, Maddie's Uncle Luke and Aunt Reagan sat with their kids and a few others. Maddie's cousin Tommy was telling a story and everyone was listening like it was the greatest thing they'd ever heard.

Maddie lifted her eyes to the sky and smiled. *Thank You, God. For letting me be part of a family like this.* There wasn't a day when she wasn't aware of how special this was. How not everyone was surrounded by love the way she was.

"Fishing on the lake tomorrow, Maddie?" Her cousin

Cole was home from Liberty University for the summer. He sat across from her where he'd been talking to Connor. Now her boyfriend gave her a quick grin. "I told him you couldn't wait to get back out on the lake."

"True." She laughed. "As long as I don't have to bait the hook."

"I remember last summer when—" Connor launched into the story about how Maddie had lost an entire container of worms when one of the little guys moved. Because how was she supposed to know they were hooked alive?

But before Cole could finish the story, the entire Flanigan family came through the back door and down the steps. Connor's sister, Bailey, and her husband, Brandon, and their two small children, along with Connor's parents and four brothers.

The Flanigans made their way over, and Connor's mother handed Maddie a card. "We're proud of you, beautiful graduate." Her tone was marked with sincerity. "Wish we could've been there."

Maddie stood and embraced the woman. "Thank you." They shared a smile and then Maddie greeted Connor's dad and brothers. "Being *here* is all that matters." She smiled at each of them as they headed for the food table.

Bailey handed her youngest to Brandon and then turned to Maddie. "I'm so happy for you." The two had been friends even before Maddie started dating Connor. "Now that you're back, we need to get coffee." Bailey looked wonderful. She sat down with Maddie and the two talked for a few minutes. The updates were all positive. Bailey and Brandon's kids were four and two now, and the couple was back to running the local Christian Kids

Theater. They were also starring in another movie together, one being filmed in Indianapolis.

"Hey . . . I'll be there at the zoo!" Maddie shared her own news, and the two made a plan to get together one day soon in the city.

As the evening played out, Maddie made time to talk to each of her family members. She had just finished a chat with Aunt Kari when Grandpa John Baxter approached. "How's my favorite grand girl?" He put his arm around her shoulders and pressed his cheek to hers.

"Papa, you can't say that." Maddie felt her eyes sparkle as she looked at him. All her life she had been especially loved by her grandfather. Like the two of them had a bond no one else could touch. "All of us are your favorites."

Grandpa linked arms with her and walked her to the dessert table. "You have a point." He winked at her and handed her a slice of Aunt Ashley's blueberry pie. "But you're my first, Maddie." He faced her. "No one else can say that."

She hugged her grandfather and took a piece of pie. No sooner had she taken her place back at her table when the background music changed. The song was an instrumental version of Newsong's "When God Made You." One of Maddie's favorites. And suddenly in the spot between the food tables, there was Connor Flanigan.

And he had a microphone.

"If Maddie could come up here for a minute." He couldn't stop smiling, and suddenly everyone was taking their seats. As if they were expecting whatever was about to happen.

Maddie's heart picked up speed and every beat pounded in her head and throat. What was this? Was he really going to ask her . . . Everyone was watching, smiling at her, waiting. Her feet started moving on cue but her heart was stuck back at the table. She wasn't ready . . . or was she?

Connor wore a pale blue button-down shirt and khaki pants. He was tanned and handsome and as she made her way to him, his eyes locked on her alone. The walk seemed to take an hour, but finally Maddie was there. She smoothed her hands over her white capris and tried to still her shaking fingers.

Then, before she could ask him what was happening, he took a deep breath. "Maddie West, I've loved you since the day we met—working that CKT show right here in downtown Bloomington."

A few people chuckled. That show had been marked by funny moments and miscues. Maddie nodded. *Is this really happening? Dear God, what am I supposed to do?*

Still Connor was talking. "There's so much I love about you, Maddie . . ." With his free hand he reached for hers. "In all my life I've never met someone so dedicated to God and family, someone who makes me laugh and builds me up. When I can't see through the haze, you can. You believe in me and I believe in you. I always will."

This was it. The question was coming. The one she planned to answer just once in her life. Maddie could feel herself smiling, feel her eyes misty with tears. But nothing about the moment felt real. Like she was watching someone else's story play out.

Connor set the microphone down. He didn't need it. Everyone was silent, waiting, hanging on every word. Even the kids. He took both her hands now and stared at her. "Maddie . . . I've asked your father's permission for what

I'm about to say. The truth is, in my heart I've asked you this question a thousand times."

The most beautiful love shone on his face.

Maddie's heart beat harder still. She forced her knees to stop knocking. Everyone was watching, holding their collective breath. Her yes was something they all expected, she could see it on their faces.

With a hush in his voice, Connor's smile faded. As if he'd never been more serious in all his life. "The question is this." Then, Connor got down on one knee. He pulled a small gray velvet box from his pants pocket, opened it and held up the prettiest diamond solitaire. "Maddie, will you marry me?"

The answer slid past her lips before she could consider the question. "Yes! Yes, of course."

He was on his feet again, sweeping her into his arms while people snapped pictures and took video. This was the moment she had dreamed of all her life with the guy she loved with all her being.

He took the ring from the box—a ring she'd never seen or discussed with him—and he slid it onto her finger. She hugged him again and he took her face in his hands. "I love you, Maddie. Forever I will."

"I love you, too." It was the truth. She did love him. And she should've seen this moment coming. And gradually, now that the time was here, she was sure. Saying yes was the right thing. Tears filled her eyes and she blinked them back. She was engaged! She was going to marry Connor Flanigan, as she had long imagined.

Then with their family members rising to their feet and breaking into applause, Connor kissed her. And just like that Maddie wasn't only about to start her dream job.

She was about to be married.

4

Dawson glanced at the driver's side of the Honda where London sat behind the wheel. She was singing John Mayer at the top of her lungs. "Life is full of sweet mistakes . . . and love's an honest one to make."

He sang along, too, and tried not to focus on the irony of the words.

This was always how they were, London and him. Wherever they went, whatever they did they had the music blaring. The two of them singing like they were performing their own private concert.

Sunlight streamed through the trees as London took the winding road ahead. The idea of hiking Multnomah Falls had been hers. No surprise. Never mind that she was dating some other guy, when London had a day off she usually called Dawson. Today was no different.

They wore sweatshirts and windbreakers because today's clear blue skies didn't begin to warm the chilly weather on the mountain. London grinned at him as the song played out, lyrics that reminded Dawson of the truth. Whatever did or didn't happen between them, London would live forever in Dawson's memory.

Indeed.

Dawson took a steadying breath. Maybe he'd tell her today. How this strange friendship they shared was crazy.

How they should either walk away and get on with their lives or admit that there would never be anyone for the two of them but each other.

No matter what she said.

A few miles up the road she pulled into the parking lot. Even from that vantage point the falls were beautiful. A ribbon of rushing water that fell from forever high and crashed onto the rocks below. The spot was a tourist destination, especially on the weekends.

"Ugh." London turned the volume down. "It's so crowded."

Dawson laughed. "Not where we're going."

Her smile found its place again. "True."

They'd done this hike before. Sure, it started up the same path all the visitors took. Along a broad path and onto the scenic bridge at the base of the falls. But just past the picture takers and onlookers was a much more narrow set of switchbacks that wound around the mountain to the back side of the falls.

Odds were only a few of the Sunday travelers had the more serious hike in mind.

A spot opened and London parked. They donned their backpacks, grabbed their water bottles and set out. Like everyone else, they stopped at the bridge and stood side by side, staring at the waterfall.

London moved closer and his arm brushed against hers. Her eyes were glued to the view. "Life feels like that sometimes."

"Mmm." Dawson loved this. Time alone with her when they could say whatever they wanted. When there were no walls and the possibilities seemed more realistic than ever. He stole a look at her. "Fast, you mean?"

"Yes." She tilted her face toward the blue sky. "The hours and minutes keep slipping over the rocks and washing away in the river below. Time we can't get back."

"Which"—he leaned his head close to hers—"is why we have to make the most of it. Before another tomorrow gets away."

"Exactly." She smiled and turned to him. "Here we are. A couple best friends seizing the moment."

Best friends. Dawson had come to hate the term, but she was right. Because if they were dating, she would have come to believe the way he did and she would understand that only the God of the universe could've created a setting as beautiful as this one.

A faint mist from the falls filled the air around them. London led the way as they moved over the bridge and up the first part of the more difficult hike. The trail was still wide enough that he could walk beside her. She took hold of her backpack straps and smiled at him. "How was church?"

"Challenging." He chuckled. "Which is good, actually. I like being challenged."

"So that's it." She lowered her sunglasses long enough to shoot him a look. "That's why you think I'm the girl for you."

He thought about telling her that this—the hike they were sharing, the intimacy between them—was why he thought that. But he didn't want to joke about it. He ignored her comment and looked straight ahead, through the mass of evergreen trees to the Columbia River Gorge far beyond. "The message was from John 16."

"John." She shifted her attention to the trail. "That's one of the gospels, right?"

"Yes. One of the four." He wasn't sure if she was still teasing. Her parents had been believers when she was born. London's mother had told Dawson that years ago. But in the two decades since, life had become demanding and their faith had grown cold.

"So?" London actually seemed interested. "Why is John 16 challenging?"

A bald eagle swept into view just ahead. They were common in the gorge, but the sight still stopped Dawson in his tracks. He pointed up. "Look."

London shaded her eyes and lifted her face to the sky. "Wow." London was clearly moved. "Only God could make something so majestic."

Chills ran down Dawson's arms. He turned to her. "You mean that?"

"I do." She started walking again. "I believe in God, Dawson. I just . . . I'm not sure about everything that goes with it." They passed another hiker and London picked up her pace. "So what is it about John 16?"

He was still stuck on her last statement. The one about believing in God. But that could wait. He focused on her question. "There's a verse that says we will have trouble in this world."

"We will?" She uttered a sad laugh. "Not very encouraging."

"There's more." He kept up with her. "It also says to be happy, because Jesus has overcome the world."

She stopped walking and faced him. "What does that mean? That He's overcome the world?"

Standing inches from her, the sunlight streaming through the trees on their faces, Dawson wondered if he had ever loved her more. Especially in light of this conversation. "Well . . ." He willed himself to remember what she had just asked. He wanted only to take her in his arms, and kiss her. With a slow sort of passion that would end the guesswork between them.

Instead he led her to a bench just off the trail. "Let's sit for a minute."

They took their spots, and turned just enough so their knees were touching. "So . . ." Her quiet laugh was prettier than any sound Dawson knew. "What does it mean?"

He leaned his shoulder into the bench. "It means no matter what bad things happen in the world, Jesus has already gained victory over them. By dying on the cross."

She thought for a moment. "Why doesn't He just stop the bad things from happening? Like with my mom's kidney?" Her pause felt sad. "Wouldn't that be easier?"

"It's a broken world." Dawson felt his smile drop off. "The only way out is by taking Jesus at His word." He could barely see her eyes through her sunglasses. "You know?"

She took a quick breath and stood. "I guess." The conversation was clearly finished. "Come on." She reached for his hand and helped him to his feet. "I have forever to think about Jesus. Right now I want to reach the top of those falls."

The rest of the hike took nearly an hour, and most of it required they walk single file. Their conversation faded, the beauty around them all they needed. But the entire time Dawson couldn't stop thinking about what she'd said. London never talked about faith. She would laugh it off and dismiss it as something only Dawson cared about. Like a hobby or a club, nothing more.

Until today.

At the top of the trail they took a selfie, the Columbia River Gorge spread out behind them, the falls just ahead. A thousand shades of green and blue. On the way back down the mountain they stopped at the gift shop and bought matching T-shirts that read: I HIKED THE FALLS AT MULTNOMAH AND LIVED TO TELL ABOUT IT.

They both laughed at the wording. As if hiking Multnomah Falls was Oregon's version of Mount Everest. "I'll wear it whenever I'm missing you." She held up the bag and skipped a few times as they left the little store. "Which is a lot lately. You're always gone. All those development deals."

He caught up to her. "And I'll wear mine every time you're out with Chuck."

"Charles." Her smile filled her face and she linked arms with him. "We broke up." She laughed. "I know, they never last. Who cares." She rolled her eyes.

Dawson's heart skipped a beat. He smiled. "Unbelievable."

London raised her brow. "You know I'd rather spend a day with you than him . . . Right?" She put her head on his shoulder as they walked. "You do know that?"

"You're crazy." He shook his head as she pulled her car keys from her backpack. He would never understand her. But with the conversation they'd had on their way up the trail, maybe they actually were getting closer to the relationship he'd always wanted.

They were quieter on the drive back. London played a ballad playlist through her phone and halfway back to Portland she glanced at him. "What's your favorite church song?"

He knew what she meant. But again, she had never asked a question like this before. "Right now? Probably 'Give Me Jesus.' It's an older song by Jeremy Camp."

"That famous guy, right?"

"Yes." Dawson stifled a laugh. "It's not really a church song. But I like it."

"Play it." She handed him her phone. "Would you do that, Dawson?"

His heart stirred. What was this sudden interest in all things faith? The topic was one she'd avoided ever since he'd met her. Whatever was happening in London, Dawson didn't hesitate. In a few clicks he found it on Apple Music and hit play.

The haunting melody filled London's car and every word seemed to mean more. As if he were hearing it through London's heart. For the first time. The song spoke about needing Jesus in the morning and when you felt all alone. And finally, in the last verse, it talked about death.

"When I come to die . . . give me Jesus." He sang along, quieter than usual. ". . . You can have all this world . . . just give me Jesus."

As the song ended, tears slid from beneath London's sunglasses and onto her cheeks. She sniffed and dabbed at her face. "That's beautiful."

Dawson wasn't sure what to say. "The words are simple." This was new ground for them. He didn't want to rush the conversation. "With the craziness of our world, He's everything that really matters."

She was still composing herself. She sat a little straighter. "I have questions, Dawson. Maybe one of these days we can talk about that." A quick glance at him. "You know, about Jesus."

This was the conversation Dawson had wanted more times than he could remember. He decided to play a few more songs by the same artist. "Walk by Faith" and "I Still Believe" and others. For a while they were quiet, lost in the serenity of the afternoon, caught up in the view of a million evergreens and the windsurfers on the Columbia River.

The lyrics were saying everything that needed to be said.

Originally they had planned to go back to her apartment in Portland, but before they reached the exit she gasped. "I know . . ." Her hair spilled over her shoulders as she turned and grinned at him. It was getting dark, so she took off her sunglasses. "Let's get ice cream."

London rarely wanted ice cream—especially when it wasn't quite sixty degrees out. He grinned at her. "How about coffee instead." He removed his own glasses and set them on the middle console. He crossed his arms. "I'm still freezing from the hike."

"Well . . . there's a little spot in Vancouver with tables. My mom and I walked by it the other day." She raised one shoulder. "Maybe we could talk a little. About my questions."

Nothing on Dawson's list this Sunday night was more important than having that conversation with London. He laughed. "Ice cream it is."

She talked about her mother's coffee shop. "We're getting new T-shirts. Pale blue. Good for summer." A slight groan came from her. "Mom's making me do a photo shoot to model them."

"The place is named after you." He imagined her face on the wall of the trendy spot. "You in a pale-blue T-shirt?" He studied her delicate profile. "Better tell her to order a lot."

"You're too kind." She drove to Vancouver's narrow Main Street and parked along the curb in front of the ice cream shop. Traffic buzzed by them inches from her car. The way it always did here.

With the engine off she turned to him. "This is it."

He peered out the passenger window at the storefront. ICE CREAM RENAISSANCE, the sign read. "I've never been." Through the glass he spotted the tables. She was right. Perfect for a long conversation. "Looks amazing."

"It is." She stared at him, her expression more serious than usual. "It's been a great day."

"For me, too." They could talk here as long as she wanted to.

"I have to say something." She took a slow breath. "Thanks for putting up with me. I know how you feel, Dawson. It's just . . . I'm not ready." Without hesitation she took his hand in hers. "I might never be. Like I told you the other night."

"I know." He didn't want to rehash that. Instead he looked deep into her amber eyes. Things were changing for her. He could see it in her face. A thrill of hope filled him. "We can talk inside."

She smiled. "Let's go."

And without giving it another thought, without checking for traffic or making sure she could even exit the car safely, she opened the door and jumped out. She was still laughing, hair flying behind her when it happened.

A pickup truck hit her square on and sent her flying down the street.

Nothing about the moment felt real. They were just on the mountain hiking to the summit and looking at the eagle. Just listening to Jeremy Camp sing about Jesus, and Dawson was just talking to her, just holding her hand.

Only now he was out of the car and running . . . running as fast as he could. And cars were screeching to a halt in all directions and people were staring and screaming and rushing toward her. Wherever she was.

"London!" He shouted her name, because she couldn't have been hit. They were going inside for ice cream, about to have the talk he'd always wanted to have with her, the one about Jesus and her questions.

The man in the pickup jumped out. "No! Dear God, no!" He put his hands to his face and fell to the ground.

Dawson kept running. This wasn't happening. They were going in for ice cream and he was going to hear her questions.

He hadn't heard her questions.

"Nobody touch her!" His words bellowed from his chest, as if that could rewind the moment, stop this scene from playing out. *Where is she, Lord? Let her be okay. Please.* His feet wouldn't move fast enough. Like he was running through glue or stuck in cement. "London, it's okay!"

Because that's what he had to say. Nothing could be wrong with her. She couldn't have flown down the road and she wouldn't be injured. Absolutely not. She was his best friend, the only girl he'd ever loved.

"London!" He yelled her name with everything in him, shouted it so that people stopped moving and stared at him. And everything was happening in slow motion. The panicked voices of strangers filled the air.

"Call 9-1-1," someone said.

"We did. We already called."

Dawson had to reach her. *Run, Dawson, you have to get to her.* Twenty feet, thirty . . . forty, fifty. Where was she? How could she have flown this far? But finally he saw her.

Lying in a heap on the sidewalk, her legs spread at a sickening angle. "No, God . . . please." This time his words were a whisper. Terror shot through him. This couldn't be his London. The girl on the ground didn't even look like her except . . .

Except her hair and her eyes.

"London, I'm here." He dropped to the ground near her head. Blood gushed from her scalp and a gurgling sound came from her throat. "London, can you hear me?"

People crowded around, staring, stunned. "Get a doctor!" Dawson shouted at them. "She needs help."

"London." His voice was soft again. He lowered himself even more so his words were next to her ear. "Can you hear me?"

Her chest wasn't moving, but she was getting air. That was the gurgling sound, so she was breathing. Everything was going to be okay because she was breathing. "London!"

With the slightest movement, she turned her head toward him and the shock of the accident seemed to lift. Her eyes found his. "I . . . didn't look."

"It's okay. We're getting you help, London. Everything's going to be okay." *Please, God . . . please.* He couldn't look at her body, couldn't bear to see how bad she really was. The damage the truck had done to her. How fast had the guy been going? Thirty . . . forty miles an hour? Maybe more? "London, I'm here. It's okay."

Sirens sounded in the distance. A reminder that this was really happening. They were supposed to be ordering ice cream, sitting at a reclaimed wood table and getting to her questions. She never got to ask her questions.

Dawson soothed his hand over the side of her head that wasn't bleeding. "Hold on, London. Please. Hold on."

More gurgling. Her eyes glazed over and her body twitched. Slightly at first and then worse and then it stopped and she was still again. She blinked and stared straight at him. "It was . . . always . . ." Every word seemed to take all her strength. No one standing around could've heard her. Just him. She uttered a weak cough. The gurgling was worse now. "It was . . . always you, Dawson."

Tears blurred his eyes. How could she be telling him this now? The sirens were getting louder.

His heart melted. "I know, London." He whispered near her face, and held her head in his hands. *Don't let her die, God, please. Don't let her die.* He ran his fingers over her hair. Hadn't he always known that was how she felt? All the Sunday hikes and jet-skiing and late-night talks? The way they held hands.

The way the air turned electric whenever they were together.

Dawson blinked and two teardrops fell from his eyes to her cheeks. "You're going to be okay, London. You have to ask me your questions."

Fear flashed in her beautiful eyes, but only for an instant. Then, as if they were surrounded by unseen angels, peace filled her face. She managed the slightest smile. "No . . . questions."

No questions? What did she mean? He didn't like this, didn't like the calm in her voice or the stillness of her body. "Hold on, London. You're going to get through this."

She winced and her body convulsed again. "N-n-no."

What was she telling him? He wanted to scream at her. Yes, she was going to get through it. They would take her to the hospital and stitch up her head and tomorrow morning she'd walk out just fine. Then they'd get in the car and come here.

To Ice Cream Renaissance.

Her breathing was worse. More noise, less air. She

struggled to look at him again. "I . . . love you . . . Dawson."

"I love you, London." His tears fell harder now. "Hang on, please."

She tried to swallow but instead she choked. So hard she cried out. He couldn't bear it. The horrific pain she must've been in. Her look grew more intense. "I asked God."

Dawson's mind was spinning. The ambulance pulled up and he could hear what must've been paramedics running toward them. "What, baby? What did you ask Him?"

"To . . ." She blinked and it took a bit before she opened her eyes and found him again. "To give me Jesus."

It was everything he'd ever wanted to hear from her. But not like this, not on a sidewalk in downtown Vancouver with her body mangled and blood spilling from her head. He pressed his cheek against hers. Time was running out. They were about to take her from him. "London . . . then you have Him. You have Jesus."

She gave the slightest nod and then she closed her eyes.

In a blur the medics were on the scene. "Excuse us. Step aside, please."

How could he tell them that he had never stepped aside for anyone when it came to London Quinn? He was always first to call, first to show up. Last to say goodbye. He was her very own and she was his. Dawson kissed her cheek and stood.

He had to move, had to let them take her. It was the only chance she had.

Someone came up beside him, a tall policeman with blond hair and big shoulders. "Dawson." The man put his arm around Dawson's shoulders. "She's okay. Jesus has her now."

What? Dawson wanted to shout at everyone to stop the entire charade. This wasn't happening. He and London were in the parlor and they were sitting at the best table in the place and she was sharing her heart. Her questions.

But the officer was still there, still holding on to him. Dawson jerked away. "I . . . can't lose her." He took a step toward the spot where London lay on a stretcher, where a medical team was hooking up an IV. "London! I'm here."

The policeman took gentle hold of his arm and pulled him back. "Don't be afraid. You won't lose her." Something warm and sincere filled the man's voice. He pressed his fingers to Dawson's heart. "London will be right here, Dawson. Always."

The officer's badge read JAG. Who was he and how come he knew Dawson's name? And London's? "Do . . . do I know you?"

The paramedics were moving the stretcher, taking her with them. When she was supposed to be sitting across from him eating ice cream.

"London!" Dawson moved to follow the stretcher, but a different policeman stopped him. Where was his friend, the blond officer? Dawson looked back for him, but the guy was gone. Nowhere. Not here or up and down the sidewalk. And the other one wasn't letting him through.

Dawson peered past the man. "London!" His voice rose against the noise of the crowd surrounding them. *God, let her hear me. Please.* They were loading her in the ambulance now, about to shut the doors. "I'll meet you there. Hold on, please hold on."

The doors closed and the ambulance pulled away.

Ten yards away the man who had hit her was still in the road, his head in his hands. Four police officers and a paramedic were talking to him. The blond one wasn't among them. Dawson wasn't sure how he was going to get to the hospital, but just then one of the four policemen approached him.

"Come on." He motioned to Dawson. "I'll take you."

On the way to the hospital, the officer was quiet. Dawson stared out the window and didn't blink. This was all a terrible nightmare. It had to be. He covered his face with his hand. His eyes were dry now, shock setting in. This was his fault. He should've told her to look for cars. Should've stopped her from jumping out without checking traffic.

If he would've done that none of this would've happened. *God, please let her live. She's everything to me. Please, Lord.*

Then it hit him and his heart slammed against his chest. Her parents! They had to know. What was he going to tell them? That she'd been hit by a truck and now . . . now she might . . . He couldn't finish the thought. Instead Dawson dialed Louise Quinn. He'd rather take the hit himself than contact London's mother, but he had no choice. He held his breath while the call rang through.

The call that would change London's parents' lives forever.

5

Dialysis days were the worst for Louise Quinn.

The process was barbaric, one she had hoped to avoid ever since her doctor found disease in her kidneys. Her dirty blood would leave her body through a thick tube and pass through a machine. Once clean, her blood would circulate back to her body.

Each time here took about four hours. Larry drove her to the center, making sure she was hooked up and covered with her favorite blanket. Then he'd run errands and she'd read a book or watch TV. If she was lucky, she'd fall asleep and the time would pass more quickly. When it was done, Larry would be back, waiting for her.

Always waiting for her.

He had loved her since they were college freshmen, a week after meeting her at Portland State University's back-to-school carnival. Now Larry was a pharmaceutical salesman and Louise ran London Coffee.

Their daughter was everything to them.

Louise leaned back in her recliner and pulled her blanket higher to her chest.

Her kidneys weren't working at all, so dialysis was keeping her alive. At least until the transplant. The one she didn't want. The surgery where her only daughter would give up a kidney to save Louise's life.

Anxiety tightened its hold on her. If a cadaver kidney came up before the transplant, Louise would gladly welcome it as a very great gift, even though the success rate was lower than with a living donor. Because a cadaver kidney would mean London would get to keep hers.

Louise had been reading, but she was at the end of her treatment and too tired to turn the pages. She set the book down and sighed. For nearly a month she had come here three days a week and watched nurses connect her to a machine. Then she would sit in this chair, feet up, while the machine drained the fluid from her blood and body. Sometimes eight pounds of fluid.

The whole thing left her freezing cold.

When it was over, she always felt weak and faint. And every time she went through the procedure, her heart got a little more worn out. Some patients didn't live past their first year on dialysis.

She tried to remember life just a year ago. When she would do Pilates every morning and run with Larry each evening. All their married lives they'd been active. The dream was to run the Portland Marathon this year. Instead—because of far too many over-the-counter pain meds, she was here. One thing was certain. When she was past this ordeal she would take up a cause greater than running a marathon.

People needed to know about the overuse of simple legal pain meds and what they could do to a body. Larry was going to help her start a nonprofit to raise awareness.

A nurse walked up and checked her machine. "Yes! Good work, Ms. Quinn." She jotted a few numbers into Louise's chart. "Just six pounds of fluid." She smiled. "That means you're consuming fewer liquids. Thirty-two ounces is the max per day. I'm sure you know."

"Yes." Louise managed a weak smile. "I'm trying." She blew at a wisp of her grayish blond hair. "I used to drink that much coffee before eight in the morning."

The nurse unhooked her and helped her to her feet. At the same time Louise spotted Larry in the lobby. He rose to meet her and with him at her side, five minutes later they were in their SUV.

Louise fell back against the seat and closed her eyes. "As much as I hate this, I'd do it the rest of my life if it meant sparing London the transplant."

"I know." Larry reached for her hand. "You've told her not to do this. We both have."

"The girl's been stubborn since before she could walk." Louise blinked her eyes open and smiled at her husband. "I'm going to sleep for twelve hours tonight."

"Here." He handed her a paper bowl with a peeled hard-boiled egg. "Gotta get your protein."

Larry had been her rock. Because of him, the hard-boiled egg had become part of the routine. She looked at him. "You love me so well."

"As long as I live." He turned his attention to the road. "Now let's get you home. Dinner's waiting."

Protein was important for a dialysis patient, but Louise had no appetite. She took a steadying breath. "Have you heard from London?"

"She's still with Dawson. As far as I know." Larry's smile came easily. "Every time they're together I think this will be the day."

"Mmm." Louise sat a little straighter. "The day she realizes how much that young man loves her." She hesitated. "How much he's in love with her."

As they were pulling into their neighborhood Louise's phone rang. Caller ID showed Dawson's name.

Louise loved that young man like he was her own. She had filled in as a second mom for him since high school. But for some reason as she reached to answer the phone she hesitated. A flash of concern shot across her mind.

"Who is it?" Larry looked at her and then back at the road.

"Dawson." Louise stared at the phone. She had to answer it. Her fears were completely irrational. Why would she be even the slightest bit concerned? Dawson was probably calling to see if he and London could stop by for dinner. Yes, that had to be it.

Larry gave her another glance. "Honey . . . answer it."

"I am." She grabbed her phone and brought it to her face. "Hi Dawson." Her tone sounded a little unnatural. She waited for good news, whatever it was.

Instead Dawson sounded upset. "Louise . . . it's . . . it's London." Yes, he was definitely crying. "She . . . she was hit by a . . . by a pickup truck and—"

"Pull over." Louise's tone was sharp. "Larry, please pull over." He did and she handed the phone to him. "Take it. I . . . I can't. I can't do this." She buried her face in her hands and held her breath. This wasn't happening. Everything was fine with London. They had worked at the coffee shop together this morning.

Larry held the phone to his ear. "Dawson . . . this is Larry." Her husband never sounded afraid. But he did now. "What is it?"

Larry's words blended together and Louise tuned

them out. She couldn't begin to imagine it was true. But what had Dawson just said? London was hit by a truck? What did that even mean? And why was Dawson crying?

Gradually the sound of Larry's conversation came to the surface. He was driving again, turning around and heading back out of the neighborhood. Faster this time. "Do you know where they took her?"

Louise sat up and looked at him. Even in the early evening shadows, Larry's face looked white as snow. She gripped his knee and waited.

"Okay. All right, we'll be there as soon as we can. Thanks for calling, Dawson. It'll be okay. We have to believe that."

The call ended and Larry turned to her. "She was still talking to him before they took her in the ambulance." His mouth sounded dry. He stared straight ahead, both hands gripping the steering wheel. "I told him she'll be okay. She has to be okay."

Twenty minutes later they parked near the emergency room and ran together through the doors to the front desk. Larry did the talking, and again Louise couldn't hear every word. She needed to see London. She would go to her side and stroke her hair and whisper a prayer over her and everything would be all right.

Someone led them through another set of doors to a small waiting room. Dawson was there. On his knees. He seemed to finish his prayer, then he stood, his eyes red, face tearstained. Louise closed the distance between them and clung to him. As if this show of support could somehow change the circumstances.

Larry spoke first. "How is she? Has anyone talked to you?"

Dawson stepped back and stared at them. "She's . . . not good. They're working on her." He struggled to speak. "The doctor said . . . someone would be in soon."

They moved to take their seats, but Louise couldn't sit. She walked to the closed door and to the far wall. The space was boxy, the air stale. Louise couldn't stop the whispered words that spilled from her lips. "I'm sorry, God. I haven't talked to You in years, but I need You. Save her, please, God. I'm begging You."

Photographs began playing across her heart, the tiny baby girl in the pink blanket the day they took her home. The purple streamers on her first tricycle and the grin across her face as she learned to ride it.

Birthdays and Christmases and first days of school. Graduations and rainy afternoons at London Coffee.

"She has to be okay." Louise turned to Larry. "Honey, she has to."

Larry was on his feet again, taking Louise in his arms. He ran his hand over her back. "Come sit down, love. You need to rest."

Louise stopped and stared at him. "You didn't say she was going to be okay. That's all you said all the way here, and now . . . now you didn't say it."

Dawson stayed seated. He lifted his head. "She might be." He wiped at fresh tears on his face. "They're doing tests. The doctor will tell us."

"Yes." Louise nodded. That was it. She still might be okay. Larry led her to the seat between him and Dawson and then she thought of something. The thing they never talked about. The facts about her birth London never knew.

"We should have told her." Louise dug her elbows into

the arms of the chair and hung her head. "Why didn't we tell her?" She sounded like someone having a breakdown. Her words weren't meant for Larry or Dawson, but for herself. "Lots of couples struggle to have a baby. So we used IVF. That's not crazy. That was never the problem, but . . . London deserves the truth." A quick pause. "I'll tell her when she wakes up. Then she'll know."

She was aware that Larry and Dawson could hear her, but she couldn't stop herself. As long as she was talking about London, her daughter had to be alive. That was it, she had to be.

"I'll tell her about the embryos. The three frozen embryos we donated after she was born." Tears stung Louise's eyes. She turned to her husband. "Why did we do that, Larry? Why didn't we try to have those babies? Those were . . . London's siblings. All of them."

Larry was still pale. He looked lost in a fog of terror and uncertainty. "I don't want to talk about this, Louise."

"I do."

Larry looked pained. "You . . . you couldn't have more babies. You know that."

"I could have." Louise was on her feet again. "I chose not to. Because of what? A difficult pregnancy?"

He apparently wasn't going to argue with her. And all the while Dawson sat there staring at the door, hearing this.

Louise dropped to her chair again and exhaled. "I struggled. But I was fine." She turned to Larry. "London wanted a sister. She always wanted a sister. And now . . . whatever happened to those embryos, Larry? Where are they?" Her heart started to race. Not a normal hurried rhythm, but a hard pounding against her chest.

This time Dawson looked straight at her. And of course. All of this would be a surprise to him. Just like it would be for London. Louise's breathing came faster. London had to wake up, right? She was going to be okay, the doctor would show up any minute to tell them so.

"Maybe we can find the embryos, what became of them. And London will have a reason to get better. So she can meet her siblings." She looked at Larry. "That's a good idea, right? We should do that."

In the hallways of her mind, Louise knew she wasn't acting rational. She was having a full-blown panic attack. Five minutes became ten and Louise was ready to burst into the hallway and find London. Even if she had to knock someone over to do it. But just then the door opened and a doctor walked in.

For the rest of her life, Louise would remember the look on the man's face. He was older, distinguished. Graying hair on a still-handsome face. But there were tears in his eyes. Tears from a doctor could only mean one thing.

"No." Louise wanted to kick a wall down and run from the room. Back to dialysis or the ride home, back to any time in her life before this minute.

The doctor pulled up a chair and sat facing them. He exhaled for what felt like a minute. "Mr. and Mrs. Quinn. Mr. Gage. I'm afraid London's injuries are very, very serious." He pressed his lips together and studied the floor for a long moment. When he looked up, he shook his head. "The impact caused significant internal injuries. All London's organs are failing. Her kidneys and liver were destroyed and her heart is damaged."

Her heart? London's heart was damaged? That wasn't possible. Louise shook her head. Her daughter had a beautiful heart. There wasn't a thing wrong with it.

Black dots swirled in front of Louise's eyes. She could hear her heartbeat in her ears, but everything else faded. She was about to pass out. She could feel it. *No,* she told herself. *You are not going to faint. Be strong for your daughter right now. She needs you.*

Louise focused intently on the doctor's mouth, on the words coming from him. "We've done what we can do." He paused. "She's . . . on life support for now." He explained that they could come in and see her. All three of them, but just for a few minutes.

Time stopped and nothing made sense. Somehow Louise stayed conscious as Larry walked beside her into the hallway. They followed the doctor, with Dawson just behind them. In a blink they were ushered into a room with a bed, and around the bed, machines.

Someone was under the sheets, but it wasn't London. It couldn't be. The person had wires and tubes coming from every part of her body and a mask covering her face. Bruises made up her cheeks and arms and her hair was the wrong color. Darker. Burgundy almost. Also she was bigger, her arms and legs and face.

Louise turned to the doctor. She shook her head and tried to keep her voice steady. "This . . . this isn't London." *Thank, God, it isn't London.* "There's been a mistake."

The doctor's look stopped her from repeating herself. He put his hand on her shoulder and nodded. Stern-like. "Your presence is very important. London may be able to hear you." He shifted his attention to Larry and Dawson and back to Louise. "Please be careful with your words."

Another look at the woman in the bed and Louise squinted. This was London? It wasn't possible. The broken, battered body before them looked nothing like her precious, beautiful daughter. Louise stepped around the doctor and moved near the woman's head. Her hair was too—

Suddenly, Louise covered her mouth to quiet her gasp. The person's hair wasn't burgundy. It was blood-soaked. Her eyes moved down the young woman's swollen, scraped arm and what she saw next made her drop to the nearest chair.

On the ankle of the woman was a small tattoo of a dove.

The one London had gotten on her twenty-first birthday.

Larry was behind her, his hand on her back. Neither he nor Dawson must've doubted that the patient was London. Dawson moved to the other side of the bed and put his hand on her arm. "We're here, London." He lowered himself so he was close to her face. "Your mom and dad and me. You're getting the best care, baby."

Tears spilled onto Dawson's face. He took hold of her hand and stood straight again. Then he squeezed his eyes shut. He was shaking, his broken heart clearly consuming him.

Louise breathed in sharply and found the strength she needed. This was her chance to talk to her daughter. Not her last chance, Louise wouldn't believe that. But London needed to hear all their voices. Even if speaking to her in this condition was the hardest thing they'd ever done.

She took London's hand. Her fingers were cold and stiff. No response whatsoever. Louise sucked in a quick breath. *Breathe,* she told herself. But she couldn't exhale. Why was London's hand so cold?

Larry was behind her, his arm around her. His presence helped her breathe out. "London, sweetheart, it's Mom." Louise was too afraid to cry. Her voice sounded dry and panicked. "Can you squeeze my fingers, baby? If you can hear me squeeze my fingers." The black dots flashed again. "Please, London."

All of them focused on the place where Louise's hand joined London's. Then in what felt like a miracle, London gave her the slightest squeeze. She actually did. "Sweetheart, I felt that. You can hear us!" Tears welled in Louise's eyes, but she fought them. "London, you're going to be okay. Jesus is here . . . He's holding you."

The words felt right, even though Louise hadn't talked with London about Jesus since she was in kindergarten. The blame was theirs. Hers and Larry's. But life had taken away the urgency of Sunday church services and there had never been time for the Bible. Success and education and politics had filled the place where Jesus used to live. But that was behind them.

Jesus was all they had now.

Larry stepped up and spoke to London. "Honey, we aren't going anywhere. We'll be here when you wake up."

The doctor was waiting for them at the door, but Louise had more to say. She moved in beside Larry and took London's hand again. "You're the best daughter. The only reason anyone comes to the coffee shop is because of you, sweetie." Another quick breath. "And I need you to model those shirts, London. So you have to get better real fast."

Once more, Louise's mind was spinning. What were they doing? Standing around a hospital bed with London on life support? How could this be happening? Tears fell from Louise's eyes. She couldn't stop them. This was real. And that reality suddenly washed over her like a tsunami.

Because what if she didn't—

Louise refused to finish the thought. "I love you, London, honey. You're the sunshine of my life. You always have been."

A slight cough came from the doctor. "She needs to rest." He pushed the door open. "You can come back later."

On the other side of the bed, Dawson still had hold of her hand. He looked over his shoulder at the doctor. "Can we pray for her?"

"Definitely." The man let the door close again.

Dawson lowered himself so his face was near hers once more. He kissed her hand, the part that wasn't bandaged. "Lord . . ." He hung his head for a few seconds. "We praise You and thank You . . . for London." A tear slid down his face. "Please, God, heal her. She needs You now . . . In Jesus' name, amen." With the crook of his arm he wiped his face. He leaned close to her face and his voice became a choked whisper. "I love you, London."

Again the doctor opened the door. "It's time. Please."

Desperation filled Louise. She couldn't walk away. How could he ask her to leave her baby girl? This was her daughter, her only child. When London woke up she'd need her mother beside her. She held tight to London's hand. Her lungs ached. How was she supposed to breathe without her girl?

Larry was beside London now, kissing her swollen cheek and wiping his tears. He turned to Louise. "Honey. We have to go . . . London knows we were here."

Tears blurred Louise's eyes as Larry led her out of the room and back down the hall.

This was a nightmare. Yes, that had to be it. A terrible, awful dream. Because London was out with Dawson, hiking Multnomah Falls. Tomorrow she and her beautiful daughter would be at their coffee shop and a photographer would come to take pictures of London in the new T-shirts.

Her modeling debut, that's what they had called it.

Louise gripped her husband's arm as they walked back to the terrible waiting room. When she sat down, Louise rewrote the story in her mind. They were not here and London was not in that hospital bed. She had certainly not been hit by a truck and she was not fighting for her life. She was out with Dawson, whole and healthy, young and lovely. Her precious London.

That's what she told herself over and over and over again. Until someone brought her a blanket and she fell asleep in the chair. Even then she continued. They weren't at the hospital. London wasn't fighting for her life. On and on it went. Not like some ridiculous, delusional story.

But as if her own life depended on it.

6

London was still holding on.

She'd been off life support for twenty-four hours, and Dawson had spent almost every one of those here. Waiting for her to wake up. Praying for a good report. Hoping this would be the time.

He was at her bedside now. She was less swollen, less bruised, but her doctor had not been encouraged by either improvement. "It's not her outside we're concerned about," he had told Dawson and London's parents last night. "It's her insides. Her organs."

She had considerable internal bleeding, too much for her medical team to stop. Even so they were less worried about her brain or lungs, crazy enough. She had flown sixty feet in the air and landed on a sidewalk and somehow she hadn't done catastrophic damage to her head. It was the reason she'd been able to talk to him in those early minutes after the accident. But since arriving here, her brain had swelled, sending her into a coma.

The machines were no longer keeping her alive, he understood that much. But her breathing sounded terrible. More labored than before. Dawson wanted to believe that was a good sign. Proof she was working to get better.

The doctors disagreed. Last night they had been clear that London's chances weren't good. Also, they doubted whether Louise really had felt London squeeze her fingers that first night. Dawson hadn't felt any response at all. He took her hand. It still felt cold and stiff. "London?"

Nothing. No movement. Her entire body was lifeless.

"I'm here, baby." Dawson's voice was a hush. His words for her alone. "Come back to me, London. I'm waiting for you."

God had done what Jeremy Camp sang about in the song. In all His mercy, He had given her Jesus. That's what she had asked for on the sidewalk. Nothing more. Not life or healing or help in that desperate moment.

Just Jesus.

Another round of tears filled his eyes. "You have Jesus now, London. You asked. So you have Him." He brushed at his wet cheeks with his free hand. "We still have so much to talk about. God, please let her come back to me."

He waited, studying her. Any small movement would do. A twitch in her cheek or a flicker of her eyebrow. Movement in her arms or legs. *Please, God . . . Please.* A minute became five and then ten.

Nothing.

Dawson released London's icy fingers and took his seat. He remembered the accident again, the way he did every hour. Who was the blond police officer? And how had he known their names? The man seemed so sure London was okay, but now . . .

Louise was in dialysis today, and Larry with her. Right by her side, where he'd been since the news about London. Dawson pictured Louise, the desperation on her face earlier as she left the hospital. She had begged Larry to stop her treatments. Anything that took her away from London wasn't worth the time.

But Louise would die in a few weeks if she didn't go. Even so, Dawson could hear the cry in her voice as her husband led her from the waiting room that morning. "Maybe it doesn't matter. If I don't make it."

Larry had stopped in his tracks. "Don't say that, love." He faced her and put his hands on either side of her face. "Don't ever say that. London needs you." He paused and brought his lips to hers. "I need you."

Louise put her head on his chest. "I'm sorry."

But those weren't the words Dawson remembered most from the last seventy-two hours.

The most crazy were the ones spoken in the hours after they arrived at the hospital Sunday. Dawson wasn't even sure Louise would remember saying them. But she had. And they'd stayed with Dawson right up until this moment.

London had been an IVF baby? She had been created in a petri dish. And then her parents had donated three embryos to someone. Which meant somewhere out there it was possible London had brothers or sisters.

As many as three siblings.

He heard a sound from the hallway, and there they were. Louise and Larry. Both of them haggard, their eyes sunken. Larry looked at him. "Dialysis took a toll."

"I'm sure." Dawson turned to London. "She's . . ." He didn't want to finish the sentence. "She's the same. Her breathing seems a little louder."

They had wiped away most of the blood from her hair. And since a lot of her swelling from the medications had gone down, she almost looked like herself. Like Snow White . . . waiting for Prince Charming to wake her up.

Two doctors came to the door. A nurse was with them.

A couple thoughts struck Dawson in that moment. First, all three looked defeated. And second, they weren't in a hurry.

No, he wanted to shout. *Do not come in here and tell us she's worse. She's getting better.* She looked better than just three days ago.

The head of her medical team, Dr. Randall, broke the silence. "Take a seat please." He had a chart with him. "We need to talk. All of us."

The other doctor and the nurse kept their eyes downward.

"Nothing's changed." Dawson spoke first. He was struck by the confidence in his own voice. As if he were the expert and they were merely visitors. "I've been here . . . four hours and . . ." He shook his head. "She's the same. Breathing a little louder, but no worse."

Dr. Randall opened his chart. "I wish that were true." He looked at Larry and Louise. "We've been monitoring her at the nurses' station." He glanced at the machines on either side of London. "I'm afraid . . . her heart rate and blood pressure have dropped dramatically."

A slight ray of hope flashed in Larry's eyes. "I've read online . . . when the heart starts to slow a little, in a situation like this"—his words came faster. Like he was desperate—"it can actually mean the patient is healing. The heart conserves energy while the body—"

"I'm very sorry, Mr. Quinn." Dr. Randall paused. "That is not what's happening here."

"She can hear us, Doctor." Dawson's tone sounded sharper than he intended. "That's what we were told. So maybe we can stay a little more positive here."

"Yes. There was a chance of that . . . before." Dr. Randall frowned. "Not anymore. We can talk candidly."

Dawson's heart pounded. London wasn't healing? What was the man saying? He glanced at London's parents. They looked pale and weak. Like they'd aged a decade in the past few minutes.

"We've all verified what's happening." Dr. Randall seemed to check with his medical team, first the doctor on his right, then the nurse on his left. "Though she's breathing . . . her brain is showing very little activity."

Dawson stared at London. Her brain wasn't showing much activity? How could that be possible? She was here and she was with them. London was one of the smartest, wittiest people he knew. It was part of what always drew him to her. And now . . .

The doctor was explaining that London's brain was shutting down because her damaged organs already had. "We believe she's experiencing a series of strokes because of blood clots to the brain."

What a terrible thing to tell Louise and Larry. Dawson wanted to run from the room and take London's parents with him. He grabbed a quick breath. "Put her back on life support, then. You have to help her so . . ."

"She's dying, Mr. Gage. Her major organs are bleeding and damaged beyond repair." Dr. Randall closed his file and crossed his arms. "She might have another hour. Maybe two." He nodded at Larry. "You can stay . . . until it happens. We've turned off the monitor alarms." He hesitated. "Take as long as you need. We won't bother you."

But shouldn't they want to bother London? Dawson couldn't stop himself from asking the obvious question. "There has to be something you can do." Desperation seized him. "What about treating the clots? Blood thinners, right?"

Dr. Randall was starting to look uncomfortable. "London cannot handle that. She still has uncontrolled internal bleeding. Life support won't help. Neither will medicine." He sighed. "This is an end-of-life situation."

Dawson stared at the man for a long moment. Then he nodded. What more could he say? The room was turning around him, and someone was talking. But Dawson couldn't hear. The medical team needed to leave so they could be with London. So they could pray for a miracle and watch God make it happen.

Finally the doctor and his colleagues walked out and shut the door behind them. Dawson and London's parents were alone with her. Dawson moved to the left side of her bed and took her hand. "London." He'd always loved her name, the way it sounded. Saying it now felt like a breath of hope. Because she was still here, still breathing.

Still his best friend.

Dawson ran his thumb along her hand. Her fingers felt even colder. A few feet away, Larry helped Louise to her feet and they took up their posts on the opposite side.

"Why aren't they helping her?" Louise buried her face in her husband's shirt. "I can't bear this."

Yes, Dawson thought. Louise was right. He wanted to step into the hall and shout at someone, tell them to get in here and give her medication. Something powerful, maybe through an IV. He watched her chest rise and fall, steady, rhythmic. Her breathing was louder, still. And too slow. Then his eyes found the monitors. Why hadn't he noticed them before? The doctors were right. What he saw was terrible. Just eight breaths per minute, her blood pressure a sickening 60 over 40. Worse than what the doctors had reported.

He stared at the numbers. The 8 became a 7. Panic pulsed through his body. They were losing her, right now in front of them. "Please, Lord . . . don't take her." His tortured words came through clenched teeth. This couldn't be happening.

But it was.

On the other side of the bed, Louise came up close to London's face. She stroked her daughter's hair and whispered near her ear. Dawson couldn't make out what she said, but tears streamed down her face. She kissed London's head and brushed her cheek against her daughter's much paler one.

Suddenly Dawson realized maybe he shouldn't be here. If this was . . . if she left them this hour, Larry and Louise might want to be alone. "I . . . I can leave." He took a step back from London's bed.

"No." Louise's answer came fast and sharp. "You have to stay, Dawson. Stand by her and pray. Please don't stop praying."

Dawson nodded. He moved back to London and took her hand again. The terrible way she showed no response made him sick to his stomach. He prayed anyway. "Please, Lord, give her life. She needs You. We all need You."

Then London did something she hadn't done in three days.

She opened her eyes.

A quiet gasp came from all three of them, and they moved closer to her bed. London blinked a few times, slow, dreamlike, and she looked at Dawson. The hint of a smile lifted her lips. "Hi." She gave his hand the slightest squeeze, then she looked at her parents. "I . . . love you . . . Mom . . . Dad."

Her parents were both crying now, silent, stunned. Louise had her hand to her mouth. "Sweetheart. We love you . . . we love you with everything we have."

Dawson's heart pounded so hard he wondered if he would pass out. Was this really happening? He looked at the monitors. Her breaths per minute were 23 now and her blood pressure was higher, too. "London." He bent low and kissed her hand. "How are you, baby?"

It took effort, but she looked straight to the part of his heart that had belonged to her for as long as he could remember. "I . . . love you, Dawson."

London recognized him! Dawson couldn't contain his joy. "I love you, too." Tears filled his eyes and he felt himself smile bigger than he had since the accident. "You're getting better! It's a miracle." There were a hundred things he wanted to say, but they'd have time for that now.

She turned to her mom and the two shared a look that held a lifetime of love and memories. Then she did the same with her dad. The sort of look a bride gives her father on her wedding day. Like there was no one else in all the world she would rather call daddy.

For a few seconds, London struggled to form her next words. She coughed a few times, heavy, terrible coughs. When she caught her breath she looked at Dawson first. "I asked God . . . and He answered me." She smiled and shifted her gaze to her mom and dad. Her words were slow and soft. "I . . . asked Him . . . to for . . . forgive me. And . . . to give me Jesus."

In all her life, London had never looked more radiant. The color was back in her face and she seemed well again, like everything really was going to be okay. "He did it,

Dawson. God . . . gave me . . . what I asked for." Tears filled her eyes, even though her smile never wavered.

Louise kissed London's cheek again. "We've been praying for you, sweetheart."

"Yes." Her dad took her other hand. "Baby girl, we love you so much."

She looked at her parents again and struggled to speak, more than before. "I . . . think I have . . . a sister." For a handful of seconds her eyes closed. When she opened them, she looked at her mother. "Did you . . . know that?"

"London." Her mom looked at Larry, then back at their daughter. "You mean . . . you had a dream?"

"I don't . . . know." Her face grew pale again. Weakness was clearly consuming her once more, but still she smiled.

Louise seemed to gather herself. "Sweet daughter . . . you were . . . conceived through IVF. There were three . . . three other embryos."

Peace seemed to come over London. "I have . . . a sister."

Dawson's mind raced. Was London talking about the embryos? And if so, how could she possibly know that? Dawson checked the monitors. Her numbers were falling. "London . . . what did you see?"

Her eyes were soft as she turned to him. "Someone . . . like me." The gurgling sound was back with her next breath. Worse now. She turned to her parents once more. "Daddy . . . Mama." She blinked and tears slid down the sides of her face. "I have to go. He's . . ." She turned her head and stared at a spot at the front of the room. Where no one was standing. That gentle smile Dawson loved so much filled her face. "He's . . . He's here."

"No." Dawson didn't want her talking like that. "No

one's here, baby. Just us. And God is healing you." He ran his free hand over her hair. "You're talking to us!"

This time when she looked at him, her eyes held an ocean of sadness. "It's okay . . . Dawson." One more soft smile, but her words were slower, quieter. "I'll . . . see you again." She moved so she could look at her mom and dad. "Jesus . . . is all you need, Mama. Daddy."

Dawson felt her squeeze his hand once more. Then her eyes closed and she fell quiet. Too quiet. He looked at the monitors. The numbers were crashing. He took a step toward the hallway, but changed his mind. Nothing could've made him leave her side right now.

Because if she saw Jesus calling her home, then—

"London, we're here." Dawson remembered the words of Dr. Randall. Her organs are damaged beyond repair. If that were true, then what were these last few beautiful minutes about? It had seemed like a miracle from God, like she was being healed. So how could she be seeing Jesus? And who was this sister she talked about?

Across from him, Louise must've realized how dire things had become. She lowered the bed rail and crawled in beside London, cradling her the way she must have when London was a small child.

"Mama's here, baby girl." She lay on her side and hugged London close. Larry put his hand on his wife's shoulder, tears streaming down his face. Louise kissed London's cheek and forehead. She stroked her daughter's hair. "I'm not going anywhere."

London drew a long slow breath and she exhaled.

Dawson waited, watching her chest. But she didn't inhale. Dawson squeezed her hand. "Breathe, London. Come on."

But then, like a rest after the final notes in the most beautiful symphony, London's monitors bottomed out. No alarms, no buzzing or warning sounds. Just the most peaceful quiet.

"No." Louise held on to her daughter tighter than before and only then did she begin to truly cry. Tears seemed to overflow from her heart and her cry became an audible sobbing, a wailing like nothing Dawson had ever heard.

Because London was gone now, her body forever still.

The miracle wasn't that London was going to live. That hadn't been God's plan. But He had given them a very great gift all the same. And even here in the saddest moment of Dawson's life he could see it. Grasp it. Appreciate it.

Dawson didn't know how he was going to take his next breath or how he would ever live without her. But he knew this much. What God had given them here in this room was a very great miracle, indeed. A miracle Dawson would cling to and carry with him until his heart stopped beating. Until he ran across heaven's fields and through eternity's evergreens, first into the arms of Jesus . . . and then into the arms of London Quinn.

The best friend he had ever had.

7

The truth was coming.

Brooke planned to tell Maddie about her adoption over lunch in downtown Bloomington in fifteen minutes. She was about to leave her office, but first she had to enter information from her last appointment into the computer. It had run a little late and now she was rushed.

Maddie deserved for her to be on time.

Patient is two years old and has human parvovirus, Brooke typed into the child's online file. *Two siblings at home are still unaffected. Mom is pregnant and needs a blood test. Recommended mom schedule an appointment with her ob-gyn. Follow-up in one week.*

Other details could be added later. Brooke had to go. She closed the file and hurried toward the front desk. On the way, her husband stepped out of a patient's room. "Meeting Maddie?" He leaned in and kissed Brooke's lips. The happy sort of kiss that said all was right with the world.

Only it wasn't.

Brooke didn't smile. She tried to slow her racing heart, stave off her frustration. "I'm telling her today." She took a small step back. "Over lunch."

"Oh." Peter's expression darkened. "I . . . didn't know."

Brooke folded her arms. "I didn't tell you." Her words

were barely a whisper. They didn't usually have personal discussions at work. She raised one eyebrow and her eyes locked with his. "You told me to handle it, Peter. I'm doing that."

"Okay." He nodded, slow and deliberate. Like he was trying to figure out her mood. "It's not like I won't be part of the discussion eventually."

She shouldn't have told him. If he wanted her to handle it, then she would. Even if she didn't like the idea. And now this conversation was only going to make her late. "Peter . . ." She kept her tone level. "You said it should just be me."

"At first." His tone grew heavy. "Of course I want to talk with her about it later. It's just . . . I think she'll open up better to you. Respond better." He hesitated. "You know?"

"Not really." Brooke tried to control herself. Peter should've gone with her to this lunch, or they should've told Maddie when they were all together. Too late now. "It's okay." Brooke walked a few feet. "I'll tell you how it goes."

"Brooke!" He caught up to her. "Don't just walk away."

"I can't be late." She was tired of the conversation. "Just . . . go see your next patient. I'm not mad." Her smile felt forced. "I've got it."

Peter didn't move. "I'm sorry. I'll talk about it tonight. With Maddie."

"Sounds good." Brooke hurried down the hall.

At the front desk, Ellen sat at her computer. The woman was in her fifties, and she'd worked for Peter and Brooke's pediatric practice for years. Ellen looked up and grinned. "Meeting with your girl?"

"Yes." Brooke remembered to smile. "Big day!" She gave Ellen a side hug. "See you tomorrow."

Lunch had been Maddie's idea, and after they ate they were supposed to visit two local bridal boutiques. It should be the best day. No way in the world Brooke would've told her daughter such life-changing news this afternoon except for one thing.

It couldn't wait. Maddie was engaged. She deserved to know the truth.

Wedding-dress shopping was probably going to have to wait for another day. At least that's how Brooke saw the afternoon going. She would explain to Maddie how she had come from a frozen embryo and how the whole thing was supposed to be a secret to anyone outside the family. And how after that she was pregnant and somehow it didn't feel like she was carrying someone else's baby.

It felt like she was carrying her own.

That was what it came down to, really. Maddie had felt like hers from the beginning. She had even asked her doctor if it was possible none of the three embryos took. Maybe the baby inside her was actually hers and Peter's.

Brooke raced to her car and set out for Uptown Café. *Hurry,* she told herself. *Don't keep Maddie waiting. Not today.* In the days after Maddie's birth, the doctor had done a paternity test, and the results were definitive. Maddie was not biologically related to them. Even then Brooke believed the impossible.

Right up until she held Maddie for the first time after hearing the news. That's when she knew her doctor was right. This baby wasn't from her and Peter. It wasn't a looks thing or a DNA test or anything definitive. The truth had simply taken root deep in her heart.

Maddie had come from another couple.

But that didn't matter, not in the beginning and not as Maddie learned to walk and talk and read. She was theirs. No biological parents would ever come around looking to meet her so there had been no hurry to explain the situation to their daughter.

Besides, Maddie would have to be older to even begin to comprehend how she could've been born from her mother and still come from other parents. Brooke and Peter had a hard time wrapping their minds around it. How in the world would their daughter understand?

Year after year they reasoned away the chance to share the truth with Maddie.

And now here she was, about to tell her newly engaged daughter the most dramatic news of her life. Brooke parked, grabbed her purse and moved quickly up the sidewalk to the front door.

The hostess led her to Maddie, sitting at a table near a pretty window. Maddie stood, her face all lit up. "Mom! Thanks for doing this!" She hugged her tight. "Can you believe we're looking at wedding dresses today?"

Brooke remembered to keep her smile in place. "So exciting!"

They sat opposite each other. Was it better to tell her now? Start out with the truth and give her daughter more time to process her new reality?

Maddie beamed at her. "I've been thinking of bridesmaids."

"Yes." So much for starting out with the news. "Tell me!"

"Well . . . Hayley of course." Maddie's eyes softened. "She'll be my maid of honor. But don't tell her." Maddie had never looked happier. "I'll ask her later today. Or this weekend."

"I won't say a word." *No worries there,* she thought. *I'm good at keeping secrets.* Brooke focused. "Hayley will be thrilled."

"It's not a surprise." A happy laugh came from her daughter. "She's my sister, after all."

Her sister. Brooke stayed intent on her daughter's news. "Who else?"

"Andrea from high school. Connor's sister, Bailey. And my cousins, of course." Maddie's eyes sparkled. "Family first." She reached across the table and put her hand over Brooke's. "That's what you and Dad always say."

"Yes." Brooke felt sick to her stomach. "That's a good plan."

"Which means Jessie and Amy, because she's fourteen." Maddie's expression grew thoughtful. "Fourteen's old enough to be a bridesmaid, right, Mom? And Cole can be one of the groomsmen. Connor already told me that."

"Definitely." There was no segue in sight. "Let's decide what to order. Then you can finish telling me."

"Right." Maddie glanced at the menu. "I love their salmon salad. With the deep-fried goat cheese. I think I'll get that."

"Me, too." Brooke couldn't eat if her life depended on it. She looked at the menu but she didn't read a word. "Okay, so . . . go ahead."

"That leaves the younger cousins." Maddie smiled. "I was thinking I might have junior bridesmaids. Have you heard of that?"

"I have." Brooke should win an award for the performance she was giving. "Junior bridesmaids would be sweet."

"I think so." Maddie leaned back. "I'll have three—Malin is twelve and Sophie and Annie are both ten. As for flower girls . . ." She took a quick breath. "Janessa is eight, is that too old?"

"Eight?" Brooke's mind raced. "No, that's not too old. She'll be great."

"That's what I thought." Maddie hesitated. "You know it took a few days for me to get used to the idea of being engaged. But I've been praying about it and Connor's perfect, Mom. Our families have been friends all this time, which means he'll get me. Because we both have very big families."

Am I being punked? Brooke forced herself to listen. *Family this, family that.* And of course that was all she talked about. Because Maddie was right, that was exactly how they'd raised their girls.

God first, then family.

The waiter came to take their order. He couldn't keep his eyes off Maddie until she picked up the menu, when he seemed to see her engagement ring. When they finished giving him their orders, she smiled at him. "Thank you."

"Is that . . ." He pointed to her ring. "Are you engaged?"

She had never looked happier. "Yes. I'm getting married next summer."

He shrugged. "Had to ask." Then he grinned at them. "I'll get your iced tea. The salads will be right up."

When he was gone, Maddie leaned over the table. "He saw my ring!"

"Of course he did, sweetie." Brooke reached across the table and took hold of Maddie's hand. "Look at it."

For a long moment they marveled at the ring. The stone was a full carat, and the band was covered in a million tiny diamonds. She released her hand from her mom's and held it to her heart. "Connor saved for a year. Can you believe that? A whole year."

"He loves you."

"So anyway, Janessa will be a flower girl and Egan, Blaise and Johnny can be the ring bearers. Then Tommy, RJ and Devin can be ushers. That way the whole family's involved." She barely paused. "Also, Mom, I was thinking about Summer, my only cousin on Dad's side. She has a little girl who's what, three?"

"She does." Brooke studied her daughter. So thoughtful. Summer had been running from her family for years. Brooke chose her words carefully. "I wouldn't count on her, but she might come."

Their iced tea and salads arrived, and the waiter seemed to do his best not to flirt with Maddie. When he was gone, Brooke saw her chance. "Can I pray for us?"

Maddie's smile came straight from her heart. "Please, Mom."

She nodded. "Lord, thank You for this food. Thank You for Maddie's excitement and her desire to include family in her upcoming wedding." Brooke paused. "Family is everything to us, Father. It's a gift we treasure. Whether related by blood or not, we're one because of You and the people around us." She took a breath. "In Jesus' name, amen."

Before Maddie could say anything, Brooke studied her across the table. The way she talked and moved and laughed. All of it reminded Brooke of herself at that age. No matter her DNA, Maddie truly had been hers from the beginning.

Brooke could feel her expression grow more serious. "Honey . . . there's something I've been meaning to talk to you about."

Maddie winced. "Is it the cost?" She picked up her fork. "Because Connor and I talked about that." Her eyes met Brooke's. "We don't want you and Dad to spend a fortune on a six-hour party. People get crazy with weddings." She shook her head. "That's not us."

"Actually . . ." Brooke felt herself losing steam. "It wasn't about that, honey. We're not worried about the cost. We can . . . talk about that later."

"Okay. Thanks, Mom. Really . . . But still, we'll be careful." Maddie hesitated. "The way I acted the night he proposed?" Her smile became sheepish. "I've been wanting to talk to you about that, too." She took a slow breath. "Everything was happening so fast. Graduation and the party and then the proposal. I could barely feel my feet on the ground."

"And now?" This was actually something else Brooke had wanted to talk to her about. If she felt ready to marry Connor Flanigan. "How do you feel about him?"

Maddie's eyes turned dreamy. "He's the one. I mean he must be, right? I love him, Mom." She looked around the scenic restaurant and back to Brooke. "And this day . . . I've dreamed about it since I was little. The day you and I look for a wedding dress." She laughed. "I can't believe it's here."

Brooke blinked. "Yes, Maddie. Me, too." She felt her heart soften. Forget the truth. That could come later. When she and Peter were together with her. Brooke took a sip of her iced tea. "I've imagined this day forever." She searched her daughter's face. "I'm so excited for you, Maddie."

"Thank you!" Happy tears filled Maddie's eyes. "We better eat. I want lots of time to shop!"

The conversation shifted to color schemes and flowers and music. In no time Brooke was actually enjoying herself. Talk of Maddie's birth, long forgotten.

"But navy for a summer wedding might not work if it's in the daytime and . . ." Maddie took a quick breath. "Or maybe pale blue for summer because . . ."

Brooke took in every word. What had she been thinking earlier? Maddie was in the middle of the happiest time of her life. Of course she couldn't ruin a day like this one with that sort of news.

Before she finished her salad, Brooke made a plan. She and Peter could tell Maddie the truth after the holidays. Plenty of time before the wedding. Yes, that's what they would do. Brooke felt good about the new plan, and Peter would definitely be on board. What she refused to think about now or later when they looked at wedding dresses was how easy it had been to put off the truth.

One more time.

When Maddie absolutely deserved to know.

8

The sun had become Dawson's enemy, waking him every morning and reminding him all over again. She would never call, never spend a day with him out on the river. He would never hear her laugh.

His London was gone.

This Sunday was no different. Dawson blinked a few times and looked out the window at the gray sky. *The rain is back,* he thought. After church he needed to go through his planner and organize the week. A big deal was closing Monday and they had a remodel meeting for an aging building in their portfolio. They needed to rework their plan to find a high-end tenant for a space with pricey square footage on the waterfront.

And then it hit him.

None of that was going to happen—not this week. Because London had stepped out of her car without looking and now . . . this morning . . . they would attend her memorial service. After that they would drive to the cemetery to bury her.

Forever.

Dawson had no idea how he got ready and climbed in his truck and made it to London's funeral. Everything about the service was a blur. The dark suits and sunglasses, the flowers at the church she never attended, the hearse parked outside.

The pews were filled with her high school and college friends, along with family from Portland, Los Angeles and Ohio. Also a few girls she had danced with, and dozens of London Coffee regulars.

A pastor said a few words about life and the certainty of death. The fragility of time, and how the days were like sand. At least that's what Dawson heard. He wasn't really paying attention. Through it all, he kept his focus on a giant framed photo of London, eyes brimming with joy, smile brighter than the sun. She was holding her dog, Bingo. The golden retriever she had loved for the last eight years.

The perfect final picture of London Quinn.

Larry and Louise spoke next. They talked about how badly they had wanted a child and how London was the one they had believed for. They shared stories about London planting her baby doll in the backyard so it would grow into a baby doll plant, and how she had thought the Mojave desert was the Mo-Jave. With the *j* sound instead of the *h*. And how she videotaped herself singing Taylor Swift's "The Best Day" for Louise one Christmas. How she had rescued a litter of bunnies one spring and how she dreamed of feeding a giraffe someday.

People laughed and cried as they listened.

All Dawson could think was that ten minutes of stories weren't enough to tell them who London was, and why she was special. Or how desperately she would be missed.

Her parents would need a lifetime for that.

They moved from the church to the cemetery and a light rain began to fall. As if God, Himself, were weeping over the brokenness of the world and the way London's young life had been cut short.

With everything in him, Dawson tried not to think about the fact that God could've prevented the accident. That was true, but it wasn't at the same time. Earth was fallen. Broken. When his cousin in Maine lost her best friend to a drunk driver, Dawson was the first on the phone, first to help her through the loss.

"Life is like that here on earth. God isn't the reason things go wrong," Dawson had told her. "He's the rescue. The only way home."

They were words Dawson had told himself a hundred times since Wednesday.

London's parents had asked him if he wanted to say a few words at the service. Dawson passed. How could he sum up what he felt for London in a paragraph at church or a few lines at a graveside service? He didn't want to try.

The rain grew harder and the handful of people who had come for this part of the memorial moved their chairs under a tent near London's plot. Dawson stayed in the rain. The same pastor was talking about man being dust to dust.

Dawson tuned him out. How could they be here, burying London? Maybe it really was a nightmare and all Dawson needed was a way to wake up. A few tears mixed with the rain on his face and he lifted his eyes to the towering evergreens in the distance, the same kind that had lined the mountainside on his hike with London just a week ago.

One week.

That was the craziest thing. That morning her whole life had stretched out in front of her. A life with him, something that looked more likely than ever that day. Her breakup with the other guy. Her questions about faith.

Dawson wiped the water from his face. They were just on the brink.

He avoided looking at the hole in the earth. The pastor asked those in attendance to put a rose on the coffin before it was lowered into the ground. One last chance to give London a flower.

No way Dawson was going to miss that.

The spray of flowers between the chairs and the casket were almost entirely white roses. Only a few red ones made up the center. Dawson took one of those. He knew the difference. Red would always be the only right color for London.

Dawson moved to the edge of the hole where the casket was positioned on a contraption that would soon lower it into the earth. He stared at the dark mahogany and his eyes blurred. For a long moment he wasn't standing graveside saying goodbye to London.

He was on a bridge watching the falls at Multnomah. And the rain on his face wasn't from the gray sky overhead, it was mist off the tumbling water. And she was looking intently at the sight and her words were like music in the air.

Life feels like that sometimes. And she was tipping her face back toward the blue sky. *The hours and minutes keep slipping over the rocks and washing away in the river below. Time we can't get back.*

She was just there, in his grasp. Their shoulders touching. The faint smell of her shampoo and perfume consuming his senses. And she was taking his hand and leading him off the bridge up the hike and they were talking about eagles and their Grad Night Anniversary and the coffee shop. He closed his eyes and let the rain wash over him.

Her voice still rang in his ears and heart. He blinked and like a reflection in a puddle the memory vanished.

It was time.

He set the rose near the top of the coffin, away from the dozen or so white roses. Because the two of them were set apart, they'd been that way from the beginning. *Don't fall in love with me, Dawson. Don't fall in love with me.*

Once more he wiped the rain from his face, then he turned and walked back to Louise and Larry. He looked each of them deep in their eyes. "I'm sorry."

They nodded and took turns hugging Dawson. There was nothing more to say, so he continued across the soggy field to his truck.

With everything in him, Dawson wanted to run back and get her, take her out of that cold, wet, wooden box and bring her home. In case maybe this was a mistake and eventually she was going to be all right. The thought was irrational, but it hit him all the same. Not because it made sense.

But because this was the first time in all the years he'd known London that he'd ever left her behind.

• • •

DAWSON COULDN'T FIND Bingo.

The other family members had left Louise and Larry's house, and the afternoon was waning, but Dawson hadn't seen London's dog since they got there. He poured a cup of coffee and moved into the living room. The yellow-haired dog wasn't near the recliner or by the front door, or at the foot of the stairs. None of his usual spots.

"Bingo." Dawson did a few soft whistles. "Come here, boy!"

Larry was sitting in his recliner, staring out a window. "Check her closet. He's been staying there."

The news was one more punch. Dawson jogged up the stairs and opened the second door on the right. London's room. He stopped at the entrance and caught his breath. The place looked the same, as if London were only out running an errand and she'd be back any minute. Even though she'd moved into her own apartment years ago.

The air here still smelled like her. He walked to the closet and sure enough Bingo was there. Curled up near a pile of her clothes.

A sob welled up in Dawson's throat, but he stifled it. Nothing good could come from standing in her room crying. He needed to get them both out of here. "Come on, Bingo, come on, boy."

At first Bingo only stared at him, his eyes droopy with sadness. Like it would take physical force to move him from London's closet. But after a few tries, the dog struggled to his feet. He was comfortable around just the four of them—Louise, Larry, Dawson and of course, London. Her most of all. London might as well have been queen of the world for the way Bingo followed her around and stayed near her. Of course he was sleeping near her clothes.

Dawson wanted to do the same thing.

Bingo took his time and the two of them walked downstairs to the living room. Dawson found his coffee and took a spot at the end of the sofa. "Come on, Bingo." Dawson patted the floor next to his feet. "Right here. Come on, boy."

Bingo hesitated but eventually he came. With London's dog nestled up next to him, Dawson took a deep breath. There. Now the Quinn house felt a bit more normal.

Louise had taken the other recliner. No music played in the background, no television. Just the silent reality that the memorial was behind them. All that was left now was the getting back to life. The moving on. The getting up each morning and learning to walk with their new reality.

"I keep thinking of everything we did wrong." Louise gazed at London's high school senior portrait on an end table across the room. "We meant to take her to Vacation Bible School every summer when she was little. But we were always headed to the pool or the park." Regret rang in her voice. "So many things seemed . . . more important."

"She's in heaven, Louise." Larry's words were low, desperate sounding. "You heard her . . . those last few minutes."

Only then did Dawson realize something. Louise and Larry didn't know the details of her final day before the accident. He cleared his throat. "London's definitely with Jesus. I know she is."

Her parents turned to him, silent, waiting.

Dawson anchored his elbows on his knees. "I never told you about that day. Before she was hit."

Tears filled Louise's eyes and she folded her hands in her lap. "I've wanted to ask so many times." She looked at Larry. "We both have."

That was all Dawson needed to hear. He took a long breath and started with the hike, the beautiful day and the way London took in the views. "She told me the waterfall reminded her of time. How it kept going, tumbling over the rocks into the river below."

Louise dabbed her fingers beneath her eyes and smiled. "That sounds like her."

"She was always talking about time." Larry sniffed.

"Halfway up the trail she asked about my church service that morning." Dawson told them about John 16:33 and their conversation about having trouble in this world, and how Jesus had already overcome it.

"On the way back down the mountain, London told me she'd broken up with the guy she was dating." Dawson smiled. He could see it all again, the sunlight in her hair, her hands on the wheel. "We were listening to music and . . . she asked me to play my favorite church song."

Louise's quiet tears fell harder now. She was hanging on every word.

From there Dawson told the whole story. How he had played Jeremy Camp's song and how London had listened intently. "She told me she had questions. Questions she was going to ask at the ice cream shop. We were . . . were going to talk about faith. For the first time, really."

This was the hardest part of the story, how London had stepped out before checking for cars, and how the pickup truck had hit her. He spared them any actual details about the accident, but he picked up with his conversation with London later, on the sidewalk.

"She told me she had asked something of God." Dawson felt his throat tighten. He would remember those minutes with London forever. But they would never be easy to talk about. "She asked Him to give her Jesus. Like Jeremy Camp's song."

A small cry came from Louise and she brought her hand to her face. Sobs took over her ability to talk, but finally she managed. "That's . . . why she was talking about Jesus . . . at the end."

"Yes." Dawson sat back in the chair. His heart ached,

but his hope was genuine. "She's safe, Louise." He paused. "She's with Jesus. I know that."

The conversation moved from London's final days to her first. Amidst moments of quiet, either Louise or Larry would share whatever drifted to the top of their hearts. The way London loved animals and how she felt most free dancing for a crowd. How badly London had wanted a sister and how strange it was that she had talked about having one just before taking her last breath.

An idea began to take hold of Dawson. He wasn't sure if this was the right time, but he had to ask. "Louise, what if she really did have a sister?" He remembered the waiting room the night of the accident. "You said something Sunday night . . . about embryos."

"She shouldn't have." Larry glanced at his wife and then at Dawson. "We weren't supposed to say anything. Way back when it happened . . . that was the rule." He sighed. "For us and for the couple who received the embryos. If that even happened."

"We signed them over to a doctor here in Portland." Louise's voice was full of regret. "We let them go and never . . . never looked back."

London's strange statement had surfaced a few times in Dawson's mind since she passed. But now he actually wanted to know. If London had a sister, shouldn't they at least try to find her? Wouldn't she want to know her biological family and the sister . . . the sister that had just died?

Not only that, but Louise still needed a kidney. Maybe . . . if there really was a sibling out there, a brother or a sister or both, they might be a match. What if they would jump at the chance to help their biological mother?

"It's been nearly twenty-nine years." Dawson paused, looking for an immediate objection. There wasn't one. "Maybe if you just gave me the name of the doctor."

Louise and Larry looked at each other and then at Dawson.

And in that single hesitation, Dawson knew how he'd spend his next days.

9

Dawson's motivation was simple: Having a sibling mattered to London. Period.

The next morning Dawson made a cup of strong black coffee and set up in his home office. London's parents had given him the name of the doctor who cared for Louise during her pregnancy. Dr. Thom Ellis.

When Dawson left, Louise had hugged him. "Be careful." Uncertainty weighed in her tone. "If there is a sister . . . or siblings . . . they might not want to be found. Privacy was important to all of us back then."

Dawson needed to be clear. "But it was at your request, right?"

"It was." She had paused. "We didn't want any surprises while London was growing up." Her eyes found the floor for a long beat before she looked up again. "I'm afraid . . . we were wrong."

Dr. Ellis had been there when Louise had been hospitalized with high blood pressure before the delivery of London. Louise nearly lost her life. It was the reason she and Larry decided not to implant the remaining three embryos. Louise delivered at Oregon Health and Science University Hospital, so Dawson started there.

According to the OHSU Hospital website, Dr. Thom Ellis still worked there. His contact information was there for the taking. *That was fast,* Dawson thought. He opened a blank email on his computer and filled in the doctor's address at the top. For a while Dawson only stared at the screen.

What was he supposed to say, and what was his reason? He couldn't presume that a stranger would want to give Louise a kidney. But maybe . . . maybe the stranger would want to know that his or her biological mother was dying.

Yes, that was it!

Dawson jotted a quick letter explaining what had happened to London and that Louise's health was quickly deteriorating. He included his cell number. Then he called Larry and asked him to write Dr. Ellis as well. "I'll need your permission along the way." Dawson was sure of that much. "Maybe copy me on your letter, and give me permission to get the information."

Larry agreed, and half an hour later Dawson's phone rang.

The caller ID showed Portland. Dawson took the call as quickly as his fingers could move. "Hello?"

A moment of silence followed. "Dawson Gage?"

The man sounded sharp, serious. *Here we go.* "Yes, sir." Dawson opened a Word doc, put the phone on speaker and positioned his fingers over the keyboard.

"This is Dr. Thom Ellis." His pause felt heavy. "I've been expecting this conversation for more than twenty years. But I didn't expect the news about London. I'm so . . . so sorry. Please tell Louise and Larry."

"Thank you. I will." Dawson stayed strong. He needed to keep his attention on the matter at hand.

"Right after your email, I received a letter from the

Quinns. Because of their permission, I would like to share what I know."

The doctor explained how he had agreed with the Quinns that the embryos were the very beginning of life, and that they deserved a chance. Whatever that might look like. "To be honest, I forgot about them." The doctor sounded frustrated with himself. "More than five years later I met Dr. David Daniels at an Indianapolis conference on infertility. The man mentioned something about frozen embryos and embryo adoption being the next frontier for couples dealing with infertility. That's when I remembered."

Dawson took notes as quickly as he could type. Dr. Ellis apparently told the Indiana doctor that if the man could find a willing adoptive couple, the rights to the embryos would be signed over. Which is exactly what happened.

"The Quinns wanted privacy. So that was part of the paperwork." Dawson could hear the sound of papers crinkling. "I have the file right here."

Dr. Ellis went on to say that on June 22 of that year, he was notified by Dr. Daniels that he had identified an adoptive couple in Bloomington, Indiana, interested in the embryos. "My notes say they were both pediatricians."

The Portland doctor added that he had a lawyer handle the paperwork to transfer rights to the doctor in Indiana, and transportation was arranged through a private airline.

Every detail was fascinating to Dawson. He glanced at his notes. "Do you have the name of the couple?"

"No. That's all." Dr. Ellis took a slow breath. "Again, please tell Louise and Larry I'm so sorry about their loss.

And about her health."

Dawson promised to do that. He thanked the doctor and even before the call ended he was googling husband-wife pediatric teams in Bloomington, Indiana.

The first result read: *Dr. Peter West and Dr. Brooke Baxter West. West Pediatric Clinic in downtown Bloomington.*

The air in his office felt suddenly thin. Dawson laced his fingers together and put them behind his head. Was this it? Had he so easily found the couple who twenty-some years ago received Larry and Louise's embryos? His heart tripped along at double time. He jotted the couple's names into his notes and did another search.

Dr. Peter West and Dr. Brooke Baxter West children.

Four links down was a press release. LATEST ZOO HIRE HAS LOCAL MEDICAL TIES. Dawson's hands shook as he clicked the story. Up popped a brief article about Maddie West, twenty-two, daughter of Drs. Peter and Brooke West. It talked about Maddie having a sister, Hayley. And that Maddie would start work at the zoo this week.

Dawson read the words again and a third time.

Maddie West. Age twenty-two. Which meant it was possible she was the sister London had talked about, however she might've known. Maybe Hayley, as well. There was no picture with the article, but finding one would probably be easy.

A quick look on Instagram and there she was, Maddie West. Her account was private, but according to the small profile pic she had blond hair. At first glance he couldn't see the resemblance between her and London. A check of Facebook and Twitter turned up nothing. *Smart girl,* he thought. *Careful about her social media presence.*

Dawson knew what he had to do. He called up Delta

and booked a next-day flight from Portland to Indianapolis. He'd exhausted his Internet search, but had he actually found London's siblings? In a single morning? Dawson thought about his flight tomorrow.

Now there was only one way to find out.

• • •

MADDIE'S THIRD DAY at the Indianapolis Zoo had started out much better than the first two. On Monday during orientation in the primate exhibit, a monkey had swung low and dropped a branch on her head.

"Part of the job," her boss had told her. The boss was Ms. Anna Barber, a straight-edged woman in her forties. Short gray hair and sturdy legs. "Stay away from the fly zones." The woman pointed at the rope hanging from the tallest tree sections. She rolled her eyes at Maddie. As if that was the most obvious thing. "Fly zones are always littered with branches."

"Yes, ma'am. Thank you." Maddie had rubbed her scalp and kept her tone polite. If only Ms. Barber had told Maddie that at the beginning.

Day two hadn't been much better. Ms. Barber had asked her to move a three-foot dwarf boa constrictor to a plastic box so his cage could be cleaned. Despite two summers of interning for the zoo and years of volunteering at a veterinarian clinic in Texas, Maddie had never held a boa. She stared at the snake. *Not too threatening,* she'd thought.

But the moment she picked it up, the snake bit the palm of her hand. Maddie had screamed and dropped the reptile into the box. The boa was fine, but Maddie was bleeding from more than twenty small holes in two C-shaped rows. Some soap, hand sanitizer and a bandage and Maddie was back to work.

She was definitely hoping today would be better.

Her first assignment that day was at the kangaroo enclosure. Visitors were allowed to take their time crossing the exhibit along a meandering path. Maddie would answer questions and have access to a bin of kangaroo kibble. Food was the best way to encourage kangaroos to stay off the walkway.

She was working with Ms. Barber today, learning the sometimes unpredictable nature of a contact exhibit. They'd been at it for an hour and already the zoo was busy. With sunshine and seventies in the forecast and school out, the exhibit would be crowded till closing.

During a lull in the action, Maddie's boss stood next to her, arms crossed. "I noticed the diamond on your left hand." She looked at Maddie's ring. "You engaged?"

"I am." Maddie smiled. Maybe she and Ms. Barber would be friends one day. "Getting married next summer."

"Well . . . good for you." The woman rolled her eyes again. "Not me. I'm single. Gonna stay that way." She released a long breath. "Of course . . . I thought about getting married when I was in my twenties. Just like you." She shook her head. Her sarcasm was abrasive. "Thought I'd found Prince Charming."

Maddie wasn't sure what to say. "It . . . didn't work?"

"You could say that." She cocked her head. "More like I finally woke up. Decided I didn't need a man telling me what to do and sharing my bathroom sink." A smile tugged at her lips. "I'm happier by myself. Do what I want, when I want." She nodded. "Very happy."

Maddie stared at her boss. She did look genuinely joyful.

A pair of small kangaroos eased onto the cement a few feet away. Maddie was glad for the distraction. Enough of Ms. Barber's views on marriage.

But her boss continued. "My only advice is this: Take your time." She shrugged. "Marriage is for life, right? Why the rush?"

Maddie wasn't sure what to say. How was she getting marital advice from her zoo boss? Also, with a full year engagement, Maddie didn't feel like she and Connor were rushing anything. The whole conversation was making Maddie feel a little sick.

"I mean . . . have you really thought this over?" Her boss wasn't giving up. "Forever's a long time." She took kibble from the can and used it to bribe the kangaroos back onto the grass. Ms. Barber turned to Maddie again. "Two years at least. That's how long I'd wait. That's nothing."

A family with four small children entered the exhibit. Maddie felt like she could breathe again. She made a mental note not to talk wedding plans with Ms. Barber. Not ever. Maddie approached the family. "Welcome!"

"Thanks." The mom was pretty with red hair and green eyes. "Is it safe? Bringing the kids in?"

"Absolutely." Maddie had memorized the answer to every question. She'd also read everything she could about the red kangaroo, the type in this exhibit. In the distance she saw Ms. Barber watching. Maddie moved closer to the mother. "These kangaroos are docile and friendly. We do ask that you stay on the path, though."

Two of the family's children had questions about the kangaroos' diet and sleep behavior. "Where are their beds?"

the boy asked. He was maybe six or seven.

Maddie smiled. "Kangaroos sleep on the grass. They do have favorite spots, though." She pointed out a few of the areas where the animals most liked to bed down.

Before the family left, two more groups entered. Ms. Barber stepped in to help and two hours went by until they had another lull.

Ms. Barber looked at her phone. "I have a meeting in the administrative office for the next half hour. You're doing fine." She saluted Maddie. "I'll be back around one."

Her approval made Maddie stand a little straighter. That had to be a good sign, being left alone in the exhibit. She counted the kangaroos in the space. Of the fourteen, all were small except two males, and they mostly stayed in separate areas.

Suddenly a low roar filled the air around them. Maddie walked toward the front of the kangaroo enclosure. Across the path were the lions. Something must've stirred up the big cats because the male was pacing along the front of his area, as close as he could get to the deep moat and stem wall separating him from the public.

The roar was getting louder, the lion clearly more irritated. Drawn by the sound, people hurried closer from all directions. Maddie glanced over her shoulder. All was still well in her area. But when she looked back toward the lion, something caught her eye.

To the left of the lions were the giraffes. And just in front of the rock wall of that exhibit stood a guy.

A guy looking straight at her.

As soon as they made eye contact he looked away. He held a notepad or sketchbook and he wore a hiker's-style backpack. Without glancing at her again, he walked toward the crowd. Lions didn't roar like this very often. The sound was loud enough that everyone at the zoo had to have heard it by now.

Maddie kept her eyes on the man. He wasn't trying to get a front-row view like everyone else. He took a seat on a bench a dozen yards back and watched from there. Then he opened his book and started to write. Or maybe he was drawing the lion.

That had to be it. She studied him. He must be an artist, searching for inspiration. Which was why he was probably looking toward the kangaroo exhibit. Hoping for something to sketch.

The lion was calming down, and the crowd began to break up. Three families walked toward the kangaroos and Maddie moved back to the center of the space.

When Ms. Barber finally returned, Maddie had almost forgotten about the artist—or whatever he was—until she had the strangest feeling.

Like someone was watching her.

She looked across the way, and once more she caught the guy staring at her. He didn't seem scary, but why was he looking at her? If he wanted to see kangaroos he should come through the exhibit.

As soon as he was caught, the man turned away again, put his book and what looked like a pencil case into his bag, and he walked the opposite way, back toward the giraffes.

Maddie watched him go. The guy was tall with strong shoulders. Dark hair, handsome features. Something about him looked familiar. She kept track of him till he moved out of sight. Where did she know him from? High school? Or maybe here at the zoo. If he was a member she'd probably seen him during one of her summers here.

But why was he watching her?

Good-looking or not, the guy seemed a little creepy. She didn't notice him for the rest of her shift. Not till she was leaving the zoo, headed out to her car. Like normal, her walk to the exit took her past the flamingos.

And there he was. Not far from the pink birds, he sat on a bench, sketchbook open. But he wasn't watching the flamingos. He was looking for her. Waiting for her. As if he had known she'd have to walk this way when she finished work.

This time he didn't look away. He locked eyes with her and started to stand. Immediately Maddie knew she hadn't seen him before. The guy was a stranger and he was staring straight at her.

Fear hit her square in the heart. *Dear God, who is he? What does he want from me?* She did an about-face and moved faster than before. There were a dozen ways out of the zoo. Maddie could get to her car before he could figure out which way she was going.

Unless he knew what car she drove.

Calm down, she told herself. The guy was probably harmless. Just here sketching animals and birds. He maybe thought she was pretty, nothing more. Even still her breathing came faster. She kept checking over her shoulder in case he was following her.

When she reached the parking lot, Maddie looked around again. No sign of him. *Good. Thank You, Lord.* She slowed her pace. By the time she was locked in behind the wheel of her car, she felt more in control. There had been no reason to panic. What was the guy going to do to her in full daylight at the zoo?

No matter how handsome the stranger was, Maddie knew one thing for sure. She wouldn't tolerate another day of being stared at. If he came back, she would tell Ms. Barber and her boss would call the authorities. Maddie relaxed against the headrest. Yes, Ms. Barber would make short work of the guy. Forget the zoo security, she'd call the Indianapolis Police and the man would be escorted forever off the zoo property, sketchbook and all.

Probably in handcuffs.

10

The annual fundraiser for the Bloomington Crisis Pregnancy Center was under way at Bryan Park, and Brooke was handing out ice-cream cones as fast as she could make them. Her sister Ashley worked beside her, while their husbands grilled hot dogs on the other side of the picnic area.

The event drew nearly fifty volunteers and it had long ago become a Baxter family tradition. Mid-seventies and pure sunshine made this the perfect day for the event. Even her dad and Elaine were here somewhere, probably manning the bouncy house with the youngest grandkids or helping with the face-painting booth like last year.

People from all over the community typically joined the fundraiser, and nearly every church in Bloomington chipped in one way or another. Bryan Park acted as a bustling hub for area families. Expansive ball fields, forever green grass, and the most beautiful sugar maple trees. This year, local businesses had donated double the cost of the event to create a windfall for the clinic.

"We need more chocolate chip cookie dough." Ashley blew at a wisp of her dark hair. "When do we get backup?"

"Soon, I hope." Brooke laughed. "Kari and Ryan should be here in half an hour."

"I thought so." Ashley dug her scooper into the chocolate ice cream. She looked at the little girl in front of her. "Nuts or sprinkles?"

And so it went without a break.

Brooke couldn't have been happier about it. Every year the fundraiser had seen more people come by for free food, games and health checkups. The community knew by now that the crisis pregnancy center did more than ultrasounds. They screened for cancer and disease and counseled women on family planning. Word was out that the clinic Brooke and Ashley ran was a safe place for women of all ages—no matter their situations.

Downtown Delight had donated the ice cream, and as Brooke and Ashley worked, the owner of the shop brought new tubs of three different flavors. "That's all we have." He wiped his forehead with the back of his hand. "Perfect day for a waffle cone."

"Definitely." Brooke smiled at the man. "Thanks again. You and your staff."

"Happy to help!" The man waved and headed for the parking lot.

Brooke grinned at Ashley. "All this ice cream makes me remember the first year we lived here." She thought for a few seconds. "You were in fifth grade."

"The infamous ice cream social disaster?" Ashley ran her scooper through the mint chip and filled a cone. "Ah, yes. I drop a whole bowl on my teacher's head a few days before school starts and . . . well, it'll be my claim to fame for always. Even if I live to be a hundred."

"You're probably right." Brooke laughed as she put two scoops of vanilla in a bowl, topped it with chocolate sauce and handed it to a small boy. She stole a glance at Ashley. "I mean, you slipped? Is that what happened?"

"I did." She shrugged. "Stepped on a napkin or something. Next thing I know Mr. Garrett is wearing my ice cream like a hat."

The laughter felt good. This night was a diversion for Brooke. A few happy hours where she didn't have to think about her daughter getting married or the truth she and Peter still hadn't told her. Brooke caught her breath. "What did your teacher say? I can't remember."

Now Ashley was laughing, too. "I believe he said . . . that particular shade of ice cream didn't match his shirt. And he stood and slowly left the building."

Kari and Ryan showed up then and the two teams swapped duties. Kari pointed to the ball field on the other side of a grove of trees. "You need to watch the kickball game. Dad's referee." She slipped a pair of plastic gloves onto her hands. "He's in his element!"

The game was another part of the tradition. The older Baxter cousins would form two teams—welcoming any community kids who wanted to play. As they walked away from the ice cream table, Brooke stretched to one side, then the other. "That scooping business is harder than it looks."

"Definitely." Ashley bent over and touched her toes. When she stood she nodded toward the field. "Let's go."

As they walked, Ashley talked about how Cole had completed his first year at Liberty University and how the other three were excited he was home for the summer. "Being together is the best." Ashley grinned at her. "It's that way for all our kids."

Brooke felt a familiar pang of regret settle in her gut. The one she had felt so often since Maddie's graduation, every time someone mentioned family. Maybe she was worrying about nothing. Maybe Peter was right. "Family goes beyond blood," he'd told her last night.

With all her heart, Brooke hoped he was right.

They kept walking, and Ashley described her newest painting. "Children playing in the foreground here at Bryan Park, parents watching nearby, as if they have all the time in the world to be together."

"Mmm." Brooke could picture it.

Ashley took a breath. "But in the far distance, stands a sweet country cemetery." Ashley lifted her eyes to the sky. "Because time is a thief." She paused. "It never stops."

Suddenly all Brooke wanted was to tell her sister about Maddie, about the lie that had been building and growing since her daughter was born. Maybe Ashley would know what to do, how to best break the news to Maddie and how to stave off any damage. After all, Ashley had been through her share of heartache.

She was one of the best listeners in the family.

They reached the field, where one team was scattered around the bases and out in the far grass, and the other was taking turns kicking the ball. Everyone on both teams was cheering. Brooke smiled when she spotted her dad. "Look at him." She pointed down the first base line. "Dr. John Baxter at his finest."

Their dad wore a bright red shirt, silver whistle around his neck. "That's two outs!" He held up two fingers. "Two outs, bottom of the third."

Dad's wife, Elaine, must've been at the face-painting booth, because she wasn't in the stands. Brooke and Ashley found seats near the top of the bleachers. A quick look to the outfield and Ashley seemed to find her son, anchored back in deep center. "I can't believe he's already finished a year of college. Seems like I was just wiping my tears as he drove off."

"Wait till he graduates. Happens in a blink." Brooke spotted her daughter playing third base. She and Cole had always been close. "Most days I can't believe Maddie's getting married."

Down on the field, Luke and his wife, Reagan, were coaching opposite teams, which only added to the merriment. Brooke and Ashley watched for a moment in silence. Was this the time to tell her sister? Brooke looked around. No one was sitting near them, and the game wasn't half over.

She took a deep breath. "Can I tell you something, Ash?"

It was too late in the afternoon for sunglasses, so when Ashley turned to her it was easy to see her eyes. The genuine love there. "Of course."

My sister has no idea what's coming, Brooke thought. She gripped her knees and rubbed her palms on her jeans. "Peter and I . . . we've kept a secret from the family." Her voice felt shaky. "For more than twenty years."

Ashley faced Brooke. "What?" She waited. "Is this . . . are you serious?"

"I am." Brooke held her breath.

"Okay." Ashley seemed to gather herself. "What . . . what sort of secret?"

"About Maddie." She met Ashley's eyes again. "No one knows this." Brooke hesitated. "It's just, ever since she graduated I keep thinking we have to move past it."

"Is she sick?" Ashley lowered her brow.

Brooke shook her head. "No." She gazed at her daughter out on the field. "But she might be when she finds out."

Ashley didn't look away. "I'm here, Brooke. If you want to talk. The lie, whatever it is. Now or later, if that works better."

"Thanks." Brooke wasn't sure anymore. How could she voice the words? Maddie was adopted? Ashley would think she was crazy. The whole family had been at the hospital for her birth. "I don't know where to begin."

Luke's son, Tommy, was up next. Brooke and Ashley watched him take his place behind home plate. Tommy was seventeen now, about to start his senior year in high school. He was tall and blond, the exact image of their brother, Luke.

Kari and Ryan's oldest, Jessie, was pitching. She rolled the ball with a little too much bounce and Dad blew the whistle. "Ball one! Keep it on the ground, Jessie girl."

Everyone in the outfield clapped. "You got this, Jessie!" someone called out.

Brooke looked at the trees beyond the park. Would Maddie still feel part of the family once she knew the truth? Finally she turned to Ashley. "It happened a long time ago . . ."

Her sister turned to her again and their eyes held. "Whatever it is, we'll get through it."

She won't believe it. Brooke exhaled. There was no easy way to say it, no words that could soften the truth. "Maddie . . . Maddie is adopted."

More cheering came from the field. "What?" Ashley leaned closer. "It sounded like you said Maddie . . . was adopted."

A feeling of doom washed over Brooke. If this was Ashley's response, she could only imagine the terrible day when they would tell their daughter. Brooke nodded. "Yes.

That's what I said." She kept her attention on Ashley. "Maddie is adopted."

"No." A half smile lifted Ashley's lips. "Brooke, that's impossible. I was there at the hospital when she was born."

This was why Brooke hadn't said anything sooner. "I know." She took a water bottle from her bag and twisted off the lid. "It's a long story."

"Okay . . . but first it has to be possible." Ashley pulled water from her purse, too. She drank half the bottle before she looked at Brooke again. "Maddie wasn't adopted, Brooke. You gave birth to her."

"It was brand-new technology." This was the first of many times Brooke would have to explain the story. She tried to be as clear as possible. "We'd been married several years and we couldn't get pregnant." She looked out at the field again. "We didn't tell anyone that, either."

"Brooke." Ashley did a slight shake of her head. "I'm so . . . sorry."

"We should've said something. Back then we didn't really believe in God or prayer. We . . . didn't think it would matter if people knew or not." Brooke looked down for a few seconds, then back at Ashley. "You didn't believe back then, either."

"True." She waited. "So what happened?"

"A doctor told us about three embryos. Donated from a couple in Portland. They'd been frozen in a canister somewhere for six years by then."

"Frozen . . ." Ashley's eyes grew wide. "You're serious?"

"Yes." Brooke gritted her teeth. "We agreed for the embryos to be implanted in me. It's called embryo adoption and today . . . well, today it's more common. Back then there were only a few cases in all the world."

"This . . . Brooke, this is crazy." Ashley ran her fingers through her hair. "Like science fiction."

"Believe me. It's real." Brooke glanced at the field in time to see Kari's son, RJ, kick the ball down the third base line deep into the outfield. His team shouted for him to run home. Which he did.

Brooke looked at Ashley again. "Anyway."

"I can't . . ." Ashley looked dizzy. "I don't believe it."

"We didn't know what would happen." Memories of that time flooded Brooke's mind. "We even wondered if she might have been ours."

"Maybe she is." Ashley sounded almost desperate.

"She's not." Brooke paused. "Because of our unusual case, the doctor did a DNA test."

Ashley put her elbows on her knees and folded her hands. For a long moment she hung her head as if she didn't have any words, or she couldn't comprehend the news. Finally she sat up straight again and turned to Brooke. "You said . . . no one knows." Ashley's face was pale. "You mean outside your family?" She hesitated. "Maddie knows, right?"

The weight of this felt like boulders strapped to Brooke's back. She shook her head. "That's what I'm saying, Ash." Tears sprang to her eyes. "Maddie doesn't know."

"You mean . . . all this time, and you didn't . . . you haven't told her she's adopted?"

Brooke looked to the sky and then back to Ashley. "No." The weight grew heavier. "We never did." She felt tears building in her heart, but her eyes stayed dry. "We always meant to. But every time . . . something got in the . . ." The excuse felt too pathetic to finish. She hung her head.

It took a while for Ashley to respond. "I think . . . think Maddie will understand." Ashley's voice was tight, like she was trying not to cry. "She was born from you, Brooke. That has to . . . it has to mean something."

A flicker of hope flashed across Brooke's heart. "Really?" She squinted. "You think so?"

Ashley reached out and took hold of Brooke's hand. "The news won't change anything." She winced. "I do wish you would've told her sooner."

"Yeah." Brooke was terrified of Maddie's reaction. "Me, too."

"But she's still yours. Your daughter." Ashley still had hold of Brooke's hand. "I really think Maddie is going to be okay."

They both turned their attention to Brooke's oldest. She was up to kick and she waved at the outfield. "Back it up!" Her laugh filled the air. "You know how we Baxters kick!"

Ashley slid closer and put her arm around Brooke's shoulders. "Hear that, girl? Brooke, she's going to be fine."

Maddie's singsong laugh was one of Brooke's favorite sounds. But what about after she learned the truth? They watched Maddie kick the ball straight up in the air. Tommy had no trouble catching it, but after he threw the ball to the pitcher, he clapped for his cousin. "Still a good old-fashioned Baxter kick!"

Brooke closed her eyes for a long moment. All she could hear were Maddie's words. *We Baxters.* Maddie had never doubted for one day that she was a Baxter.

Sure, she was a West, too. But Peter's parents lived far away and his only brother never came around. So these days

Peter thought of himself as a Baxter. And of course that's how Maddie felt. She was proud of the fact. Which meant no matter what Ashley said, Brooke's greatest fears were about to be realized.

Maddie was going to hate them.

11

He had found her.

Dawson had found London's sister. He was sure about it. Maddie West was a breathtaking blond replica of London. She moved like her and stood like her. Dawson could only imagine how the girl might talk like her. Even laugh like her.

All of which raised a handful of urgent questions. What was he supposed to do next? How could he approach her about something that happened before she was born? What if she didn't want to know about her biological parents? And the biggest question, of course.

Why was he really here?

The answers evaded him. For his second day at the Indianapolis Zoo, Dawson set up camp at the rhinos. Far enough away from the lions and kangaroos that Maddie wouldn't see him. Because he was pretty sure she'd be looking. At least twice yesterday she had caught him watching her and by the end of the day when she turned and practically sprinted the other direction, one thing was clear.

Maddie was afraid of him.

So today he had to be careful. Dawson found an empty bench, pulled the sketchbook from his bag, and stared at his giraffe drawing from the day before. He chuckled. The animal had squatty legs and a too-thick neck. Huge eyes. Sort of a squashed giraffe. This was why his dad hired architects to handle their blueprints. *Come on, Dawson, what are you doing? No drawing rhinos today.* He had to make a plan.

A family with six kids walked past him and up to the front of the rhino area. "Mommy!" The littlest girl was maybe five years old. She looked up. "I want to work at the zoo when I'm older."

And suddenly the words didn't belong to the child. They belonged to London, the year after they graduated from high school. She had already made it clear to him that she didn't want to date, didn't want him falling in love with her. But nothing could stop their friendship. That July morning had been chilly, and the outing, London's idea. A day at the zoo.

Dawson had been a few times with his mom, back when he was just a kid. But not for a long time. Where London was concerned, it didn't matter what she suggested, the day ended up unforgettable.

That Tuesday at the Oregon Zoo was no exception.

They wore sweatshirts and jeans and from the moment they walked through the front gates, London was giddy. They saw monkeys first that day, three of them swinging through the trees, chasing each other.

"Those are spider monkeys." London stopped at the railing—as close as she could get. She turned to him, those amber eyes. "Did I ever tell you, Dawson? My dream growing up?"

Even now he remembered the way his heart pounded in his chest from the closeness of her. He smiled. "Which one?"

"The zoo!" She looked at the monkeys again. "I always wanted to work at the zoo!"

Her exuberance had been childlike and all Dawson could think was there never would have been a more beautiful zoo worker. But he kept his thoughts to himself, the way he usually did.

Instead he had grinned, playing along. "It's not too late."

"It is." Her shoulders slumped a little. "I have a plan now. It's fine." She sighed and found his eyes again. "I dance . . . and I help at the coffee shop. But I would've been good at zoo work, Dawson. You know that."

"Yes." He had laughed. "You would've been the best."

Dawson blinked and the memory vanished like April snow. Every shared moment with London was a treasure now, locked away deep in his heart like so many diamonds. Every now and then when he wanted London more than his next breath, Dawson would lift up one of those gems and marvel at it, turn it around in his mind and relive it.

So he could have one more minute with her.

And now . . . now he had found a surreal blond version of her. Younger, but so much the same. The article had mentioned a sibling. Hayley. Was she London's sister, too?

A gentle wind played in the trees near the exhibit. This part of the zoo was less crowded. More space to think. He narrowed his eyes and drew a deep breath. So what was his next step? He couldn't just walk up to her. *Hi. You don't know me but I was best friends with your sister in Portland.*

No. He sighed. That would never do.

Or maybe it would.

Dawson shifted on the bench and remembered the

girl, the way she looked talking to visitors in the kangaroo enclosure. Maddie West. Certainly Dawson wasn't going home without talking to her. Which meant at some point he'd have to approach her. Right? He could walk up to her, introduce himself and laugh a little. Something to set her at ease.

And then he'd tell her the truth about why he was there. Yes, he could do that. Nothing strange about conveying news to someone. Maddie might want to know about her biological parents. His thoughts picked up speed. *I'd want to know. If I were in her place. Not like her life has to change over this. It's just news. Important, very sad news.*

News Maddie deserved to hear.

The wind picked up and Dawson lifted his eyes to the gray sky overhead. *What am I doing here, Lord?* The question wasn't one he wanted to answer. On the face it made sense. He had come here to tell Maddie West that she might have a biological family in Oregon, and if that was true . . . then she needed to know about her sister.

But did he have other reasons? Was the search about finding someone like London? Maddie looked so much like her and she—

Enough. He took his phone from his backpack and dialed Louise. She would have something to say about the situation. One ring, two. Three. The call went to her voicemail and Dawson hung up. None of this could be summarized in a message. Besides, it didn't matter what Louise said or thought or what advice she might give.

An urgency came over him. What was he waiting for? He slid his things back into the bag and stood. He was going to talk to her.

Then he could fly home and get on with his life.

• • •

STORM CLOUDS COVERED Indianapolis that afternoon, a precursor to the severe weather forecast for later. Maddie was glad for the change. The kangaroos were more active when rain was in the air. She'd been hand-feeding them pellets for the past hour trying to keep the visitor path clear.

"Okay, Joey, come on." Maddie patted the head of the smallest kangaroo. She held out a handful of food and led the baby off the walkway. "There you go. Good boy."

Her boss must've decided Maddie could handle the work, because she was alone in the enclosure today. Not that it was busy. Only three visitors had walked through the exhibit since lunchtime.

Maddie turned to the wash station and cleaned her hands. As she did she heard the gate of the exhibit open. *Good,* she thought. Patrons made the time go by faster. She turned back toward the fenced-in grassy field. Only instead of a couple or a mom and dad with kids, it was him.

The stranger from yesterday.

Maddie took a step back. He was still fifteen yards off, but he was looking her way. Straight at her. She glanced around. If he threatened her she would run out the back gate and scream for help. He couldn't do anything to her here. Not out in the open like this.

Why are you afraid? she asked herself. Determination welled up. She didn't have to be nervous. Maybe the guy only wanted to know about kangaroos. He was getting closer, walking up the winding path toward her. Maddie held her ground. As she did she sucked in a soft breath.

Wow. The guy was gorgeous. Tall, broad shoulders and short dark hair. Deep blue eyes, eyes that held hers so completely she almost looked away.

"Hey." He stopped a few feet from her and smiled. "I . . . I wanted to apologize if I scared you yesterday."

Maddie felt her shoulders relax. Maybe he wasn't a creeper. Still . . . She took a half step back. "I thought you were—"

"Following you?" The stranger slid one hand into his jeans pocket and shook his head. "I know. I was worried you'd think that."

His kindness caught her off guard. There was an easiness about him, despite his obvious strength. Maddie let her attention fall to his sketchbook. She nodded at it. "You're . . . an artist?"

"Sort of." He slipped the book into his backpack, and slung it over his shoulder again. "I'm . . . studying animal behavior for a report I'm writing." He looked at her again. "So yeah, I've been doing a little sketching and—" He stopped short and held out his hand. "I'm Dawson Gage. Again . . . so sorry. I didn't mean to scare you."

The moment her fingers were in his a chill ran through her. She shook his hand. "Maddie West." She cleared her throat. What was this crazy attraction? Like she'd known him all her life. She pulled away and folded her arms. Why did the stranger have such an effect on her? "Thanks . . . for the explanation."

"Definitely." He chuckled once. "I couldn't finish my work today and not tell you."

"Right." She narrowed her eyes. "So yesterday . . . you were interested in the kangaroos?"

"Yeah. I mean . . ." He glanced down for a moment and

his cheeks grew a shade redder. "I guess . . . it's just . . ." The guy was definitely struggling. "Okay. Here it is." He held his hands out to the sides. "You're really pretty, Maddie. I wanted to meet you, but I never worked up the courage." He hesitated, his eyes on hers again. "Until now."

The stranger thought she was pretty! Maddie started to smile but then she remembered Connor. Her fiancé! What was she supposed to say? She fiddled with her engagement ring. "Uh . . . thanks." She uttered an awkward laugh. "I'm . . . engaged." She held up her hand. "Thought I should get that out there."

"Oh." Disappointment darkened his face, but he rebounded fast. "Of course you are." Both hands were in his pockets now. "Sorry." He pointed to the exit. "So . . . I guess I'll be going." A sheepish grin flashed on his handsome face. "Had to try." Once more his eyes held hers. Respect marked his expression, but his interest hadn't lessened. That much was clear. He gave a slight nod. "Nice meeting you, Maddie."

Before she could say anything he turned and sauntered toward the bottom of the path and the exit. Outside the exhibit, he turned right toward the lions and after a minute he slipped out of view.

Maddie felt flushed and her heart beat faster than before. Part of her wanted to call out to him, talk to him a bit longer, find out more about his report. More about him, whoever he was.

This Dawson Gage.

Maddie squeezed her eyes shut. What was she thinking? She was in love with Connor Flanigan. Some stranger couldn't turn her head. She exhaled. Everything was fine. The whole moment had been so sudden, that was all. Just fear and relief coming together in an encounter she hadn't expected.

Yes, that had to be it.

The rest of her shift passed quickly and her boss arrived to take her place. She left the kangaroo enclosure and looked both ways. Like she expected to see the stranger again. But he wasn't on any of the benches near her exhibit. She walked toward the parking lot. Just as well.

She was practically a married woman. No reason to be looking around for a handsome stranger she'd only just met. But when she passed the flamingos she heard her name and turned.

He was on a bench near the lemurs and as she stopped, he stood and came to her. This time he didn't saunter and his expression seemed more intense. What was so serious?

Never mind how handsome he was. She loved Connor with all her being. She would tell this Dawson Gage there wasn't a chance, and that would be that. He could stop chasing her around and go back to wherever he came from.

The distance between them closed and he set his backpack on the ground. "Maddie."

She held her purse tight to her body. "I'm sorry." She shook her head. "I told you . . . I'm engaged to a guy I love. Very much."

He searched her eyes. "I . . . I don't want to ask you out. There's something else." Whatever he wanted to say, he must've thought about it since their meeting earlier. "I have information for you."

Maddie started to turn around. Maybe the guy *was* a stalker. No one ever said a bad guy couldn't be handsome and charming. "I have to go. My fiancé is expecting me and—"

"Wait. Please." He took a step closer. "Don't go. Hear me out."

Maybe if she gave him a chance to speak his mind, he'd leave her alone. "Fine." She wasn't smiling. "Tell me."

His expression softened. "I lied to you earlier. I'm sorry."

She looked around but they were alone on this part of the path. As if the zoo were deserted except for the two of them. "About what?"

He didn't break eye contact. "I'm not here doing a report." His words were slow, deliberate. "Maddie, I'm a developer from Portland, Oregon. I came to Indiana looking for you."

Her head started to spin. He was going to kidnap her, threaten her family and take her back to his home. And then who knew what he'd do to her. Again she backed away. She could still run. Race down the path until she found someone, anyone who would help her.

But he took a step closer. "The news, Maddie . . . it's about your biological family."

A few seconds passed while his words registered. She faced him. "Biological?"

"Yes." Now he seemed in a hurry to get the details out. "Your biological parents are good friends of mine. Their daughter is . . . was one of my best friends."

Maddie shook her head. She felt the hint of a sympathetic smile lift her lips. "I'm sorry, Dawson." Poor guy had wasted all this time looking for her and now he had the wrong girl. "My family lives here." She hesitated. "You must be looking for someone else."

Without saying a word, Dawson pulled a slip of paper from the pocket of his backpack. "Here. It's my number."

She shook her head. "I can't help you. Whoever you're looking for, I don't know her."

"Maddie . . . I'm looking for you. Maddie West. Bloomington, Indiana. Daughter of Doctors Peter and Brooke Baxter West. Your biological family lives in Portland. Near me." He exhaled, clearly discouraged. The piece of paper was still in his outstretched hand. "I thought you'd want to know about your sister. That's all."

Anger rippled through her. "What do you know about my sister?" She'd had enough of the stranger and his crazy words.

"I loved her." His words rang with passion, conviction. "Not Hayley." He took a slow breath. "London. Your biological sister."

"What?" How did he know where she lived? Or her parents' names? How did he know about Hayley? Maddie's knees began to shake. What did he mean, *her biological family*? Who was this London girl?

Maddie's hands trembled. The nerve of this stranger to say these things. "I'm not adopted. Don't you think I'd know?" Her words sounded fierce. She started to turn again. "I have to leave."

"Here." He held the paper out again. "Just take it." He paused. "That way you can call me. If you ever want to talk."

Maybe it was Dawson's sincerity or maybe her curiosity over how the guy could've confused her with whoever he was looking for. Whatever in that instant compelled her, Maddie stopped and took his number. "I need to go. You have the wrong person." She was a few yards away from him now. "Don't come after me again."

"Wait." He called after her. "Maddie, I'm telling you the truth. I promise."

Before she could scream or break into a full sprint, she glanced back and felt the slightest relief. He wasn't coming after her. Maybe he was biding his time or making a plan for another day. But he wouldn't trick her into talking to him or going anywhere with him.

Clearly he knew who she was, where she lived and her parents' names. He even knew about Hayley. Maybe he didn't have her confused with someone else. This might just be his way of stalking her, so she'd spend more time with him.

Fear pushed her faster toward her car. The nerve. Telling her she was adopted. Of all things. She looked back several times on her way to the parking lot, but the guy wasn't chasing her. He was nowhere in sight.

Good. *Thank You, God.* She climbed into her car, threw the piece of paper on her passenger seat and started the engine. First thing tomorrow she'd report him to administration and zoo security. The way she should've done yesterday. After that she wouldn't have to worry.

Dawson Gage wasn't going to bother her again.

She could hardly wait to get home and tell her parents about the whole thing.

12

Maddie thought about calling Connor on the way home, but her mind was still spinning. What would compel a stranger to come from the other side of the country to the Indianapolis Zoo, all so he could tell her some fabricated story about some fictitious adoption?

He was either dangerous or terribly confused.

Either way, Maddie still felt uneasy when she pulled into her family's garage and walked into the house. She set her purse and car keys down on the floor just inside the foyer and found her mom in the kitchen. "I'm glad you're here." Maddie went straight to her and hugged her. "I had the worst day."

Her mother held her for a long moment and then slipped a meat loaf pan in the oven. Maddie must've looked terrible, because her mom seemed worried. "Honey . . . you're pale. What happened?" She felt Maddie's head. "Are you sick?"

"Only because of what happened." Maddie dropped to the nearest kitchen chair. "Wait till you hear this."

Her mom took the chair beside hers and reached for Maddie's hand. "Did someone hurt you?"

"No." Maddie took a deep breath. "The craziest thing."

Before she could tell her mother about the stranger, her dad joined them. His smile faded when he saw Maddie. "Sweetheart, what's wrong?"

"She was just about to tell me." Her mom patted the chair next to her. "Come sit."

Hayley was at her piano lesson, so it was just the three of them. *Breathe,* Maddie told herself. *You're okay.* She looked from her mother to her dad. "This guy . . . he was at the zoo yesterday. All day. And every few hours I caught him looking at me."

Her father leaned forward. "We need to contact the police."

"It gets weirder." She folded her hands and set them on the table. "He was back again today and he came up to me. Introduced himself. Dawson Gage, he told me."

"Maddie, you should've called for help." Her mother looked outraged. "Someone stalking you at your workplace? That's against the law."

"I know." Maddie sighed. It felt so good to be home, away from the stranger. "I will. Tomorrow."

"So what did he say?" Her dad looked ready to take care of the situation. "Was there more?"

"Yes." Maddie paused. "He was clearly delusional or dangerous. Or maybe he had me mixed up with someone else."

Her mom reached out and put her hand over Maddie's. "This is very serious, sweetie. Thank you for telling us."

Maddie nodded. "At first he made up this elaborate story about writing a report on animals and just, you know, coming up to me because he thought I was pretty." She held up her left hand. "I told him I was engaged. But then later . . . later he stopped me on my way to the car. Near the flamingos."

Fury built in her father's eyes. "I don't like this."

"Me, either." Maddie still couldn't believe it. "That's when he told me the whole report thing was a lie . . . and that he had come here from Portland to find me." She started to shiver. "He knew your names . . . and Hayley's."

"We need to call the police." Her mother reached for her cell phone. "I want to make a report before—"

"Hold on." Maddie wanted to finish. Her parents might be less worried once they heard the rest. Because maybe the guy had simply confused her with someone else. "He said he came here to give me information. About my biological family." She looked from her dad to her mom and a single laugh came from her. "See what I mean? The guy might just be confused, but it scared me."

Suddenly, at the same time, her parents sat back in their seats. Their anger and concern disappeared. Her mother spoke first. "Did . . . did he explain himself?"

"Mom." Maddie blinked. "He didn't have to explain himself. I told him he had the wrong person. Clearly." She uttered another solitary laugh, but there was nothing funny about the change in her parents. "I told him . . . I'm not adopted."

Then her father did something Maddie could never have expected. Never imagined. Something that tilted her entire world off its axis. Her dad didn't chuckle or shrug off the situation or agree that the guy probably had her mixed up with another Indiana girl. Instead he stared at his hands and sighed.

The heaviest, longest, gravest sigh Maddie had ever heard.

• • •

BROOKE WANTED TO freeze time, send Maddie back out to the car so that when she came inside from the zoo today the telling of this terrible story would be her's and Peter's idea. Not something they were forced into.

But here they were. And without warning or planning or praying about the situation an hour before the discussion, they had no choice but to tell Maddie the truth.

"Honey." Brooke looked long at Maddie and then at Peter. "Your father and I . . . we need to talk to you."

"What?" Maddie pushed back from the table. She shook her head. "Why are you acting like this? Did you hear me?" Her voice was louder than before. "The guy thought I was adopted. But I'm not adopted." Panic filled her tone. "I have pictures . . . pictures of you in the hospital, Mom. Holding me in your arms. Minutes after I was born."

Peter took over. "Sit down, honey." His voice was broken. "Please."

Something in his tone seemed to make Maddie obey. Slowly, as if she were in a trance, she sat back down and stared at them. "Are you saying the guy was telling the truth?" This time she didn't laugh. "That's impossible. What's wrong with everyone?"

"The truth . . . is something we've wanted to tell you for a long time, Maddie."

Their daughter blinked. "Tell me?" Her words were barely a whisper. "Tell me what?"

"The man was right." Peter leaned closer. "Your mother and I . . . we tried for a few years after we married. But we couldn't have a baby."

Brooke covered her face with her hands for a long moment. Was she trapped in a nightmare? This wasn't how she wanted to tell Maddie. Again she found her daughter's eyes. "Someone reached out to us about three frozen embryos."

Maddie shook her head. "Three . . . ? I don't believe this." She sounded more shocked than angry. "Tell me you're making it up."

Brooke didn't say anything. Peter, either. Finally Brooke pressed on. "We're not making it up, sweetheart. We've always looked for the chance to tell you."

"When a couple uses in vitro fertilization," Peter began, "sometimes they have extra embryos. Tiny, tiny babies that can remain viable on ice for years."

"I was a . . . a frozen embryo?" Maddie's voice was loud again. "Are you kidding me?"

Help me, God . . . I'm the worst mother. Please help me. Brooke took a deep breath. "I agreed to have the three frozen embryos implanted in me. Your dad and I believed those little babies deserved a chance at life."

"Only one of the embryos survived the process." Peter stood and walked around the table to Maddie. He sat beside her and put his hand on her shoulder. "Maddie, you've been our child from the day we found out your mother was pregnant."

Maddie moved Peter's hand and pushed her chair further back. "Wait, you're serious?" She stared at Peter and then at Brooke. "You're saying I really am adopted?"

Brooke reached for her, but Maddie jerked away. "Don't touch me." She spat the words. "You lied. About . . . about my whole life!"

And in that moment, Brooke knew she was right before. Maddie wasn't going to be okay. They had done a terrible thing by not telling her and now they would all pay for it.

Help us, God. This is all our fault. Brooke's silent cries echoed through her heart and soul. *Let this pass, Father. Please. Help her understand.* Maddie's reaction was more upsetting than anything Brooke had imagined. Their daughter was reeling, her whole world falling apart before their eyes.

Peter tried first. "You have to understand, embryo adoption is different, Maddie. You are our daughter. No question about that. You were formed in your mom's uterus."

"But my . . . biological family"—bitterness made every word sound heavy, like poison to Maddie's tongue—"is in Portland, Oregon?"

What could Brooke say? "We . . . we always wanted to be that family, Maddie. We've been that family."

"No." Maddie stood again, eyes blazing. "If I came from a . . . a frozen embryo . . . then you're not my biological family." She was breathing harder. "It's science, Mother. The sperm and egg came from two other people. You should know that."

"Maddie. Of course I know that." Brooke stood, and Peter did, too. "But I birthed you." What could she say to help the moment? "You've . . . you've been ours from the time you took your first breath."

"I haven't." Maddie had never looked more angry, more upset. Then something seemed to occur to her. "Hayley, too? She came from a frozen embryo?"

Peter shook his head. "No." He took a slight step closer to Maddie. "After we had you . . . a few years later your mom got pregnant."

The news seemed to hit Maddie in waves. Like an atomic bomb. She put her hands over her face and stooped down for a long moment. When she straightened, furious tears filled her eyes. "So . . . so Hayley isn't . . . my real sister?"

Brooke wanted so badly to take Maddie in her arms, but she couldn't. That much was clear. "In every possible way that matters, Hayley is your real sister, Maddie. She's always been your sister."

"No!" Maddie shook her head. Slowly at first and then harder. "She's not my sister." She glared from Brooke to Peter. "And you're not . . . you're not my parents." A realization seemed to hit her. "I thought the guy was stalking me." Her anger burned brighter. "He was only trying to help."

"Honey, we didn't want to tell you this way. We planned to—"

"Stop." Maddie took two steps back. She held up her hand, like she didn't want Brooke or Peter to come any closer. "Don't say another word. You're both . . . you're liars." A tear slid onto her cheek. "Don't you remember what you always told us girls, Mom?" She looked at Peter. "Dad?"

There was nothing they could say, no excuse they could give her. Brooke had a feeling she knew what was coming.

Maddie glared at them. "You told us you don't lie . . . to someone you love." She was seething now, her eyes furious and heartbroken. "And you don't love . . . someone you lie to."

Every word cut like a knife. Peter was clearly feeling the same thing. Maddie was right. All their years as a family they had taught their daughters to be honest. *Tell the truth. God is pleased with honesty.* And to drive the point home, time and again they had told the girls the simple adage.

You don't lie to someone you love. And you don't love someone you lie to.

"I'm sorry, Maddie." Brooke moved a half step closer. But the action only made Maddie back up further.

"We're both so sorry, honey." Peter stayed frozen in place.

"I don't forgive you." Maddie was shaking now. "Not now. Not ever." She put her hand over her heart. "Can you imagine how this feels? My whole life is a lie. All because . . . all because of you two." She shook her head. "I'm leaving."

Brooke and Peter followed Maddie to the foyer. Brooke reached her first, and for the slightest moment she put her hand on her daughter's arm. "Honey . . . please. Don't go."

Maddie jerked away. "I said . . . don't touch me." She grabbed her purse and car keys from the floor, opened the door and stormed out.

Peter stepped onto the porch. "We need to talk, Maddie."

"No." Maddie didn't turn around. "There's nothing to say."

God, how can this be happening? We failed so terribly, please, help us. Help Maddie. Brooke felt sick to her stomach. She called after her daughter. "Maddie, please."

Their daughter looked back just once, halfway down the sidewalk. Her words came like so many bullets. "All . . . this . . . time?"

Their daughter shook her head once more and hurried to her car. Like Maddie was being chased by the ghost of a past that had died in a single conversation. She slammed the car door shut and started the engine. Then she peeled off down the street.

"I'm going after her." Peter started to head back into the house. "She isn't safe, driving like that. So upset."

"Don't." Brooke took her husband's hand. "There's nothing we can do. She . . . she needs to process. She'll probably go to Connor's house."

For a long moment they stared down the empty road in the direction Maddie had gone. Then Peter turned to her. "Brooke. We made a terrible . . . terrible mistake." He took her in his arms and they held on to each other. Like they might drown if they let go.

Brooke closed her eyes and pressed her forehead into Peter's shoulder. "She deserved to know. She's going to hate us the rest of her life."

The possibility wasn't just something dramatic that hung over the here and now. Maddie was furious with them, and she had a right to feel that way. Every detail of their daughter's entire reality had just been altered. Decimated. The platform of her existence had been eliminated in a single conversation. And now Maddie really did hate them.

Just like Brooke had feared.

13

Maddie nearly ran a stop sign before she forced herself to slow down. She pulled into the parking lot at Bryan Park and found a spot as far away from the entrance as possible.

With too much force she slammed the gearshift into park.

Then she leaned her head against the steering wheel and tried to breathe. She had to be dreaming. That was it, she would wake up and all this would be an unbelievable, impossible nightmare.

Of course she wasn't adopted.

People always told her she looked like her little sister, Hayley. She didn't look just like her mom, but most girls didn't. Her mind raced back in time. How often had she heard her father say, "Maddie is the mirror image of my mother."

A grandma Maddie rarely saw because they lived overseas.

Her heart pounded and she tried to grab a deep breath. She hadn't gotten one since the bizarre conversation played out at the kitchen table. She had only told them about the guy at the zoo because she was worried he might be dangerous.

She wanted her parents' opinion.

Forever she would remember the blank stare on her

parents' faces when Maddie laughed at the strangeness of Dawson Gage thinking she was adopted. The way her parents had looked at each other. Their hesitation and guilty eyes. They had lied to her about everything.

How did they expect her to respond?

Chuckle a few times and brush it off? *Interesting, Mom and Dad. I never knew that. Anyway, what were you saying about your day?* Like really?

Was that how they thought she'd handle this?

Maddie lifted her head and stared out the windshield. Everything about her life was different now. She wasn't a Baxter or a West. Hayley wasn't her sister, and her parents weren't her parents. They had lied to her all her life. Her eyes settled on a pretty oak tree across the street.

Why hadn't she noticed the tree before? Even Bloomington looked different.

Her eye caught the piece of paper on her passenger seat. The one with Dawson's phone number. What if the stranger hadn't come to the zoo this week? Her parents said they were planning to tell her, but when?

A year from now? A decade?

Maddie left the park. It would be dark in an hour or so and she didn't want to be alone. Not when her entire past had unraveled in a matter of minutes.

Big questions took the place of her anger. Who actually was she? What was this biological family Dawson had spoken about and what did he want to tell her about her real sister? London, right? Wasn't that her name?

Maddie drove as fast as she could to Connor's place, an apartment downtown where he lived with a few buddies. She waited till she was parked outside the building before she called him.

He answered on the first ring. "Hey!" People were talking in the background. "How was the zoo?"

Where was she supposed to begin? She breathed out and closed her eyes. "Connor. I'm out front." *Don't cry*, she told herself. *Stay calm*. "Can you come down? I . . . I need to talk."

"Sure." Connor knew her well enough to know something was wrong. Her tone couldn't hide that much. "Is everything okay?"

"Please . . . come down." She dabbed at a stray tear. "I'll tell you then."

Three minutes later, Connor hurried out his apartment door. He was still tucking in his shirt as he slid into the passenger side of her car. "Maddie?" He took her hand and searched her face. "What . . . what happened?"

"Can we go somewhere?" The busy street had a stream of pedestrians and any minute one of Connor's roommates might come out and see them. "Lake Monroe, maybe?"

"Of course." He searched her eyes. "I'll drive if you want."

"Actually, yes. Please." Maddie shielded her face with her hand and then let it fall to her lap again. "I can't focus."

Only then did Connor look worried. "You're scaring me."

She shook her head. "This isn't about us." She held his hand more tightly than before. "You're the only one I can count on right now, Connor."

"Okay. It's just . . . I haven't seen you like this." He brushed a tear off her cheek. "Let's go."

They switched places, and fifteen minutes later they pulled into the parking lot at Lake Monroe. Connor took her hand again and they walked to a picnic table at the water's edge. The place where Maddie and her family had shared so many Fourth of July picnics.

The people she used to think were her family.

For a long moment neither of them said anything. There was no easy way to share this, no gradually getting to the truth. "Connor . . . I'm adopted. I just found out."

For a few seconds he only stared at her, not moving. The single sound was the lake water lapping against the shore. He shook his head, clearly worried about her. "Maddie." He leaned in. "You're not adopted."

The two of them had looked through Maddie's family photo albums. Connor had seen the same pictures Maddie had seen. Her mom holding her in her first few moments of life, her parents standing together with her in their arms as they brought her home from the hospital. Maddie still didn't quite get it. Explaining it to Connor would be difficult.

But she had to try.

For the next ten minutes she told Connor the story of the guy at the zoo, how he had come to Indiana looking for her and how he wanted to tell her something about her biological family. Her sister London in particular.

The whole time Maddie talked, Connor didn't say a word. Probably because it seemed too unbelievable for him to do anything but listen. So Maddie told him how she'd been scared by the guy and taken his number as a way of getting rid of him.

"Then I came home and told my parents." Tears filled her eyes again. "I expected them to laugh. You know, brush it off. The guy obviously had me confused with someone else. But that's not what happened."

For the first time since they sat down, Connor looked

nervous. Like the story she was telling might actually be real. He wrapped his fingers around hers. "What'd they say?"

"I . . . still can't believe it." She lifted her eyes to his. "They said it was true, Connor."

"But what about the pictures at the hospital? Your parents brought you home when you were two days old." The sun was starting to set and pink streaks colored the sky. "How do they explain that?"

This was the weirdest part. "I was a . . . frozen embryo." She took a deep breath and tried to explain the situation the way her parents had explained it to her. "So I came from another family."

"Wow." Connor still had hold of her hand, but he sat back against the table and stared at the lake. "I can't believe it."

"I know." Maddie sniffed a few times and wiped the wetness from her cheeks. "Like everything about my life is a lie." The bitterness in her tone grew more intense. "Those aren't my parents and Hayley isn't my sister." She hesitated. "I'm not a West and I'm definitely not a Baxter."

Connor faced her. "Now wait a minute." He put one hand on her cheek. "You can't think like that, Maddie."

She felt herself stiffen. "What?"

"This is a big deal. I get it." Connor searched her eyes. "Sure, you might have different DNA, but they're your family. Absolutely."

"Seriously?" Maddie pulled away from him. "That's how you feel?" She stood and crossed her arms. "My parents tell me, 'Oh, hey. By the way, you're adopted. You were a frozen embryo from some other couple.'" She stared at him. "And you tell me it's no big deal?"

He stood. "Maddie, I'm on your side. I'm just . . . trying to be a voice of reason."

A scream was building on the inside and Maddie couldn't do anything about it. "I need to go." She stepped away from him and held up her hands. "You don't understand. No one does."

"You can't leave." His smile faded. "You're my ride."

She loved him, but he didn't understand. Not this time. Her knees shook, and the cool breeze off the lake made her teeth chatter. Her mind was spinning. "Connor." She sat back down on the bench. "My whole world is caving in." She looked up at him. "Don't you see?"

Concern flashed in Connor's eyes, but he shook his head. "To be honest, no. You were born to your mother." He squinted. "So I don't see why you're so angry. You belong to the family you're in." He put his hand on her shoulder. "But I love you, Maddie. And I'm here for you. Whatever that looks like."

Maddie should've been thankful. But that's not how she felt. She wanted Connor to get upset along with her, to accuse her parents of betraying her and basing her whole life on a lie. But he didn't understand.

The sky was getting dark, the air cooler. After a minute Maddie stood. "I need to go."

"Okay." He wove his fingers between hers like before but they weren't close to connected. She drove this time and neither of them talked on the ride back. When they pulled up in front of his apartment Maddie realized something. None of this was Connor's fault. She couldn't be upset with him. She wasn't, really.

She was numb.

"I made things worse. I'm sorry." He leaned over and tried to kiss her, but she pulled back.

"I just . . . I need time." Maddie's heart skipped a few beats. She couldn't wait to leave.

"Maddie." He sat back in his seat. "You said this wasn't about us."

She didn't know what to tell him. "My world's falling apart. I need to be alone." She reached out and put her hand over his. "That's all." Her words felt hollow, but she wanted to get away from here. What else could she say?

Connor turned to her. "So I blew it tonight. Okay." He opened the car door and put one foot on the curb. "But I stand by what I said, Maddie. Your family loves you. This news today . . . it doesn't change anything."

Words wouldn't come. The silent scream inside her grew and all Maddie could do was nod. "Goodbye, Connor."

"I love you, Maddie West. I loved you yesterday same as today. I'll love you tomorrow and always. Nothing has changed." He slid his other leg out of the car. "Don't forget that."

"Sure." She tightened her grip on the steering wheel. "I'm sorry, Connor. I have to go." She should tell him she loved him, too. But she no longer knew who she was, let alone how she felt about Connor Flanigan.

Everything was upside down.

After a few seconds, Connor gave her a final look and he walked back to his apartment.

Only then could she finally breathe.

Where am I supposed to go, God? She stared into the night. *And how come You let this happen? Why didn't they tell me when I was little?* It was the first time she'd thought about the Lord, and His role in all this. She had followed

Him, believed in Him since she could talk. Her parents' faith had been a daily example for her.

Until now.

She drove for half an hour up and down the streets of Bloomington. Every few minutes her phone buzzed in her purse, but Maddie didn't care. There was no one she wanted to talk to now. *Help me, God. I don't know who I am.* She pulled over and parked along Main Street.

Again her phone buzzed, and this time she took it from her purse. Eight texts from her mom, three from her dad. One from Connor. She read his first.

I can't get my mind around what just happened between us. You found out you were adopted as an embryo and now you don't tell me you love me? I'm worried, Maddie. Call me tomorrow and tell me you're okay. We can work through this together. But you're a Baxter, no matter what you think right now. I love you.

Her heart warmed. She didn't have to take it out on Connor. He had nothing to do with what happened. From his perspective nothing had truly changed. He loved her whether she had biological parents in Portland or not. No difference.

She texted back her response.

I love you, too, Connor. I'm sorry about earlier. You don't understand what I'm going through, but that's okay. Just pray for me.

There was no hesitation before she hit send. She didn't want to leave Connor wondering about their relationship or the wedding they were planning. She still wanted to marry him, but she had no idea how long it would take before she'd feel like herself.

Or if she'd ever feel that way again.

Never mind the texts from her parents. She didn't want to read them. What could they say at this point? She remembered her younger sister. Poor Hayley. How would Hayley feel once she knew that Maddie wasn't her actual sister? The blame could go nowhere except to their parents.

She looked at her passenger seat. The information the guy had given her was still there. Crumpled up and overlooked. The way she felt about herself tonight. What was it he had wanted to tell her about her biological sister? A person Maddie hadn't known existed until today?

The scrap of paper called to her. On the other side of the lies her parents had told her was a real flesh-and-blood family. Parents who had leftover embryos and gave them to someone who gave them to the people she thought were her parents.

She'd never heard of something like this. But it had happened to her. She picked up the small handwritten note. Then before she could change her mind, she dialed the number. Because in this moment she wanted to talk to just one person. The guy who had braved her outrage to give her the last thing she'd expected from him: the truth. The only person kind enough, bold enough to explain her past was a stranger from Portland, Oregon.

Dawson Gage.

14

The voice of God had been loud for the past twenty-four hours and John Baxter was doing his best to heed it. He wasn't sure exactly what was happening or whom it was happening to, but someone in his family was in trouble. John knew that much.

Because as far back as he could remember, there was an unsettling in his soul, a persistent push to pray down on his knees whenever one of his kids most needed help. Last night he had told Elaine about the feeling. "God wants us to pray. Something's wrong."

Not that they only talked to Him then. He and Elaine had built their marriage around praying for their kids and grandchildren, their friends and their community. Even the nation. "I might be getting older," he would tell his wife. "But as long as I draw breath I can pray. And prayer changes things."

That's how he felt now. Sunshine spread as far as the eye could see over Bloomington that day, and he and Elaine had taken their usual early Saturday morning trip to the farmers' market. Blueberries and apples, fresh eggs and milk. But through every step, every few minutes he heard it.

Pray, John . . . pray for your family. Pray without ceasing.

And John's response was as easy as his next breath. *Yes,*

Lord. Whatever You ask of me, I'll do. Please guard and protect my family. Whoever is in need, help them. Surround them with Your loving protection.

Then he'd walk another few yards and the voice would come again.

My son, pray for your family. Don't stop. The enemy seeks to kill, steal and destroy. I have come that they might have life and have it to the full. Don't stop praying.

So back home just after noon when the call came from his oldest daughter, Brooke, John wasn't surprised. In His time, God always filled in the missing pieces of what was happening. Which was why praying mattered so much.

John took the call and moved to the front room. He sat on the sofa and faced the window. The big oak and blue sky outside eased his anxiety. "Brooke." He took a slow breath. "How are you?"

"Dad . . ." She stopped short, and John knew.

As certain as his heartbeat, he was sure this was why he'd been praying. Brooke was crying. "Honey . . . take your time." He lifted his eyes to the sky. "I'm here. Whatever it is."

Her tears took more of her voice. "Peter and I . . . we need to talk to you and Elaine. To the whole family. Tonight. P-p-please."

John's heart sank. "Okay, honey. Absolutely." Was this about their marriage? They'd had trouble before, but had something worse happened? John had only heard Brooke this upset a handful of times and always the situation had been very serious.

Brooke grabbed a jagged breath. "I've asked the others to come. Even Luke and Reagan." A soft sob sounded through the line. "After dinner. At Ashley and Landon's house."

John and Elaine had dinner scheduled with their

neighbors. But they could cancel that. Nothing was more important than this. "We'll be there." He paused. "Brooke, is there anything I can do for you between now and then?"

"No." Her answer was quick. "It's too late for that." Her pause felt heavy. "We'll explain it all tonight."

The call ended and John found Elaine in their bedroom sorting laundry. She must've seen his expression because she dropped the towel she was folding. "John . . . what is it?"

"I'm not sure." He came to her and pulled her into his arms. "I told you . . . how God has had me praying constantly since yesterday."

"Yes." She studied his eyes. "Did you hear something?"

"Brooke called." He told her about the meeting planned for that night.

Elaine nodded. "I'll let the neighbors know. They have a few other couples coming. They'll understand."

This was one more reason John loved Elaine. She would never replace his first wife, Elizabeth, the one he had married as a young man and raised five children with. The one he had lost to cancer when she was far too young.

But Elaine was the one he loved now. She cared for his family as if they'd always been her own, and she understood the importance of being with them on a day like this. He gently kissed her lips. "Thank you."

"Of course." Her smile melted his heart. "Brooke needs us."

They spent the rest of the afternoon and early evening doing their usual weekend vacuuming and sweeping, cleaning bathrooms. With every passing hour John prayed longer, more intently.

Whatever it is, dear God, please go before us.

Finally it was seven o'clock and the family was all together at Ashley's house. The adults gathered in the big living room—the one where John and Elizabeth had raised their family before selling the house to Ashley and Landon.

The kids went out back to catch fireflies and fish the stream. Landon made it clear the adults needed time. "Give us an hour." He smiled from the doorway, his warm voice loud enough to carry across the back porch. "Then we'll join you!"

Landon returned to the living room and joined Ashley on one sofa next to Brooke and Peter. On the opposite one sat John's second oldest daughter, Kari, and her husband, Ryan. And next to them was John's youngest, Luke, and his wife, Reagan. His oldest son, Dayne, was with his family in California this month working on a major feature film.

Whatever the news, Dayne would have to hear it later.

John and Elaine took the pair of rockers situated between the sofas. A hush fell over the room. All eyes were on Brooke and Peter.

Pray, my son. Don't stop praying.

Yes, Lord. John held his breath for a long moment. *Let Your presence be here tonight. Please.*

The tearstains on Brooke's cheeks made it clear that something desperate had happened. But for now her eyes were dry. Peter took hold of her hand, and John felt himself relax, even just a little. They looked too united, too close to be struggling in their marriage. This had to be about something else.

John waited along with the rest of the family.

Brooke took the lead. "This is my fault."

"And mine." Peter was quick to include himself.

"Yes. Both our faults." Brooke looked at Peter, and then around the room. Her hesitation seemed to last a long time. Finally she drew a deep breath. "Maddie is adopted. She isn't our biological daughter."

Concern flashed across John's heart. Was Brooke having a breakdown? Was she unwell? Maddie was definitely not adopted.

No one said a word for half a minute. Luke was the first to break the silence. "Brooke . . . I love you." His tone was gentle, kind. "But with all due respect, Maddie couldn't have been adopted." He looked at the faces around him. "We were all there . . . at the hospital when she was born. I have pictures."

"I have them, too." Brooke nodded and held her hand up. "Of course. I know what you're all thinking. I gave birth to her so how could she be adopted." She paused. "But this is real."

"It's a long story." Peter slipped his arm around Brooke's shoulders.

And then, taking turns, they told it. How they couldn't have children and after a few years they were contacted by a doctor friend who specialized in fertility. He'd come to possess three frozen embryos and—though it was cutting-edge science back then—he had surgically implanted them into Brooke.

"Only one of them took." Brooke's eyes looked damp again. "That's why we have Maddie."

Now the room seemed quiet for another reason. If John had to guess by the looks on the faces around him, everyone was stunned. Him most of all. He pressed his elbows into his knees and looked at Peter and then Brooke. His voice fell to a whisper. "Why didn't you tell us?"

Brooke hung her head and Peter cleared his throat. He struggled to speak. "It seemed crazy. We . . . didn't think it would work, and when it did . . . when we were pregnant . . . all we wanted . . . was to celebrate." He sighed. "We thought we could tell you later."

Suddenly John thought about his granddaughter, and he felt the blood leave his face. "You . . . you told Maddie, though. Right?"

Again Peter and Brooke waited. Shame came over their faces and Brooke shook her head. "We wanted to tell her." She looked at her husband. "Every time we made a plan, the timing seemed off." Her voice broke. "I kept thinking there would be a . . . better opportunity. When she was four or when she went to school. When she became a teenager or when she started high school."

A crushing weight filled the room.

Brooke looked at Ashley. "I told Ashley a few days ago."

"Yes." Ashley sat a little straighter. "I said Maddie would be okay, and she and Peter just needed to tell her."

"Instead"—Brooke glanced around the room—"a stranger told her." And then she explained how a man had come to the Indianapolis Zoo from Portland. "He walked up to her and told her he had news about her biological family."

John put his hand over his face for a few seconds. "Dear God, help her." His words were barely audible. *Poor Maddie. She must be feeling blindsided*. No wonder God had wanted him to pray.

Peter explained how Maddie came home and told them about the stranger and his ludicrous claim that she had biological parents and a sister, London, and how he claimed to have news about her. "She thought the man had her confused with someone else."

A sick feeling came over John. Why in the world hadn't Brooke and Peter told Maddie sooner?

Kari folded her hands and turned her attention to Brooke and Peter. "So you told her the truth then?"

"We had no choice." Two tears slid down Brooke's cheeks. "She's very, very angry with us."

Elaine reached for John's hand. He felt tears in his own eyes. "I'm so sorry. For all of you." *All of us,* he wanted to say. But he kept that last part to himself. Brooke and Peter clearly felt bad enough. They needed to find a way to move forward. Not wallow in what should've been.

"She's still your daughter." Ashley looked from Brooke to John and then around the room. "That's what I told Brooke last week, and it's true. Never mind that she came from someone else at the beginning. She was born into this family. She belongs here."

Luke and Kari nodded, and the others followed suit.

John found his voice. "Of course she belongs. She was knit together by God inside *you*, Brooke." *But she deserved to know the truth a long time ago*. That much was true, too.

There was no real way for John to wrap his mind around the news. Of all the things he had thought might be said tonight, this wasn't on the list. Not even close. Never for a moment had he doubted that Maddie was Brooke and Peter's biological daughter. He couldn't imagine how broken Maddie must feel.

How devastated Brooke and Peter must be.

Peter sighed. "Hayley knows. She's at home tonight, in case Maddie comes back." He pinched the bridge of his nose, his voice thick with emotion. "She didn't come home till after we were asleep last night and she was gone when we woke up this morning."

"Wow." Luke's sigh was as heavy as the air around them. "I can't imagine."

"We wanted to tell you." Peter still had his arm around Brooke. "So the family can pray. And so you can know the truth." He paused, clearly fighting his emotions. "The way everyone should've known from the beginning."

Another silence followed.

Remind them of my Word, my son. They need certainty.

There it was again. The voice of God, John was so familiar with. He steadied himself and looked right at Peter. They needed their heavenly Father's unchanging truth. "There will be healing through all this. We will pray for that and believe it will happen." He saw Ashley nodding.

Then he turned his eyes to Brooke and Peter. "Nothing is impossible with God. All things work to the good for those who love Him. God is faithful and true and He will not let this destroy your family." John felt his strength gather. "That's what the Bible says and that's what we believe."

"Yes. We've always come back to that." Luke took Reagan's hand. "It's all we have."

They shared awhile longer. Kari used her phone to read aloud a few Bible verses on God's healing power. Then Reagan talked about impossible situations in her life where God had worked a miracle. Before the discussion ended, John looked at his kids and their spouses. "Let's pray. Where two or more are gathered in His name, there He is, also." He paused. "So . . . He is here. He sees us."

Then, as John had been doing since he felt the prodding yesterday afternoon—as he'd done all his life—he prayed for his family. For Brooke and Peter and Maddie and Hayley. That God would shower each of them with love and mercy and certainty in the days ahead, and that He alone would have the final say about Maddie's future.

About her very identity.

After the prayer, Brooke and Peter thanked everyone. "We gave you no warning."

"You needed us." John looked around, proud of the people in the room. They had dropped whatever plans they'd had to be here. "That's how love responds."

When they were finished and when Elaine and the others were out back with the kids, John went to Brooke and Peter and wrapped his arms around them. "We'll get through this." His tone was gentle. "Christian counseling might be a good idea. For all four of you."

"We've thought about that." Peter looked slightly more encouraged. "When she comes home we'll suggest it."

"The thing is . . ." Brooke rested her head on John's shoulder. "I never wanted to tell her she wasn't a Baxter." She closed her eyes for a moment. "Being part of this family means so much to her."

"Listen." John took a deep breath. "She will always be part of this family. As long as she lives. This information cannot possibly change that."

Brooke nodded. "I want to believe that."

"Thank you." Peter put his hand on John's arm. "We needed this." His eyes welled up again. "It feels good to be honest. Finally."

Later that night when they were back home and Elaine was asleep, John found his favorite spot in the front room again. He had been praying constantly for Maddie, that she wouldn't run away from her family, but toward them. Now more than ever.

I'm here, Lord. He looked to the night sky over Bloomington. *How can I help my granddaughter? Where is she right now?* A part of him wanted to get in his car and search the city for her. Make sure she was okay. Brooke and Peter had heard from her. A brief text indicating she was okay, but she wasn't ready to come home.

Not for a long time.

Those had been her words. So they didn't have to call the police or file a missing person's report. But still they wanted to find her, and John thought maybe he could help. Take a drive to the schools and parks and parking lots. Wherever she might be.

But then he stopped himself. That wouldn't help. Maddie needed to work through her feelings with God. He was the only one who could assure her of who she was. Whose she was. *Still, Lord, I'm willing. Send me to her if that would help.*

My Son, you will be needed in this. Be ready. Keep praying.

Be ready. Was that really the voice of God telling him that? Would the Lord use him to help make things right with Maddie? John would keep listening. Keep watching and waiting for a time when he could help. Until then he would pray that Maddie never forget she belonged in this family. She was Brooke and Peter's daughter, and she was Hayley's sister. She was a West.

And most definitely she was a Baxter.

15

The missed call had come from Indiana sometime during his flight home, which gave Dawson Gage just the slightest slim thread of hope. Maybe Maddie had changed her mind. Maybe she wanted to talk to him.

By now she almost certainly knew the truth.

Dawson felt terrible about how things had played out at the zoo. How could she not have known about her past? Had her adoptive parents actually not told her? Or had she just been too afraid to give him any information?

Whatever it was, Maddie had wanted nothing to do with him.

Even though it was Saturday, he sat in his office, facing the floor-to-ceiling windows and his view of the Columbia River. He had fallen behind in work because of his time in Indiana. And all for what? Maddie had probably tossed his number in the trash on her way to her car that day. Yes, his time in Indianapolis had been a complete waste.

Unless the call had been from her.

But Dawson doubted that. Probably just his Uber driver telling him he'd forgotten his sweater. Dawson didn't care. He was a Pacific Northwest boy. His closet was full of them. What he wanted was a call from Maddie.

He started an overdue email but after a few lines he looked up again. The river was deep blue today, dark because of the clouds overhead. This was the type of day he and London loved. They would jump on their Jet Skis or set out down the river in his speedboat.

Seeing Maddie West hadn't done anything to help him stop missing London. He ached for her. Even if Maddie called, what was the point? He could tell her about London and Larry and Louise. He could share stories and photos with her. But at the end of the day nothing would change.

London would still be gone.

Music. That's what he needed. He put a list of songs on shuffle and hit play. Sometimes he liked nothing more than the old songs. "The Old Rugged Cross" and "How Great Thou Art." Songs that had stood the test of time and still brought a person closer to Jesus.

An hour later he had sent four important emails. It was time to meet his dad for lunch across the river. Work was busy all around, so his father had been at the office catching up. They chose a quiet steak house, and Dawson was glad. He knew his father had concerns about his trip.

Once inside the restaurant, he saw his dad already at a table. Dawson crossed the room and the two of them hugged. Then Dawson slid into the spot across from his father. Dawson spoke first. "Caught up on some work today."

"Me, too." His dad nodded. "Closed the Williams deal."

"Finally." Dawson smiled. He took hold of his water and drank it half down. His eyes focused on the distant window. "Looks like rain."

"Son." His father's eyes were on him, not wavering. "I don't want to talk about the weather." He took a slow breath. "Did you find her?"

Dawson didn't have to ask what his father meant. Better to get the conversation over with. "Yes." He finished his water. "She works at the Indianapolis Zoo, like I thought."

"And?" The serious look in his dad's eyes softened. "Did you talk to her?"

"Briefly." His smile felt sad. "She was afraid of me. Thought I was stalking her."

His father nodded. "I can imagine. You were there two days."

"It took me that long to approach her." Dawson sighed. "Dad . . . she's a blond London. Looks just like her. Talks like her."

"I wondered." He anchored his forearms on the table. "Did you tell her about the Quinns?"

The waiter stopped at their table and told them the specials. He seemed to sense he'd interrupted. "I'll give you a few minutes."

"Thanks." His father smiled. Then he turned his eyes back to Dawson. "Did you?"

"I tried." Dawson glanced up from the menu. "Dad . . . she didn't seem to know she was adopted."

His father sat back hard. "How could she not know?"

"Maybe her parents didn't tell her." Dawson felt terrible about the possibility. "Anyway, she knows now. I'm sure she left the zoo and called them on her way home. Told them about this weird guy who stalked her at work . . . and who wanted to talk to her about her biological family."

"Poor girl." His father clenched his jaw, the muscles working one way then the other. "Dawson . . . what if she wasn't supposed to know? What's the point?"

This was where Dawson had feared the conversation would go. "Louise and Larry have the right to find out what happened to their embryos." He kept his voice calm.

Anything much more than a whisper and the whole restaurant would hear him. "Don't you think?"

"Let's choose our lunch." His dad pushed his glasses back up his nose and lifted the menu. "There's more to talk about here."

A minute later the waiter came back and they ordered.

His father leaned close across the table again, his voice soft. "Dawson . . . you can't replace her." He reached out and squeezed Dawson's hand for a few seconds. "I think . . . if you're honest with yourself . . . that's at the heart of this whole thing. Finding London's sister . . . tracking her down." He paused. "Otherwise, I can't see the point."

This was the one thing Dawson hadn't wanted to think about. The possibility that he had gone all the way to the Indianapolis Zoo to find a replacement for London. The very idea was appalling. He tried one more time. "I'm serious, Dad." He smiled, as if that might help his case. "London's parents deserve—"

"Dawson." His father shook his head. "You told me Louise and Larry signed a deal. They would never go after the embryos, never try to find the family who adopted them. Right?" He hesitated. "Wasn't that it?"

"Sure." Anger tinged Dawson's voice. "But that was before their daughter died. Now it just seems . . ." What was he thinking? That finding Maddie and telling her about her biological family was somehow his right? That his curiosity and determination to do this for the Quinns mattered more than Maddie's feelings?

"Look." His dad stared straight at him. "I know how much you miss her, Son. But now somewhere in Indiana, London's sister must feel like the world is collapsing around her." He paused. "Maybe just let it go. You said the girl didn't want to talk." He shrugged. "End of story." His hesitation was long enough to let his words sink in. "Don't make this about you, Dawson. Please."

Dawson didn't want this conversation, didn't want to reason away the hope of connecting with Maddie West. Even now. But his father was right. Louise and Larry didn't need to meet her. He had called the Quinns when his plane landed yesterday and told them the news. He had found her. London's sister.

But neither of them had said much. The reality of having another biological daughter had only seemed to confuse them and make them more sad. "We should've tried again," Louise had said. "Then this girl would be ours."

So if it didn't help Louise and it exposed a terrible lie to Maddie, what was the point? Dawson stared at the table. "Maybe you're right." It was the last thing he wanted to admit. That he might've gone to Indiana looking for someone to replace London. Dawson lifted his head. "She's engaged. If that helps any."

His dad's lips curved in a partial smile. "It does. Because maybe you'll let it go." He put his hand over Dawson's once more. "I'm sorry, Son. I'm so sorry. We all are."

Dawson nodded. His dad was sorry because he was right. London was gone. And no one could ever replace her. Dawson did a few slow nods. "I know." He pursed his lips. "Thanks, Dad. I didn't want this talk . . . but I needed it."

"Yes." His dad exhaled. "Sometimes God helps us face the very thing we're running from."

Like going after Maddie West.

Understanding filled Dawson. Their lunch arrived and they talked about the deal his dad had just closed and the prospects in the coming week. They left together, and his father stopped near his truck. "Glad you're back." The two hugged. "Not just from Indiana."

Dawson could feel the sadness in his eyes. Because this conversation had an air of finality about it. "Thanks, Dad." He patted his father's shoulder. "I mean it." Dawson smiled. "See you tomorrow."

"Sundays are the best. Going to be a good message at church!" His dad grinned. "I have a feeling about that."

"Save me a seat."

They waved and Dawson climbed into his Chevy. His dad had been spot-on today. Dawson never should've gone to Indiana. He thought about his father's words. *You can't replace her . . . you can't replace her.*

Was that really what he'd been trying to do? In his desperation after losing London?

A light rain began to fall. He didn't want to replace London, right? That wasn't it. He had no delusions that the girl would want to talk to him and that somehow they'd find the same sort of friendship he'd shared with London. That wasn't it.

The truth hit him then.

He didn't want Maddie to fill London's place. He wanted London. Just a few more minutes with her. He had hoped being with the girl at the zoo would give him that gift. Hearing Maddie's voice, watching the way she tossed her hair and walked across the kangaroo exhibit.

And he had been right.

Sitting on the bench by the lions and giraffes watching her, when she didn't know he was looking, he had allowed himself to pretend. London had a blond wig, but she was there and she was whole. She hadn't died, after all.

Dawson shuddered at the reality. What a terrible thing

to do to the Indiana beauty. Projecting his own brokenness on her as if the girl could ever be London Quinn. Yes, his dad had been right about almost everything he'd said at lunch. But one thing wasn't correct.

He had never intended to replace London.

Since Maddie didn't want to talk to him, the entire ordeal was behind him. He could get on with accepting the situation as it was. As it always would be. London was gone and she wasn't coming back.

The rain came down harder. Dawson was halfway home when he remembered the missed call from the Indiana number. If it had been Maddie, she would've left a message or called back. Through the afternoon and evening that's what he told himself. Anytime recent memories of Maddie came to mind, he pushed them out.

His heart had no room for them.

But just before eight o'clock, he was sitting at the edge of his dock, remembering London, seeing her racing ahead of him on the river, when his phone rang. A single glance told him it was the same Indiana number. For a few seconds he only let it ring. This wasn't Maddie. That was all a big mistake.

But before the call could go to voicemail, he answered it. "Hello?"

Silence filled the air.

"Hello?" He gritted his teeth. "I think you have the wrong number."

Then he heard a sharp breath. "Dawson Gage?"

It was her. He had known that voice since high school.

"Maddie?" He didn't want to scare her, didn't want her to run. There wasn't a single smart reason why he should continue the call, but he did. *Please, God, give me the words.* "Is . . . that you?"

"Yes." She sounded unsure. "You were right." The words seemed hard for her to say. "I was adopted. As . . . as an embryo."

There it was. The dots were connected, but only because of him. He felt terrible. "You didn't know? Before I showed up?"

"I didn't." Her tone sounded a bit more relaxed. "My parents told me everything." She paused. "The people I *thought* were my parents."

Oh, man. Dawson felt his heart drop. *What have I done to this girl?* "Did . . . they say why they hadn't told you? Before?"

"You know . . . they always wanted to say something . . . they kept waiting for the perfect moment." Bitterness flashed in her voice. "All the things you say when you're caught in a lie."

Dawson squeezed his eyes shut for a brief moment. "I didn't mean . . . to cause any trouble, Maddie. I didn't."

"It's not your fault." Maddie rushed ahead. "I called because . . . I'm coming to Portland, Dawson. I want to meet the biological family you talked about." So much about her voice reminded him of London. But the sound was different, too. She was her own person. He had to keep reminding himself of that.

The girl on the other end of the call wasn't London.

Then her words hit him. Wait. What had she said? She was coming to Portland? The wooden dock beneath him seemed to give way. What was he supposed to tell her? "They respect your privacy, Maddie. You don't have to come."

"I already booked my flight." Her voice softened. "I want to meet my sister. London, wasn't it?"

Dawson's heart broke in half. He had to tell her, had to make the situation clear. "Maddie . . . She isn't . . ." They were the toughest words he would ever say, now and forever. "London was killed in a car accident a few weeks ago."

Maddie's gasp was quiet, but Dawson could hear it all the same. She didn't say anything for a full minute, and Dawson didn't either. Then he could hear her. Maddie was crying. How could he comfort her? After another few seconds, Maddie did a quick cough. "That's . . . what you came to tell me?"

"Yes." If only it weren't. Dawson stood and walked closer to the water. She was just right here, standing beside him. He could feel her still. London would've been thrilled to know she really did have a sister. He pictured Maddie on the other end of the phone. "I . . . thought you should know."

She didn't speak for a bit. When she finally did, she sounded like she was suffocating in sadness. "I can't believe it. I just found out about her and now . . ." After half a minute, she took another deep breath. "Now she's gone."

"So you don't have to come." Dawson didn't want her to feel obligated. She belonged in Bloomington with her family, no matter how badly her world had been rocked. "I just . . . wanted you to know . . . what happened to her."

It took time, but eventually Maddie seemed to find control. "I want that, too." She paused. "I'll be there tomorrow." She told him the details of her flight and asked about a hotel near the airport.

In a matter of minutes Dawson had given her the information she needed. He offered to pick her up and then he said the only thing he could say. "I'm sorry, Maddie. I didn't mean any of this to hurt you."

"I know. You were only trying to help." She seemed more stoic now. "See you tomorrow, Dawson."

He hung up and took his seat again. He would have to tell Louise and Larry. And his father. The ordeal had taken a dramatic turn. Most of the day he'd tried to convince himself that he was impulsive for going to Indiana and definitely wrong for approaching Maddie West. But now she was coming to Portland. Not as a replacement for London. Of course not. But as a girl whose entire world had just been turned upside down. He checked the time on his phone. She'd be here in eighteen hours.

Dawson had a feeling he'd be counting every moment.

16

There was one thing Maddie had to do before boarding the plane to Portland. She packed early that Sunday morning and then went down the hall to her sister's room. Hayley was still asleep, but Maddie couldn't wait. She needed to leave in fifteen minutes to make her flight.

She opened the door and stepped inside. At first she just stood there, watching Hayley sleep. The girl had their mother's nose and cheekbones. Same pretty hair and profile. She had their father's sense of humor and his long fingers.

Why hadn't Maddie seen it sooner, the way Hayley looked just like their parents?

Her parents.

The truth was out now for everyone, even Hayley, Mom had said that much on text. But Maddie hadn't talked with her sister yet. She had no idea how Hayley would treat her given the situation.

God had been kind to Hayley, healing her a little more every year from the near-drowning accident she had when she was three. But she still struggled with processing complicated things. And nothing was more difficult than this. Either way, whatever her reaction, Maddie knew one thing.

Hayley would always be her sister.

She moved to the edge of Hayley's mattress, sat down, and put her hand on Hayley's arm. "Hey . . . wake up."

Gradually Hayley opened her eyes. When she was fully awake, tears gathered and she sat straight up. "Maddie!" Hayley threw her arms around Maddie's neck. "Where have you been?"

Tears came for Maddie, too. She hadn't seen this happening. Rather than confusion or hesitation, Hayley only wondered where she had been. "I stayed at my friend Andrea's house." Maddie tried to find her voice. "I needed to think. That's all."

"You needed to pray." Hayley pulled back and looked at her. Sunlight streamed through the window and caught her innocent blue eyes. Baxter eyes. "Is that what you mean? Because now you have two families. And . . . that's a lot to pray for." Hayley was talking as fast as she could, as if she'd been saving all this up for the moment she might see Maddie. "Also you have another sister. But I'm your sister first, right, Maddie?"

If Maddie didn't have to be strong for Hayley, and if she didn't have a plane to catch she would've collapsed on the floor in a pile of tears. *Dear sweet Hayley.* Maddie took her hand. "You're my only sister. Now and forever."

Hayley looked confused. She took a few seconds to formulate her next question. "I thought . . . don't you have another sister, too? A new one?"

"I don't." Maddie tried to smile. "I have the best sister in the world because I have you." She leaned close and kissed Hayley's forehead. "You're all I'll ever need."

"Okay." Hayley nodded. Her uncertainty dissipated and her expression held only a guileless joy. Because Maddie was here and that was enough.

But now Maddie was leaving, and she had to explain

why. "Okay . . . so I'm taking a trip, Hayley. I wanted you to know."

"A trip?" In a single breath, her eyes turned fearful. "I want to go!"

"You can't." Maddie stroked her sister's hair. It had been blonder when she was little, back when everyone always commented how the two girls looked so much alike. "I have business to do."

Hayley leaned back on her pillow. She reasoned at about a fourth-grade level. But it was so much better than what her doctors once expected of her. That she'd never walk or see or talk again. "Why, Maddie?" Her lip quivered. "Business where?"

Maddie didn't dare tell her she was going to Portland to meet the other family. She searched for the right way to explain herself. "The West Coast. I'll be there for a week, maybe longer." She thought of an idea. "Remember when I was in college, how I was only home for Christmas break and summers?"

Hayley nodded. "I remember." The slightest sparkle flashed in her eyes. "We always had so much fun when you came home."

"Exactly." Maddie relaxed a little. "We'll have the best time, Hayley. As soon as I get home."

Hayley hesitated. "Do Mom and Dad know you're going?"

"Of course." Maddie had told them last night. They had begged her not to leave, but Maddie cut the conversation short. "Everyone knows." She shot a look at her phone. It was time to go. "I wanted to say goodbye before I left."

Hayley sat up straighter. "Thanks, Maddie." She flung

her arms around Maddie's neck once more. "I'll miss you every minute."

"Me, too." Maddie blinked back her sorrow. She put her hand on Hayley's cheek. "Thanks for understanding."

"That's what sisters do." Hayley grinned. "I'll pray for your flight."

Maddie waved one last time before leaving the room. By then tears streamed down her cheeks. Yes, her parents knew she was leaving today. But not at this hour. She wasn't about to wake them and tell them goodbye.

Her Uber arrived a few minutes early. Two hours later Maddie was buckled into her seat at the back of a 737. Whatever was ahead, she was ready for it. She couldn't leave Indiana fast enough. It wasn't really her home, anyway. Portland was, apparently.

She checked her phone. Eight texts from her parents. Mostly from her mom. Maddie decided to read them.

Honey, where are you? I thought you said your flight left this evening?

Maddie, Hayley told us she talked to you . . . and you left. So your flight must've been earlier. Why didn't you say goodbye?

Then one from her dad.

You're hurting, we get that. But to leave on a cross-country flight without telling your mother and me goodbye? Maddie, this isn't like you at all. We're very worried. Please let us know you got to the airport okay. You took a ride with a stranger, when I would've been happy to drive you.

Each word pressed into her, ripping at her heart. If the people she thought were her parents loved her so much, if they were going to miss her so much, then she had one question for them.

Why hadn't they told her the truth?

Maddie, I'm panicking here. We wouldn't know if you got kidnapped. You haven't told us who's picking you up or where you're staying. Portland can be very dangerous, honey. Please . . . text back.

That was all Maddie could take. She didn't want them worrying about her. She was old enough to leave the state and go somewhere for a week. Even for a year. Whatever it took. But to make them overly concerned wasn't fair. The flight attendant made the announcement. No more cell phones.

Maddie typed as fast as she could.

I'm sorry for not saying goodbye. I have a lot to work through. Yes, I'm safely on the plane, and Dawson will pick me up when I land. I'll be fine. And Portland's no worse than Indianapolis. Tell Hayley I love her.

With all her heart she wanted to say the same thing to her parents. If only all of this was a bad dream so she could go back to being Peter and Brooke West's daughter. Back to being part of the Baxter family.

But that simply wasn't the case. This was her new reality and she had to walk in it. Even if that meant putting distance between her and the parents she had back in Bloomington. Maddie sat in a window seat, and she stared out as the plane taxied down the runway. Next to her, in the center spot, an older woman looked, too. "Beautiful day." She smiled at Maddie.

"Yes, it is." *Patience,* Maddie told herself. The last thing she wanted was mindless banter on the flight. Maybe if she played the conversation out now. Before they took off. "You from Bloomington?"

"Originally, yes." The woman was maybe sixty-five,

seventy years old. Her expression grew sad. "I came home to bury my mother." She sighed. "Dad died last year. We knew it wouldn't be long before Mom went, too."

The details caught Maddie by surprise. "I'm . . . so sorry."

"It's okay." The woman smiled despite the obvious pain in her eyes. "They loved Jesus, so I know where they are." She angled her head, like she was remembering a million happy moments. "And we had the best relationship. All our lives. The absolute best." She did a slight shrug. "No regrets."

Her words hit hard. Maddie nodded. "That's good."

"What about you?" The woman's question seemed genuine, like she really cared about Maddie. "You live in Bloomington?"

"I do. My family's here." She said the words before she could stop herself. Not that it mattered. She didn't want to get into specifics now, or before she knew it she'd be crying with a stranger. "Taking a trip to Portland to see . . . friends."

"Nice." The conversation fizzled and the woman yawned. "Well . . . I need to catch a little sleep on this one."

"Me, too." Maddie hesitated. "Nice talking to you."

"Yes." The woman smiled. "You seem like a sweet girl. Your parents must love you very much."

If she only knew, Maddie thought. "Yes . . . I'm sure they do." As complicated as things were, that much was the truth. Maddie's adopted family did love her. They had just left her with a lifetime that wasn't real anymore.

Maddie stared out the window as the plane took off. She half expected that if she turned back to the woman, she'd be gone. An angel, sent to deliver a message from

God. The importance of loving family and living without regrets.

Maddie had spent all her life that way. It was her adoptive parents who had changed everything by not being honest with her. And maybe the parents who really loved her were the ones waiting for her in Portland. The ones who cared enough to spare her life.

The parents she didn't know.

Indiana disappeared behind them. Something about that made Maddie feel free and at peace for the first time since hearing the news. It was still unreal that she was on a plane headed to the Pacific Northwest.

Like all of this was happening to someone else.

She closed her eyes and leaned back.

The one bright light through the past few days had been Connor Flanigan. She spent yesterday at his house in the backyard, helping his family plant summer flowers and in the kitchen, cooking dinner with his mother. Connor still didn't get it, how the news of her adoption could shake her so badly. But he was trying.

She pictured the moment last night when she sat with him on his family's porch and told him she was going to Portland. They were on the swing, and as soon as her words were out of her mouth, he stopped rocking. He had just one word for her.

"Why?" He didn't blink.

"Because." Maddie had rehearsed her answer. "I want to meet them. My biological parents."

By then Connor knew that Maddie's blood sister had died. Maddie had no idea how or what had happened. There were many things she wanted to talk to Dawson about. That was one of them.

"Who will you stay with?" He didn't give her time to answer. "Don't tell me you're hanging out with the guy who came to the zoo?"

"I am." She hadn't wanted to upset him or make him think things were rocky between the two of them. They weren't, not anymore. Maddie had overreacted that first night, but since then Connor had been extra sensitive. "He knew my sister very well." She hesitated. "I'd like to hear about her, what she did for fun, what was important to her. Everything I can learn."

He nodded. "I get that."

Maddie slid closer to him. "This isn't about me and you." She turned to him, their faces a breath from each other. "Believe me?"

"I do." He worked his fingers through her hair and kissed her. "And I can't wait till I say those words in front of a packed church."

"Mmm." Maddie felt the same way. "Me, too."

"How long will you be there? A few days?"

"Well . . . probably longer." She eased back so she could see him better.

"Probably?" He laughed, but it sounded nervous. "Don't you have a return flight?"

Maddie winced. "Not yet. I thought it would be better to keep it open."

The light left his eyes. "Oh."

She searched for the right words. "What I mean is, I might want to come home tomorrow." Her smile felt weak. "My boss at the zoo told me to take my time. So who knows?"

"Or stay a month." Connor ran his hand over her hair again. Peace seemed to return to his spirit. He filled his lungs and studied her. "You know what? I don't care. Stay as long as you need to stay, Maddie. You're going for answers . . . you need to find them."

"Really?" Maddie felt a burst of relief. She had never loved Connor more. She studied him, making sure he meant the words.

"Yes." He grinned. "You just graduated and your job isn't full-time yet. Why not? Go figure things out. Then come back." He kissed her again. "Ready to be my wife."

The way Connor said it, she could hardly wait. She would go to Portland, meet with her biological parents and hear the story of London—the sister she would never know. Then—after a few days—she would return home and get back to planning a wedding with Connor.

Maddie opened her eyes and gazed out at the vast blue. There was one problem. Where was she going to live when she came home? Connor's parents knew the truth now. But it wouldn't feel right moving in with them. Andrea couldn't take her long-term, either. Every room in her place was filled. Maddie certainly didn't want to stay at the home she grew up in.

She had a lot to work through. But at least she had Connor.

He was the only one who even remotely understood. Maddie smiled. Connor was such a good friend. Telling her she could be gone as long as she needed, and that it was important to figure this out. All so she would have no questions or hesitations when they moved forward with their marriage.

Yes, Connor was great. She was blessed beyond words to have him.

Maddie slept the last two hours of the second flight,

and then suddenly they were landing. This was Maddie's first time to the Northwest. What she saw out the window made her catch her breath. Portland was stunning. Crisp towering mountains covered in forests of dense pines. Rich, deep shades of green set beneath a beautiful bright blue sky. Picturesque rivers wound their way from the mountains through the city. The landscape was how she pictured heaven looking.

As far as the eye could see.

She could hardly wait to be on the ground and feel the cool air. A thought occurred to her. Maybe she was drawn to the city because she should've grown up here. What would life have been like living in this beautiful place, without the heat and humidity of Indiana? Would she have been a mountain climber or a windsurfer on one of the rivers? Maddie had no answers for herself. She would probably never have answers, because she had missed growing up here. Missed getting to know London.

Of course, if she'd been raised here she wouldn't have her family in Bloomington. And she wouldn't have Hayley. The wonderings were enough to make her head hurt.

Once she was off the plane, she texted Dawson. *I'm here. Headed for baggage.*

He replied almost immediately. *Welcome to Portland. I'm out at the curb. Look for the Chevy truck.*

Maddie read his text again. This was really happening.

But as she walked the concourse a wave of anxiety hit her. Dawson would be waiting for her. A guy she didn't even know, which made this whole trip seem a little crazy. What if he was only making up the story about knowing her biological family? Maybe he really was going to kidnap her?

Maddie stepped into a bathroom and gripped the edge of the sink. Dawson was not going to kidnap her. How could he possibly have known she was adopted unless he was telling the truth? That would be the weirdest guess a person could ever make. *Breathe, Maddie. Just breathe. Please, God, protect me.*

She touched up her face and hair and headed to baggage claim. When she had her two suitcases, she took a deep breath and walked through the double doors to the outside. The air was cold and clean-smelling. A hint of evergreen tinged the breeze.

Just as she began looking for his truck, she felt someone behind her. Maddie spun around and jumped. "Dawson! You scared me."

"Sorry . . . It seems to be a pattern." He stood there, a goofy grin on his face. "I guess that's the effect I have on you."

"No . . . I'm okay." Maddie's laugh caught her off guard. "I thought you'd be in your truck. That's all."

He took both her bags. "I figured you might need help."

If Maddie had thought he was handsome the first time they met, she had underestimated him. She could hardly wait to hear about the connection this guy had shared with her sister. The thought reminded her that despite the laughter from a minute ago, Dawson had to be grieving London's loss.

He held the door open for her, and once they drove off, Dawson spent the first ten minutes asking about her flight and about Connor. "I'm happy for you, Maddie." His smile was more melancholy. "I always thought I'd be married by now."

Maddie wondered how old he was. She had a thousand questions. Once they hit the interstate she started with the most important one. The most urgent. "Do you have a picture of London?"

"Here." He tossed his cell phone to her. "The code's all ones." His eyes stayed fixed on the road. "Pictures of London are about all I have in my photos."

For a few seconds, Maddie stared at him. "You were in love with her."

He glanced her way. "I was." He worked the muscles in his jaw. "She only wanted to be friends."

Which meant Maddie knew exactly one thing about her sister.

The girl was crazy.

Maddie took Dawson's phone and opened his photos. The first batch of pics was of the two of them on Jet Skis. They showed Dawson and a girl who must've been London racing down a beautiful, vast river. Maddie couldn't make out the girl's features.

But the next was a selfie of Dawson and the girl, and after that an up-close picture of what had to be London. Time stopped. It was like looking in a mirror. Maddie's heart began to pound. She brought her hand to her lips. "She . . . she looks just like me."

"Yes." Dawson looked over long enough to catch Maddie's attention. "That's why I kept staring that day."

Maddie understood now. She looked at the photos again. London was so pretty, long layered dark hair and beautiful eyes. In these shots it was hard to tell what color they were. But in more ways than Maddie could count, they shared an uncanny resemblance.

And of course they did. She and London were sisters, after all. Fertilized in the same petri dish.

"So . . . how old was she?" Maddie still had no idea.

"Twenty-eight." Something in Dawson's expression told Maddie this was hard on him. Talking about London. "We were the same age. Became best friends our senior year of high school."

Maddie nodded. *Twenty-eight*. Did that mean she and her embryo siblings sat in some doctor's freezer for more than five years before being brought to life? The idea seemed outlandish. How could tiny babies last that long in a freezer? Another question for later.

For a few minutes, Maddie fell quiet. She watched the city pass by out the window and she felt the strangest sensation. Like she was home. She'd always wondered what this part of the country looked like, always wanted to visit and now she understood why. Portland was quaint with buildings of vintage gray and black. The place beckoned her soul. Again she caught a quick look at Dawson. He had turned Christian music on the radio. Another thing she hadn't asked—whether her sister was a believer.

"Dawson." She studied him. It was time to find out. "What happened to her?"

He drew a quick breath. As if even the mention of losing her caused him more pain than he could handle. But after a few seconds he narrowed his eyes. "She died in an accident." That was all he said. All he seemed able to say. "We'll talk about it at dinner, if that's okay. We'll be there in five minutes."

"Of course." Maddie settled back in her seat. Because she just remembered something else. In three hundred seconds she wasn't only about to hear the story of what happened to London. She was about to do something she had never imagined doing.

Maddie was going to meet her biological parents.

17

Ever since Dawson told them about Maddie West, Louise's emotions had been all over the place. And now that the girl was about to walk through the door, Louise didn't know what to do or how to act.

Homemade lasagna was in the oven and the salad was ready to be tossed. Already Larry was in the living room watching out the front windows. She wanted to join him, but then . . . she wasn't sure. The girl hadn't known she was adopted until just a few days ago.

Who knew how she would feel meeting them now?

Louise leaned against the kitchen counter and remembered the evening when Dawson called with the news. Larry had been at the office and Louise was at the computer, paying bills.

"I found her." Dawson had sounded tired. "I just landed in Portland, but I had to call. It was definitely her."

He told her how Maddie had thought he was a stalker and how she'd had no idea she was adopted. "She's beautiful. Just like London."

"How old is she?" It was one question that mattered. Because if Maddie had come from the embryos she and Larry had donated, then she would probably be in her twenties.

"She just graduated Texas Christian University. I found

that out before I flew to Indiana." Dawson sighed. "I guess she couldn't be any older than twenty-two or so."

Dawson explained that he'd given the girl his number, but he hadn't expected to hear from her. "She was very upset." He'd gone on to say he thought the girl would eventually figure out he was telling her the truth. But that didn't mean she'd want to connect.

When the call ended, Louise had gone into London's room. Her daughter hadn't lived there for years, but it was still hers. The posters of adorable kittens and puppies, and her cheerleader pom-poms pinned to one wall. Her old high school clothes still lay in a heap on her closet floor. She'd been sorting through them a week before the accident. Finally ready to give them away.

A project she never finished.

Louise had turned to the other wall. Hanging there were sketches she'd done of monkeys and lions and giraffes. On the dresser stood a framed picture of the two of them. Louise and her precious London, the day she graduated high school. London had gone to college in Portland for one reason.

So she would be close to Louise. Her daughter loved being home, loved working with her mother at the coffee shop on Twenty-third. She was an only child and other than Dawson, her parents had always been her best friends.

Right until the end.

Then Louise had curled up on London's bed and rested her head on London's old pillow, and for nearly an hour Louise had grieved.

Not only the loss of London. But the loss of her sister.

Why hadn't she and Larry tried again? Sure, her pregnancy hadn't been easy. But that didn't mean a second one would be as bad. Louise had clenched her fists, breathing in the scent of London's teenage perfume, the one that still lingered on her comforter.

I should've been brave, she thought to herself. *We should've demanded they implant those embryos in me. And then Maddie would be my daughter . . . and London would've had a sister.*

Larry had found her there when he came home. Louise told him the news. "Dawson found London's sister."

Then, without a word, Larry had done something he'd never done. He crawled into London's bed with Louise. For the next half hour they held on to each other. Every doubt plaguing Louise had battered Larry's conscience that night, too. The endless what-ifs, the choices that could've changed everything.

"Maybe if she'd had a sister, she wouldn't have been so . . . free-spirited." Larry had wiped a few tears from his cheeks that night. "She might have settled down and married Dawson and by now . . . by now we'd be grandparents. We'd at least have London's child."

The sad possibilities were all too much. Despite the windy rain that day, they had gone outside for a walk. By the time they returned home, they had talked out all the scenarios and let it go. What was done was done. They couldn't go back and change things. "Besides, the girl doesn't want anything to do with us." Louise explained that Maddie hadn't known she was adopted. "Best to just move on."

Larry agreed, and that was the end of it.

Until Dawson called with the update. "She's coming to Portland."

"Who?" Louise had no idea what he was talking about.

He hesitated . . . and that was her first clue. When he spoke, he sounded dazed. "Maddie West. She . . . wants to meet you. She wants to know about London."

So now, any minute, the girl who could've been theirs if Louise had been more brave, would walk through the door to find out about the sister she missed out on knowing. If Maddie hated them, Louise couldn't blame her. And if that was the case, they would have a civil dinner and—

The doorbell.

Louise waited for only a few seconds. Then she brushed her hands on the dish towel and hurried to the entryway. Already Larry had the door open and in a blur, Dawson and Maddie walked into the house.

Tears weren't part of the plan tonight. Louise and Larry had talked about it, nothing that would make Maddie uncomfortable. This needed to feel like any other dinner, a meal with friends. A simple, sweet time of food and conversation. That was the plan.

But facing Maddie West, Louise had no control over her reaction.

The resemblance between this girl and London was astonishing. Louise brought both hands to her mouth and then dropped them. "Hello." With hesitant steps, Louise approached the girl.

"Maddie." Larry gave the girl a side hug. "Please, come in."

"Thank you." She looked from him to Louise. "Thanks for having me. I know . . . it's not . . . it's not the best circumstances."

Louise still couldn't breathe. She followed her husband's example and gave Maddie a side hug. But as she did, her tears spilled down her face. No amount of determination could've stopped them. Maddie stood there, like she wasn't sure what to say.

"I'm s-s-sorry." Louise pressed her fingers to her cheeks. "You . . . look so much like her."

Maddie gave the hint of a smile. "I do. I looked at pictures on Dawson's phone."

As they moved into the kitchen, something else took Louise's breath. At the sound of Maddie's voice, Bingo came trotting into the room. He stopped and stared at her, then he wagged his tail. Just a bit.

"Oh . . . he's beautiful." Maddie stooped down and nuzzled the dog's face. "I love goldens. What's his name?"

"Bingo." Louise looked at Larry and Dawson, and then back at Maddie. "He was London's dog." Louise wondered if she might pass out. The retriever never went to strangers. Not ever. But something in Maddie's voice must've made him think . . .

Louise couldn't finish the thought.

The uncanny similarities continued when Maddie offered to toss the salad, and she set the croutons in a side dish—something London always did. "Do you have balsamic?" Her tone was polite and cultured. Whoever had raised her, they'd done an exquisite job.

Italian hurt Maddie's throat? Louise had to steady herself against the counter to keep from reeling back. How many times had London said the same thing?

As Louise pulled the dinner from the oven, Maddie's eyes lit up. "Lasagna! My favorite."

The similarities wouldn't stop. "It was London's, too." Louise looked at Maddie and their gazes held. And for the first time it occurred to her—she was looking into the face of her daughter.

"I usually get lasagna when we eat out. Because no one in my family likes it." Maddie seemed to catch herself. Her smile faded. "No one back home, anyway."

Louise had a sudden, fierce sympathy for the parents Maddie had left back home. They must've been suffering over all the uncertainty and changes now that Maddie knew the truth. The girl was clearly upset about all of this.

Like she wasn't even sure she could call her adoptive parents her family.

We'll talk through that later, Louise told herself. Because no matter how badly she wished things were different, the truth remained. Maddie's real family lived in Bloomington. They were the ones who had given her life in every way that mattered.

Not till they finished dinner did Maddie pop up and clear the plates. Something London rarely did. Louise smiled. It was good to see something that was exclusively Maddie. They moved into the family room and Maddie took the chair. Almost at the same time, Bingo curled up at her feet. Like the dog had known her all his life. Dawson sat on the love seat and Louise and Larry settled in on the sofa.

"I know I just met you." Maddie looked sad and tired. "But please . . . could someone tell me what happened to London?"

Dawson slid to the edge of his seat and for a moment he looked down at his hands. Then he took a deep breath and turned his eyes to Maddie. For the next ten minutes he told her everything about the day of the accident—starting with the hike at Multnomah Falls.

Again Louise couldn't stop her tears, but she didn't mind. She would never hear the story of London's accident without crying. Next to her, Larry was brushing away tears, too. If only they could have that one day to do over.

When Dawson got to the part about London losing consciousness on the sidewalk outside the ice cream parlor, Maddie held up her hand.

"I have a question." She looked like she wasn't sure she wanted to ask it. "Did . . . did London have faith in Jesus? Because I do, and I've wondered ever since . . . you know."

Louise exchanged a quick look with her husband. It was the only question that mattered. She had to say something here. "We dropped the ball with London's upbringing . . . at least when it came to faith." Louise fought against her guilt. "Dawson tried. Over and over again."

Across the room, London's handsome friend looked down once more.

Louise continued. "No matter what Dawson said to her . . . London wasn't interested." Her tone was heavy with regret. "And we did nothing to help that."

Maddie didn't say anything. Her eyes welled up.

"But . . ." Dawson looked at Maddie. "There on that sidewalk everything changed." He told Maddie how London had asked about Jesus on the ride back down the mountain and how she wanted to talk about his faith over ice cream. "She had questions."

Every word held Maddie. She barely blinked as she listened.

"The last thing she said to me was that she had asked God to give her Jesus." Dawson raked his fingers through his hair. "Second toughest day of my life."

Of course, the most difficult was the one that came later. The day London took her last breath. "And even then"—Dawson's voice sounded more hopeful—"she talked about going home to Jesus. So . . . to answer your question, yes." He smiled at Maddie. "At the end, she had faith."

Larry picked the conversation up. "You would've loved her, Maddie. I can only imagine . . ."

Maddie brushed the tears from her cheeks and nodded. Larry stood to give her a tissue from the box on the end table. She pressed it beneath her eyes. "I can't believe I missed her."

Dark accusations shouted at Louise. *It's all your fault. This whole thing could've been prevented and maybe London would still be alive. If only you hadn't given away those embryos.*

The moment passed and Maddie stood. "I brought a photo album. Pictures of me growing up. It's in my suitcase." She pointed to the door. "Can I get it?"

"Of course." Louise wasn't sure she was ready for this. Larry gave her a sympathetic look, like maybe he wasn't ready either.

Dawson was on his feet now. "Let me help." He and Maddie left the house without saying a word.

When they were both outside, Louise put her head in her hand. "Larry."

"I know." He put his arm around her. "Here with her . . . it's like . . . Like being with London."

"Every word, every glance."

"Looking at pictures of Maddie as a baby . . ." Larry's voice trailed off.

Louise lowered her hand. "It'll be like looking at every season and stage we missed."

"Well." Larry stood and walked to the bookcase. "Let's show her London's baby photos. That's what she came for . . . to learn more about the sister she never knew."

Louise nodded. "I like that." At least if they had London's pictures out, too, the discussion would be more about how the two looked alike.

Not about the daughter Louise and Larry had missed out on.

Dawson and Maddie returned and for the next half hour they compared photos, Maddie's growing up pictures with London's. Time and again they found similarities in the photos. London sitting with a pumpkin on a hay bale when she was two years old. And then Maddie in almost an identical pose.

They were pictures of a happy childhood. In that sense, Louise was thankful. Maddie hadn't been theirs, but she had clearly been raised by people who loved her.

Next, Maddie told them about her family. Her parents were doctors and she had one sister, a sister who had suffered a near-drowning accident when she was little. She talked about identifying more with her mother's side of the family. "I always thought I was a Baxter." Her voice fell. "Until . . . I found out."

Louise wanted to take the girl in her arms and comfort her. Clearly she was confused. Like she had nowhere she truly belonged. Not the family back home and not Louise and Larry, who she'd only just met. One day soon, Louise hoped she might feel comfortable enough to go deeper on the subject.

It was after nine o'clock when the evening wore down. Maddie yawned. With the time change and emotion of the day, she was bound to be tired. The one thing they hadn't talked about was Louise's health, but she was glad about that. It was a detail that could wait. If it came up at all.

Just because Maddie wanted to meet them didn't mean she would become part of their lives.

But oh, how Louise wanted that. And when Dawson left to take Maddie to her hotel, Louise collapsed against her husband. "How did we miss her?" The ache wasn't ever going to stop. They had lost the chance to have this wonderful second daughter. All out of fear of the unknown. If Louise had it to do all over again, she never would've hesitated and Maddie would be theirs.

Her thoughts stayed there long after she went to bed. Sleep wouldn't come and Louise stared at the ceiling. Maddie had been kind and talkative, friendly and thoughtful. So much about her was like London. If Louise would've chosen to give birth to Maddie, the two girls would've been best friends. By the time she closed her eyes, Louise was sure that giving up Maddie hadn't only been a selfish choice.

But the worst decision she and Larry had ever made.

18

Dawson stopped by the office that morning to pick up a file. By then his dad knew about the change of events with Maddie and this time he didn't have a list of questions for Dawson. Just two words.

"Be careful." His father gave him a quick hug and a lingering look.

His dad didn't need to worry. Maddie had told him yesterday that she and her fiancé were doing great. Better than ever. Dawson left the office and headed for the hotel. He had one job today as he took Maddie around. It was what London would've wanted him to do.

Tell the Indiana girl everything he could about the sister she would never know.

And all the while try to ignore his broken heart. *This is not another day with London*, he told himself. *That's a lie*. Maddie was a totally different person, and after her few days or a week here in Portland she would go home to her fiancé and her parents. No matter how her time here went.

Because that was the right thing.

Then Dawson would get on with healing, learning how to live without the only girl he'd ever loved. He studied the clouds as he pulled into the hotel parking lot. More rain today, most likely, but he didn't mind. The truth was, today would be good for him. Maddie was her own person and by the end of their time together that would be more evident.

She was on the phone in the lobby when he entered the hotel. Dawson stayed back a few feet so she could finish her call. It didn't take long. She dropped her phone in her purse and smiled at him. "Sorry."

"No worries." He walked with her out to the truck and held the door for her. After last night he felt like he knew her better. Enough that the air between them didn't feel awkward. "How'd you sleep?"

"Well." Maddie buckled her seat belt. "I just can't . . . I can't believe I had a sister I never met. I can't stop thinking about it. Especially after all those photos last night." She sighed. "And now it's too late."

No one hurt more over London's loss than her parents and him. "You would've loved her." He stared again at the gray sky overhead. "After today you'll know that a little better."

"Thanks." She settled into her seat and looked out the window. "It means a lot, Dawson. That you would do this."

And there, in that moment, was the first major difference between Maddie and London. Dawson smiled to himself. Maddie was more polite. London was sarcastic, something Dawson had always thought would soften someday.

He worked to keep his head clear. "Let's start at University of Portland. That's where London went. She graduated with a business degree."

"Business . . ." Maddie's voice trailed off.

"Yes." It was hard to know where to begin with Maddie. She knew nothing about London, not the reasons she attended business school or her hopes and dreams. Nothing. He understood how Maddie must feel. Hungry for anything that would help her know London.

He would spend the next few hours seeing to that.

On the drive to the university Dawson kept stealing glances at her. Maddie was stunning, so like London. But she had a beauty all her own, too. He focused. "London grew up here. All her life." The zoo exit was coming up. "Her dream was to work with animals. The two of us . . . we were at the zoo a while back. She was ready to throw away the coffee business and start working with monkeys."

"So . . . she loved animals." The news seemed to hit Maddie hard. She looked out the window and watched as they passed the sign. Then, as if she were talking to the memory of her sister, her voice fell to a whisper. "I wish we could've talked about that."

Dawson waited a few minutes. Maddie needed time today, space to process everything she was learning. All she had missed out on. As they pulled off toward the university, he picked up again. "London loved working with her mom at the coffee shop. It was something they did together." He stopped at the light at the bottom of the off-ramp. "They were planning to open another one in Vancouver, across the river. Because the shop in Portland is so popular."

"Can we go there?" Maddie sounded hopeful. "Later today. I bet we liked the same coffee, too."

"We will." He chuckled. "It's on the itinerary."

"Perfect." They climbed out of his truck and she fell in beside him as they walked. "I have a feeling you'll be a very good tour guide."

He smiled and the sensation was wonderful. More like his old self than he'd felt in far too long. Just then the sun cut through the clouds, and Dawson lifted his gaze. "Don't be alarmed." He grinned at Maddie and switched to a mock tour guide voice. "If you look up just overhead, that's the sun." Another laugh caught him by surprise. "People in Portland are often frightened when the sun makes an appearance."

"I jumped a little. Yes." She played along as they walked, peering up at the sky. "The sun. I believe I've heard of it."

"I wondered." Dawson grinned and joy filled his heart. Who was this delightful young woman? And why couldn't he have met her before? He pushed the random questions from his mind and they continued down the pathway. Maybe today wouldn't be so sad and heavy after all. Losing London wasn't something personal to Maddie. The two never knew each other so for her, it was okay to have a little fun on the journey.

"Oh . . . I read up on Portland." Maddie's eyes sparkled as she turned to him. "Is it true you have two seasons here? Winter and August?"

"Nice." He allowed a quiet chuckle under his breath and he winked at her. "Which . . . is why it was kind of the sun to show up. Just for you. God lets that happen sometimes . . . when we have a special visitor to the city."

"I see." She did a slight curtsy. "Very kind." She glanced up. "Thank you, God."

London wouldn't have said that. Dawson studied the girl walking beside him. No, London would've teased him. *There you go. Always talking about God, Dawson. The sun is always in the sky, not just for one person.* How often had London said things like that? He glanced at Maddie again.

Whatever ways she was like London, there were clearly many more ways she wasn't.

The sun streamed through the evergreens that lined the path. Any rain in the forecast must've moved on. God truly was giving them a day fitting for remembering London. All sunshine and blue skies.

Dawson walked Maddie to the business building where she pointed to a bench near the front entrance. "Could we sit, please?" Her pretty face reflected the light. "For a few minutes."

"Sure." *She's engaged,* he told himself. *Keep your distance.* He let her take the lead. When Dawson sat down, he was careful to keep a few inches between them. He ran his hand over the bench. "I bet London never sat here."

Maddie turned to him. "Why not?"

"Because." He looked at Maddie. "Your sister never . . . she never stopped moving." He could see her again, hair flying behind her as she ran. "London was a free spirit. She didn't always make great choices, but she loved big."

So big, he told her, that the last time he had visited her on campus they had shared lunch in the cafeteria across the lawn. "She stayed with me till the last possible minute, asking about my work and telling me how she wanted a London Coffee shop in every city on the West Coast. Then she was going to expand to New York City."

"Ambitious." Maddie raised her eyebrows. The breeze caught her long blond hair and she tucked it behind her ear. "I can be that way. But not always."

"That's just it. The conversation wasn't so much about ambition . . . as it was about her heart." Dawson leaned back and looked across the campus. "She was so busy sharing her dreams with me, she almost missed class. When she left, she had to run to make it." He pointed to the sidewalk they'd just come up on. "I still see her, sprinting across the path, racing into this building."

"Mmm." Maddie nodded. "Which is why she probably never sat here."

"Right." Dawson pulled his North Face jacket closer around his body. "It's cold."

"Not for me." Maddie breathed in through her nose. "I like it. No humidity." She stared straight ahead. "I like that. Now . . . I can picture her rushing this way, headed for her business classes." She paused. "I feel connected to her here."

"Yes. I mean . . ." There were so many other places where Maddie was bound to feel a stronger connection. "London . . . well, she wasn't very studious." He laughed. "She got by, but her greatest classroom"—he pointed to the mountains—"was out there. Hiking and sailing. Riding Jet Skis. Working in the shop with her mom. Getting coffee with her dad."

"And being with you." Maddie's voice grew soft. She pulled one knee up on the bench and looked at him. "Is this too hard for you, Dawson? Walking where she walked today? Talking about her?"

"I thought it might be." His eyes met Maddie's and held. "But I'm having fun." He shaded his brow. "And the sun's out."

"True." She laughed, and the sound was music in the cool air. "So take me to her favorite places. How about that?"

They each wore tennis shoes and a jacket warm enough for a short hike. "Ever heard of Multnomah Falls?"

"Yes!" Maddie's eyes lit up. "It's on my list of places to see."

"Well." Dawson stood. He almost reached for her hand to help her up, but he stopped himself. "Multnomah Falls was one of London's absolute favorite places."

An hour later they parked at the lower lot and Dawson cut the engine. "Here we are."

"It's beautiful." Maddie peered out the window and looked up at the distant falls. "This is where you came that day?" She didn't seem in a hurry to get out. "The day . . ."

"Yes." Dawson had wondered how he would feel when he came back here. If he came back. But he wasn't sad now. Maddie brought too much light to the moment for that. He opened his truck door. "Come on."

Without thinking, Dawson hurried around to Maddie's door and opened it. "The walk to the falls isn't long."

As they made their way, Dawson noticed something. Maddie had the same skip in her step, something Dawson had loved about London from the beginning. But the pretty blonde was shorter than London, just an inch or two.

Maddie zipped her jacket a little higher. "I can see why she loved it here."

"Rain or shine." Dawson slid his hands in his jeans pockets. "You hike much in Indiana?"

"We have Lake Monroe." Their pace was slow and easy. She told him about the dark blue water and the walking path around the shore. "My family has a boat at the club. I love being on the water."

Dawson made a mental note. If the weather held up, and if Maddie were still in town, Jet Skis might have to be on the schedule for later that week. They walked to the bridge at the base of the falls and stopped. Mist from the water hit their faces, much as it had done that day a blink ago when he was here with London.

For a long time neither of them said anything. Then Maddie pointed to the path on the other side of the bridge. "You and London walked that trail?"

"All the way to the top." He grinned. "Like I said, she never stopped."

"This is far enough for me." She lifted one foot and pointed to her white Adidas tennis shoe. "Unless I had my hiking boots."

"Really?" He raised one eyebrow. "You have hiking boots? For Lake Monroe?"

"No." She laughed and gave his shoulder a slight push. "Indiana is flat. But sometimes I go to Los Angeles to visit my aunt and uncle. We hike the Santa Monica Mountains."

Dawson nodded. Who was this mysterious girl? Part London and so much more her own self. "Sounds amazing."

"It is." She turned her back to the falls and leaned against the railing, her eyes on his. "It starts out desert, but by the time you reach the crest you can see the entire Pacific Ocean. I love it."

Dawson took in every word. He couldn't get over the fact—Maddie liked hiking, too. The realization was still making its way through Dawson. Her kindness and polite demeanor had at first made him wonder if she was maybe a less interesting version of London. But that wasn't true at all.

"So . . . tell me about you." Maddie looked at him, her expression open. No walls between them. She grinned. "Other than the whole 'writing a report on zoo animals' thing."

"Don't forget my sketching ability." He laughed. "I never showed you my giraffe."

She tipped her head back and laughed, lighter than before. Then she leveled her gaze at him. "I can see why my sister liked you."

The moment grew quiet. He still faced her, the two of them a breath away. Dawson had almost forgotten London was the reason they were here. As if Maddie were some amazing girl he'd just met and this was how they were spending the afternoon. Dawson turned his attention to the falls. "I'm a developer."

"Right. You did say that." Maddie didn't break eye contact. He could feel her stare.

Don't do this. He had to keep reminding himself. She belonged to some other guy. "I work with my dad here in Portland. We develop riverfront properties on both sides of the Columbia. Buy old buildings and fix them up. Then lease them out or sell them."

"For more money." She never looked away. "Sounds interesting."

"It is." Dawson hadn't expected her to want to know about him. "We're talking about expanding in the next year. Maybe moving into another city."

A gust of wind caught the mist and made their faces wet. Dawson wiped his forehead and nodded toward the parking lot. "We better keep going. The tour isn't over."

On the drive back she asked about his family and he told her about losing his mother. She was quiet, maybe processing that. "I'm sorry."

"It was a long time ago." He smiled. "Just me and Dad now."

Maddie told him about her cousin Amy losing her entire family in a car accident. "Doesn't matter how many years go by, the loss still hurts."

Dawson narrowed his eyes. It was like she had known him all her life. But he didn't say that. He just nodded. "Yes . . . it's always there."

Next they went by the high school where Dawson and London first met. They got out of his truck and leaned against the side facing the entrance. The sun felt warm on Dawson's face and he took a long breath. "I fell in love with London on Grad Night at Disneyland." He grinned at Maddie. "She told me not to fall in love with her."

Maddie angled her head. "No." She shook her head. "She couldn't have meant it. You two spent all that time together. I'm sure she was in love with you, too, Dawson."

"Actually, she wasn't." Dawson shrugged. He was coming to accept the fact. "I always thought I could convince her." The way they were standing, side by side leaning on his truck, Maddie's shoulder was barely touching his arm. He moved a few inches away. This day wasn't real. She'd be going back home soon. Where she belonged. He remembered what they were talking about. "London had this thing she would always say to me. Whenever the subject came up . . . you know, the two of us as a couple."

"So . . . you talked about it?" Maddie angled her shoulder into the truck and looked straight at him. "And she still wasn't sure?"

"No." The story was complicated. "We saw faith differently. She . . . thought it was a crutch. Honestly, she wanted nothing to do with God." He paused. "Till the day of her accident."

"What did she used to say? When the subject came up?" Maddie was clearly curious. Like she genuinely wanted to know about whatever Dawson and London had shared. "That one day she'd open her eyes and see . . . the guy right in front of her?"

He was flattered, but he didn't want her to see that. *Don't fall for her. This isn't real,* he told himself. *Be the tour guide.* But Dawson couldn't help himself. He had thought about London's favorite comeback more than once since Maddie arrived. He just never planned to share the detail.

Until here. Now, with Maddie.

Against his own advice he let his eyes hold hers for a long moment. "She told me the right person for me was out there." He paused. "And that one day I'd meet her and I would know." He smiled. "She always said that this . . . girl I was going to meet . . . wouldn't be her. But someone like her."

Someone like you, he wanted to say. A girl with faith and a gentle spirit, but all the adventure and beauty of London. Maddie was that girl, no question. But she was taken and she was going home in a few days. Dawson caught himself and the moment broke. "We still have coffee to get."

Maddie wasn't in the same sort of hurry. She didn't move, still leaning against the truck, her blond hair spilling over her shoulders. "Someone like her." She nodded. "Because of your faith differences."

"I guess." Dawson couldn't look in her eyes. Otherwise he'd never look away. "Come on. Louise is expecting us."

But the change of topic did nothing to ease the way Dawson felt. The entire ride to the coffee shop, he could barely draw a full breath. They parked in the side lot next to the shop. Just out front Maddie stopped and looked at the sign. "London Coffee." She smiled. "I like it."

"The whole city does." Dawson laughed as he held the

door for her. Inside, they said hello to Louise, ordered coffees and found a table near the window. The place was bustling with people and theirs was the only open spot. "See what I mean?"

"Yes. Wow." Maddie's cheeks were red from the sun and wind. "And I see why." She looked around and ran her hands over the reclaimed wood table. "I'd be here every day."

Dawson studied her as she looked out the window at bustling Twenty-third Street. "Maddie . . . tell me about that day at the zoo. What happened . . . after you left."

Her eyes found his and a chill ran down his arms. Again it was like he'd known her all his life. She put her hands around her coffee mug. "It was . . . one of the worst days of my life."

"I hate that you didn't know." He took a sip of his coffee. "I never expected . . . I wouldn't have come."

"I believe that." Her smile was warm with understanding. "You had nothing to do with what happened to me, Dawson."

"And how about now? Are you . . . still upset with your parents?"

"Well . . ." she sighed. "They aren't exactly my parents, you know? They're my adoptive parents. And they lied to me all my life."

Nothing about Maddie was hard or jaded. But that last revelation sounded bitter. Every word had an edge to it. Dawson looked at her for a few seconds before speaking. Maybe this was why he was here with her today. So he could help remind her who she actually was. "They're still your parents, Maddie. Bloomington is your home and those people are your family. No matter where you came from."

"That's just it." Maddie looked deep into his eyes. "I'm not sure who I am now. All my life I've thought I was blood related to my family, and now I know I'm not. So am I more a part of Louise and Larry? Would London have been my best friend? I feel . . . disconnected from everything back home." She raised one slim shoulder. "I'm not sure how long I'll feel like that."

"So . . . you and your parents . . ." He tried again. "Things aren't good?"

"No." Her single laugh was empty of any humor. "We aren't talking, really. They know I arrived here safely. That's about it."

Dawson let the reality work through him. How awful for her parents back home. He would make a point of bringing this up later. Maddie couldn't hate her parents. Embryo adoption was cutting edge back then. Most people still didn't know about it. How would you tell a child she was adopted when she was formed in her adoptive mother's womb?

After coffee they stopped at the store for flowers. Maddie's idea. They were having dinner at Louise and Larry's again and she thought a bouquet would be a nice touch. "Yes!" Maddie seemed to know what she wanted from the florist. She skipped ahead to a pretty display. "Yellow roses. They're my favorite."

His heart missed a beat and he blinked. Because for a few seconds he could only see London, delighting over a bouquet in this very store. How could they be so similar? When they'd never even met? He took the spot beside her. "Yellow roses were London's favorite, too."

Maddie reached for the flowers and stopped. She turned to Dawson again. "Thank you. For telling me that."

She took hold of the bouquet and faced him. “I would’ve been good for her. I believe that.”

No question, Dawson wanted to say. If London had been close to Maddie, maybe she would’ve understood Dawson’s faith sooner. He let the thought pass. It was all speculation, at this point. Maddie would’ve been younger, and maybe she would’ve been as wild and free spirited as London. That’s how it worked with younger sisters.

The night was less awkward, less emotional. They played spades after dinner and when Dawson took Maddie back to her hotel, they laughed about how long they’d stood at the falls. “My shirt was damp for an hour.” Dawson kept his attention on the road. He hadn’t had this much fun in a long time.

Maybe ever.

They made a plan to ride the Jet Skis the next day. Dawson parked in front of the hotel and faced her. “When do you leave?”

“I’m not sure.” Again, she didn’t look away. “I didn’t buy a return ticket.”

The news shocked Dawson. “But . . . your family. Your job.”

“I know.” She smiled. “I just need to be here. I’m not sure how long.”

His heart beat a bit faster. “Okay.”

“I asked Louise and Larry if I could stay with them for a while.” She looked up at the hotel sign. “This is my last day at the Hilton.”

Dawson nodded. “All right, then. I guess the tour’s going to last a little longer.” He climbed out of the truck and got her door once more.

When she stepped out she grinned up at him, and

then, without hesitating, she eased her arms around his neck and hugged him. Not for too long, and not in a way that was inappropriate. But for Dawson, the feeling lasted long after she let go.

She smiled. "Thank you." The temperature had dropped, and she shivered in the cold night air. "For today, Dawson." She seemed to look straight to his soul. "It was a gift from God. More than I could've imagined."

He only hesitated a moment. "For me, too."

"And you don't have to be my tour guide after today." Her laugh was easy and light. Now that he'd had a full day with Maddie he could tell the sound was her own.

"You're firing me?" He had to be careful. There was no room for mixed signals. Not when the situation was already so complicated. "What if I like the job?"

Again she tipped her head back and laughed. As if he were the funniest guy she'd ever known. "I didn't say I don't want to hang out." Her eyes sparkled. "I just don't need a tour."

"Okay." Dawson felt his smile fade. What was she saying? And how come she looked at him that way? "I guess you should . . . you know, go in and call your fiancé."

The reminder seemed to put her off. She took a step back. "I guess so." She held up one hand. "Thanks again."

He watched her walk through the doors. When she was gone he stepped back in his truck and drove away. Maddie West was the most wonderful girl he'd ever spent a day with. They'd had no fighting about God, no jokes about Dawson being a monk. No hopes dashed once again.

Maddie believed the same way he did.

Every minute of the day had been unforgettable. By the time Dawson got home he had to work to remember his own words. *Maddie wasn't London. She was only here for a short time and then she would go home to her fiancé.* But none of that changed the way she had looked at him. Not once but throughout the day.

When he turned in that night he couldn't wait to see her again. Whether she went home in a few days or a few weeks, he would enjoy the time he had with Maddie West. She was her own person, and Dawson wanted only to be with her again. She wasn't London. But in the craziest, most uncanny way she was someone like her.

And as he fell asleep Dawson couldn't imagine going a day without her.

19

She was falling for him.

The one thing Maddie didn't see happening on this trip was actually happening, and there was nothing she could do about it. Dawson's green eyes were a world she had spent the whole day exploring and all she wanted was more. More hours to talk, more places to see, more time with him.

As wrong as it was.

Back in her hotel room she sat on the edge of her bed and covered her face with her hands. What was she doing here? She never should've left Indiana. Connor loved her with all his heart, and since early that morning he would've been thinking of her, praying for her. *Figure things out,* he had told her.

She was the world's worst fiancée. And even so all she could think about was Dawson. She had expected today to be melancholy and informative. She would learn about London and at the end of the day she'd feel closer to the sister she never met.

That had happened, definitely. But somewhere on the path at University of Portland, Maddie had realized something startling. She was enjoying herself far too much. How could she go home to Connor and plan a wedding when she'd never felt this way around any other guy? She wasn't sure if Dawson felt it, too, but something between them was electric.

Maybe because she wasn't the same person she'd been before Dawson walked into her life. Who was she? Now that she wasn't related to her family? And was she determined to destroy everything about her past, walking out on her parents and betraying Connor? Even just in her mind? She didn't want to do that. Hurting the people back in Bloomington made no sense. Especially when it came to Connor.

But she couldn't help herself.

Maddie lowered her hands. Suddenly all she wanted was to call home and talk to her mother. Her mom would understand what she was experiencing and why she wasn't feeling the same about her fiancé. But she couldn't call home any more than she could make sense of her crazy attraction to Dawson. It wasn't just his looks or his beautiful faith. She was drawn to something deeper.

Like she really had known him all her life.

Lord, why do I feel so much when I'm with him? Is it because of London?

She waited but there was no quiet whisper from heaven. Instead a Bible verse came to mind. Something she'd read that morning before Dawson picked her up.

Come to me all you who are weary and burdened, and I will give you rest. Take my yoke upon you and learn from me, for I am gentle and humble in heart, and you will find rest for your souls. It was from Matthew, Chapter 11, and always the words brought her peace.

Come to me all you who are weary and burdened, and I will give you rest.

Maddie breathed out. Gradually the words soothed

her anxious heart. There was only one thing to do next. She grabbed her phone and called Connor. He was at his parents' house helping his dad put together a new backyard table. He asked her about the day and then he wondered why her answers were short.

"I'm sorry." She stood and paced the room. "I thought you needed to get back to work."

Connor didn't say anything.

Maddie's pacing wasn't helping. Her mind was back at Multnomah Falls. She sighed. "Hello? Connor?"

"Forget it, Maddie. Whatever." Now it was Connor's turn to sound short. "Maybe you're right. My dad still needs my help."

"I said I was sorry." Maddie couldn't wrangle her errant thoughts. She couldn't tell Connor that her promise to him was being tested on every level. She sighed. "It's been a long day, that's all."

"Maybe tomorrow will be better." Connor was definitely trying to rebound. "I love you, Maddie. Try to get back to the hotel earlier. We can talk then."

"Oh." She hesitated. "Actually . . . I'm staying at Louise and Larry's house tomorrow. Until I come back."

Again Connor said nothing. Nearly a minute passed before he spoke. "Until you come home, you mean?"

"Right. Home." Maddie dropped to the bed again. "I love you, Connor. We can talk longer tomorrow. I'm not even making sense."

That night Maddie took two hours to fall asleep. When she did, she dreamed about Dawson.

The next day was sunnier still and ten degrees warmer. Dawson seemed to know from the moment he picked her up what he wanted to do. He took her to breakfast and then to his house. A mansion on the Columbia River. Dawson gave her London's wet suit and a room where she could change. The house was stunning, but warm. *Like him,* Maddie thought. The wet suit was a little long, but otherwise it fit perfectly. No surprise.

Maddie had jet-skied before on Lake Monroe, but the experience was nothing to how it felt riding alongside Dawson down the scenic river. The strong current made the adventure that much more exciting.

Ten minutes into the ride, a swell from a passing boat nearly capsized Maddie's WaveRunner. Maybe she was over her head riding on the Columbia River. Dawson must've seen her uncertainty because he motioned for them to go back to the dock. They idled in the water a few feet from each other. "Sorry." He was breathless, same as her. "That was a little dicey."

"At least I stayed on." Maddie tried not to stare at the way his arms looked in the wet suit. "I'm not a pro like you."

He moved closer to the dock and grabbed the rope. "I have an idea." He looked over his shoulder at her. "Park yours. You can ride with me. I want to show you something."

Maddie couldn't think of a single reason to object.

Dawson tied the rope around his Jet Ski and anchored hers to the dock. Then he climbed on again and helped her onto the spot behind him. He reached back for her hands and eased her arms around his waist. He looked back, his voice warm against her face. "We might go fast." His grin melted her heart. "Don't let go."

"I won't." She shivered, but not because the cold water was getting to her. With her arms around Dawson, the warmth from his back spread through her body. She hoped the ride would last an hour. At least.

He took her upstream under the 205 Bridge. If they went much farther they'd wind up in the gorge. The same section of the river they'd driven past to get to the falls yesterday. Instead, Dawson turned the ski around and glanced back at her. "Hold on!"

She tightened her grip on him just as he took off flying across the river. The current was working with them now and the ride was faster than any she'd ever taken. She could feel his ab muscles working beneath his wet suit as he angled the machine one way and then the other.

When he slowed to an idle she finally exhaled. Her heart raced and they were both breathing fast. She leaned her face alongside his. "Do it again!"

"In a minute." He idled to the right and she saw a strip of land she'd missed before.

"An island." She wiped the spray from her face. "Is this what you wanted to show me?"

"Yes." He drove a few feet up onto the shore and took her hand. "Come on. I love this place."

The sun was warmer now, and once they were off the Jet Ski, Dawson peeled back the top half of his wet suit. He had a tank top underneath, but it did nothing to hide the way he looked.

Maddie left her wet suit on. She was still wearing Connor's ring, after all.

They sat on the sand, side by side. Dawson seemed careful to leave a few inches between them. *Good guy*, Maddie told herself. On top of everything else she liked about Dawson Gage, he had character. Faith was action to him. That much was clear.

"This is as close to a deserted island as we'll get in

Portland." He grinned at her. "It's just a little strip of land, but I like to think of it as mine."

"And mine." She nudged his elbow and then regretted the fact. *Contain yourself.* She aimed for a less flirty tone. "At least today."

"Yes." He looked at her and his smile dropped off. "At least today." Those beautiful eyes of his. So much wisdom and empathy. Like he knew her every thought.

They spent an hour on the island. Dawson talked about his high school and college days and how he'd managed without his mother. And she told him about Hayley and her drowning accident and how for the longest time she'd thought the terrible ordeal was her fault. "I was supposed to watch her."

"I'm sorry, Maddie. For you and Hayley." He shook his head. "But you were a child." Dawson worked his toes into the sand. Somehow they'd moved closer to each other and now his elbow brushed against hers. "Your sister wasn't your responsibility. It was an accident."

"I get that better now." Every time their arms touched it was electricity for Maddie. She tried to concentrate. Then she remembered she was wearing a ring on her left hand and that she was officially engaged. Planning a wedding. "Connor was the first one to help me see I wasn't to blame." There. She had brought her fiancé into the conversation. "Connor's always been good for me that way."

Dawson did a couple slow nods. But he didn't say anything. Like maybe he wasn't sure how to respond. Instead after a few minutes he asked if she was looking forward to staying at the Quinns'. "They're the nicest people." Maybe it was Maddie's imagination, but his tone seemed a little cooler. "I'm sure Louise is glad to have you."

The mention of Louise made Maddie remember something. "Is she sick? Louise?" Maddie shifted toward him and her toes brushed against his. Like her body had a mind of its own. She inched away and looked at him. "She seems tired. A little slow when she walks."

Dawson took a deep breath and stared across the river. "Yes." He turned to her again. "Louise is very sick." She works at the coffee shop because it's something she shared with London. She always said her time there . . . would be the last to go."

"What?" Maddie sat cross-legged and faced him. "Why didn't you tell me?"

"She asked me not to." Dawson rubbed his neck. "She's in kidney failure, Maddie." He clenched his jaw and looked at the sand between them. When he lifted his face to hers again his eyes were damp. "London was going to give her a kidney. But neither of hers survived the accident."

Maddie's heart pounded. She was still trying to understand. "So . . . she's on a donor list? And after a transplant she'll be fine?"

"She's been on the list for more than a year." He sighed. "She'll be mad I told you . . . but Louise has three months, maybe four without a new kidney."

What was this? "You mean . . . she's dying?"

"Yes." He looked out over the river. "London was a perfect match. And honestly . . . I'm not sure Louise is upset about dying. She'll get to be with London again."

Maddie shook her head. "No." She patted Dawson's knee. "We can't let her think like that." Her mind raced. If London was a perfect match, then . . . "Wait!" She stood and stared down at Dawson. "If my sister was going to give her a kidney, I should at least be tested."

Dawson was on his feet now, too. "Louise would never allow that." He took both Maddie's hands in his. "Don't even think about it."

She should let go, slip free from his tender grasp and step five feet back. But she couldn't. And here on their own private island in the middle of the Columbia River, Maddie had no idea what that said about her.

Instead she held his hands more tightly. "She gave me life, Dawson." Maddie's voice fell to little more than a whisper. With the wind off the water she wasn't sure he could even hear her. Conviction filled her tone. "Louise had three leftover frozen embryos. Do you know how many people would've given the okay to throw them down the sink?"

Dawson locked eyes with her and for a long few seconds Maddie wondered if he might kiss her. They were only a foot apart. Instead he shook his head. "You don't know what's involved, Maddie."

"I do." Maybe this was why she was here. Because her biological mother needed her. Maddie was suddenly sure. "My parents are doctors. One of their friends just gave a kidney to his brother. It's no big deal."

A single laugh came from Dawson. He let one of her hands go and gently brushed the hair from her face. "I hear London in your voice." Imperceptibly he moved nearer, closing the distance between them just a little. "Every word you just said . . . she would say." He paused. "She did say."

"Take me tomorrow, please Dawson." She felt so comfortable around him. There was no understanding that except for the fact that London had loved him. The nearness of him was pulling her in, making her forget every promise she'd ever made. She dug her heels in the ground so she wouldn't move any closer to him. "Whatever clinic London was connected with. They can test me."

He couldn't refute her logic. "I'm telling you . . . Louise won't want you to do this."

"It doesn't matter." She put her hand alongside his cheek. "Maybe this is why I'm here. Have you thought of that?"

Dawson looked like he could barely think. "Okay. I'll take you." He covered her hand with his and then he stepped away from her. "Come on. We need to get back."

No mention of the reason he maybe suddenly wanted to leave except the one obvious to both of them. Here on this strip of land, with no one to see or know or wonder what was happening, it would have been easy for him to kiss her. But that couldn't happen. After all, she wasn't here forever. Just for a while. Dawson was part of a make-believe life Maddie hadn't even known she'd had until last week.

She held tight to him on the way back, and this time he didn't race across the water. He took his time, like he never wanted the ride to end. Which was exactly how she felt.

Back on the dock, Dawson exhaled. "Let's get you some hiking boots."

Her laugh seemed to break the intense connection and bring things back to a more easygoing feel. "I'd like that." She thought for a moment. "Dawson . . . first, would you take me to the cemetery? Where London is buried?" She paused. "I mean . . . I know she's not there. But I'd like to bring flowers."

"Yellow roses." Dawson looked at her as he peeled off his wet suit. It wasn't a question. He knew her better now. Not just because of London.

An hour later they were back in his truck headed north.

Maddie had the roses. The cemetery was a twenty-acre park of rolling green grass and a few dozen evergreens. Dawson turned in and took a winding paved road to the top of the highest hill. "London loved a pretty view," he explained as he parked. "Her parents chose this spot."

All this time Maddie hadn't cried about losing London. She'd never known the girl and though they were alike in some ways and their baby pictures practically matched, Maddie wasn't sure the two of them would've been friends.

Or maybe they would've, and Maddie would simply be different. More like London. Or London might be more like Maddie. Either way, being here at the cemetery made everything about London more real. Less than a month ago London was the one riding Jet Skis with Dawson down the Columbia.

And now . . . now she was here.

They walked a few yards to a modest grave marker. It looked painfully new. Maddie stopped and stared at the words. LONDON MARIE QUINN. Then her birth and death dates. Beneath that it said simply:

SHE LAUGHED. SHE LOVED. SHE LIVED. BECAUSE OF JESUS, SHE LIVES STILL.

Dawson stood back while Maddie set the flowers alongside the flat stone. Then, with her toes at the edge of the marker, the floodgates gave way. Buried in the ground here was her blood sister. The only other person on earth who had shared her DNA, the same mother and father.

And Maddie had never even had the chance to hold her hand or hug her.

Tears flooded her eyes and ran down her cheeks. Dawson moved up beside her and put his arm around her shoulders. No words were needed. The loss was great for both of them, in their different ways.

After a long while they walked back to the truck. Maddie was even more convinced about being tested tomorrow. If she could give Louise a kidney, if she could do something to save her biological mother's life, then this loss and heartache would all be worth it.

She might even call her mom back in Bloomington. They could talk about the reasons she wanted to be tested and the risks of donating a kidney. A call would be the right thing to do.

When Maddie had more control of her emotions, Dawson started the truck. He still didn't say anything, not until they pulled into the parking lot of Academy Sports. Then he took her hand and ran his thumb over hers. "I was serious about the boots."

Again the chemistry between them was like a physical force. Maddie smiled. "I'm serious about hiking with you."

"Good." He released her hand and the two headed for the store entrance.

The air between them lightened when they were in the store, and from there Dawson took her to a longer hike half an hour past Multnomah Falls. This time they talked about their faith, and how maybe culture was moving back to God. Pop music and films. Books. Everywhere, there were signs of people believing again. "Jesus is everything to me." Dawson looked to the sky. The path was wide enough that they walked side by side. "He always will be."

And Maddie knew she would remember him for the rest of her life.

20

Brooke had tried to call Maddie every day since she left. Twenty days in a row, three times a day, sometimes four. Not once did her daughter pick up. So Brooke would text, and she wasn't the only one. Her dad and Elaine and all Brooke's siblings had tried texting Maddie.

So far the only person in the house Maddie had texted back was Hayley. She still loved her sister. One thing Brooke was thankful for. Because in their darkest moments, Brooke and Peter truly believed Maddie was so confused, she no longer loved them. As if what they had done by not telling Maddie the truth about her identity was too much to forgive.

But then Brooke and Peter would hold hands and beg God to soften Maddie's heart, to bring her back home. Never had Brooke imagined that in the fallout of telling their daughter the truth about her identity she might leave. That she would be gone three weeks and move in with her biological parents, or that she would reject everything about her real family.

Today Brooke's appointments had been a blur of colds and ear infections and one broken arm. The whole time, every little girl was Maddie. The one Brooke had carried inside her, the one she birthed and held and loved from her first minute of life. Oh, to go back and do it all over again. She and Peter would've told Maddie from the time she could talk.

Different DNA, but still our child. Adopted as an embryo but always a West. Always a Baxter. Those would've been their words as often as Maddie needed to hear them. Yes, they would've made that clear even if little Maddie couldn't possibly have known the meaning of DNA or embryos. Never mind.

They would've told her.

Lunch was at the same time each day for Brooke and Peter. It was one of the joys of sharing the pediatric practice. No appointments noon to one. Instead they would take a walk and get coffee or lunch. Today they walked to Chopt, a new salad place a block from their office.

Just as they were about to go inside, Brooke's phone rang. She had stopped hoping the call might be from Maddie, but just in case, she checked the caller ID. "Peter!" She dropped to a bench near the front door. "It's her."

The sidewalk outside the restaurant was quiet. Peter joined her and Brooke put the call on speakerphone. "Maddie? Maddie, thank God."

Silence. And then only the most faint sound of someone breathing on the other end.

"Maddie?" Peter tried this time. "Honey, we're both here. Please . . . talk to us."

"Okay." Maddie's voice sounded beyond broken. "I . . . wanted to tell you a few things."

Brooke's heart raced. She was calling them, talking to them. No one could've forced her, so this could only be God working in her heart. "Yes." There was a breathlessness in Brooke's tone. She couldn't help it. "We're here, honey. We love you."

"We miss you." Peter seemed as desperate as Brooke to get the words out, tell her what she needed to know. "Every day we're praying for you, sweetheart." His voice choked up and for a few seconds he struggled to speak. "We're so . . . so sorry."

It took a long pause, but finally Maddie spoke again. "I know." Anger still tinged her tone, but she was calling. That's all that mattered. "First . . . Dawson has been helping me with forgiveness." She was still fighting for control by the sound of her voice. "He's been showing me Scriptures, praying with me."

Dawson. Brooke's mind raced. "The guy who came to the zoo?"

"Yes. He was in love with London. My . . . sister who died." Her words held an unspoken accusation.

Only then did Brooke realize the gravity of the situation. "London . . . she's . . ."

"She was killed in an accident. Almost two months ago." Maddie paused. "That's what Dawson came to tell me."

The weight of this landed hard on Brooke's shoulders. She could tell by the pain in Peter's face, the same was true for him. He slid a little closer to the phone. "Honey . . . I'm so sorry."

Brooke had no idea what to say. Had they told Maddie sooner, she might've found these people and enjoyed a friendship with her biological sister. Instead . . . "We're both sorry. Your . . . her parents must be devastated."

"Yes." Maddie seemed a little calmer. She told them the names of the people she was staying with. Her biological parents. Another detail Brooke and Peter hadn't known till now. "Louise and Larry Quinn. They have a guest room. And they're letting me work at their family coffee shop a few days a week." She paused. "But I'm spending most of my time with Dawson. When he doesn't have to go to the office."

Maddie was helping out at her biological mother's café? Questions filled Brooke's mind, but they could wait. The entire conversation felt like something from a nightmare. Maddie was living with strangers in Portland and spending most of her time with some man they didn't know. She wanted to ask her daughter about Connor. But that could wait, too.

Choose your words carefully, Brooke told herself. "Okay. So . . . you and Dawson . . . you were saying?"

"He's been wonderful." This was the best Maddie had sounded since they answered her call. "Every day he tells me . . . 'Call your parents. Forgive them. That's what God would want.' "

All this time she had been frustrated at the guy who had flown to Indiana from Portland just to ruin their daughter's life. But now Brooke understood. Her opinion of Dawson had been completely wrong.

The young man was on their side. How would he have guessed that Maddie didn't know the truth about her birth?

A slight relief came over her and she felt Peter relax some. He sat a little straighter. "Thank you for sharing that, Maddie. We know . . . how hard this is for you."

"Not really." There it was again, her quick tongue and hard tone. She sighed, like she hadn't wanted to sound that way. "So . . . the other thing is going to take a minute for you to understand."

Brooke braced herself. What else could be coming? Peter put his arm around her, and together they huddled over the phone. Waiting.

"So . . . my biological mother is dying of kidney failure." Maddie sounded resolute. "London was going to give her a kidney, but the accident . . . her organs didn't survive the trauma."

No, Lord. Brooke pressed her hands against her knees. This couldn't be happening.

"Anyway." Maddie seemed in a hurry to get to the point. "Dawson took me down and I'm a match. I've been through the testing and everything's approved. I'll be giving Louise one of my kidneys in mid-August. I'd do it sooner if the doctors would let me."

Peter's face was pale, a reflection of how they both clearly felt. He spoke first. "Honey . . . there are ramifications for someone who donates a kidney. They . . . haven't done enough research." He sounded desperate. "Years from now when . . . when you go to have babies there could be—"

"I grew up with two doctors, Dad. Three if you count Papa." Maddie sounded doubly determined. "I've done the research. None of those studies has been verified. I'm healthy and it's perfectly safe to live a long life with one kidney. I can have ten babies if I want."

Most research backed what Maddie was saying. Brooke knew that. But no scientific study mitigated the risk of anesthesia and infection. All sorts of problems were possible with such a serious surgery. Brooke closed her eyes. Her perfectly healthy daughter was going under the knife to give a kidney to a woman she hadn't known until this summer?

My daughter, you taught her to think of others better than herself. You taught her because I taught you.

Brooke's eyes flew open. She didn't have to wonder

where the voice came from. The reminder was from God Himself. Because it was true, the most important truth she could have heard in this moment.

"Mom?" Maddie sounded concerned, even just a little. "Are you there?"

Peter looked at Brooke. "I think . . . what your mom and I want you to understand is that there *are* risks. Whenever you have surgery of any kind." He paused. "Also, if you go through with this . . . please, let us fly there. To be with you, honey."

"Yes. Please, Maddie." Brooke felt stronger now. Her fear was gone and a strange pride took root inside her. Despite the risks, Maddie was about to do a heroic thing here. Even if Brooke wouldn't have chosen it. "We would love to be there. And as for the risks . . . you already know about them, don't you?"

"I do." Maddie's tone was unshakable. "I won't change my mind." She sighed. "And . . . I don't want you to fly here. This . . . it's something I have to do on my own."

For a quick moment, Brooke looked at her husband. Their daughter was going to have major surgery and she didn't want them there? In the hospital, praying for her? Standing by here? She felt sicker than before, but she gave a slight nod and he seemed to understand what she was saying. They needed to affirm this decision, or they would lose Maddie again. Besides, God would be with her. Whatever happened, Maddie was only acting in faith and love.

Peter took over. "What you're doing, Maddie . . . it's a beautiful thing. Your mother and I both think so."

"Yes." Brooke felt the sting of tears. "We're supposed to love others. Even more than ourselves."

"Exactly." A hint of indignation remained in Maddie's tone. "Thank you."

"The Lord will walk this journey out with you, Maddie." Peter had tears now. "Does that mean . . . you're not coming home yet?"

"No." She drew a deep breath. "Not till after the surgery. Even then . . . I'm not sure."

Brooke worked to keep her panic at bay. "Honey . . . what about your job? You worked so hard to get that position."

A group of noisy, happy people walked past them. Brooke had to work to hear their daughter's answer. "I talked to my boss. She said I can start up again the first of October." Maddie hesitated. "If I want to come back."

Was she really considering not coming home? Brooke didn't trust her voice. She shook her head and motioned to Peter.

He cleared his throat. "Maddie." His tone was heavy with sadness. "We will pray for your return. Every day. Just like we've been doing." He hung his head for a moment. "Again . . . we're very . . . very sorry."

"I know." Maddie sounded a fraction softer. "I'll call again. Sometime."

Sometime soon, Brooke wanted to add. But she wouldn't do anything to push Maddie away. Not at this point. "We miss you, Maddie." Brooke fought the tears. She didn't want her daughter to hear her so upset. That would only make Maddie less likely to call again. "Thank you . . . for reaching out."

"And for telling us about your decision." Peter straightened and turned his face to the sun. "If there's anything we can do . . . let us know. We'd be on the next flight."

"Yes. We love you so much." Brooke put her hand on Peter's knee. They would have to get through this together. "Thank you for the call."

Brooke wasn't sure, but it sounded like Maddie was crying. A quiet, subdued cry. "Okay." She sniffed. "Talk to you later."

The call ended and Brooke put her phone back in her purse. Then she fell into Peter's arms. How had things gotten so broken? Never mind that another group of patrons was walking past them. Tears came for both of them.

"Lord," Peter whispered. "Thank You for the call from Maddie. Thank You for the love she's willing to show to her biological mother." There was a catch in his voice. "Heal her heart, Father. Please . . . work through this Dawson friend of hers so that one day . . . one day soon . . . she might forgive us." He massaged his brow. "And come home . . . In Jesus' name. Amen."

"Amen." Brooke could barely get the word out.

Maddie was supposed to be home planning a wedding. Instead, their new reality was something they would have to accept. Maddie was living with her biological family, grieving the loss of a sister she'd never met and planning for a surgery to give one of her kidneys to Louise Quinn.

No wonder she had called. She'd had a great deal to say. On top of that she wouldn't be home for a very long time. She'd made that clear, too. But right now Brooke's greatest heartache wasn't what she'd said. It was the words Maddie didn't say.

She didn't say she loved them.

• • •

CONNOR FLANIGAN BOUGHT the ticket to Portland late that night. He'd only heard from Maddie every other day, and their conversations were getting more strained all the time. She spent most of the time asking about him. Mainly about his new job as communications director for Luke Baxter's law firm in Indianapolis.

Maddie was well aware of how badly Connor had wanted the position. He'd been waiting tables in Bloomington, hoping for the job to open up. Luke had told him it was coming, and that there would be a number of qualified applicants.

Three rounds of interviews later, just last Friday, Connor had been hired.

It was as much a dream position for him as the zoo was for Maddie. So these days should've been spent celebrating their new careers and their upcoming wedding. Instead, Connor was barely connecting with his fiancée, and because her parents hadn't told her the truth, she had all but moved to Portland.

Their conversation that Friday felt like something he might share with a stranger.

"I got the job at Luke's law firm."

"Wow, that's great. When do you start?"

"Not for another week. And what about you? Are you working?"

"Some. I'm picking up shifts at London Coffee, where my sister worked before the accident."

"That's nice."

"It is nice."

And on it went. Sickeningly shallow with none of the heart they'd shared just a month ago.

So Connor had made up his mind. He would board a plane tomorrow—while he still had time before his job started. Whatever was going on in Portland, Connor was sure of one thing. He was about to lose Maddie. He'd talked about his concerns with his parents, and they agreed. Maddie wasn't the girl he had known before. Her life was upside down and there was a good chance she wasn't coming home.

Connor was terrified of the possibility. He loved Maddie West with all his heart, even now. When things were so strained between them. Seeing her in person was the only option, the only chance he had to connect with her again. His early flight would get him there by eleven in the morning with the time change. His return flight was late that same day. Just long enough to see if what they once shared could be salvaged.

The plan was simple. He would land in Portland, rent a car, drive to London Coffee and find his fiancée. Then he would take her somewhere quiet where they could talk. Where he could look her in the eyes and ask what was happening to them.

And maybe . . . just maybe he could talk her into coming home.

21

The sadness in Maddie's heart wouldn't let up, not since her phone call with her parents. Yes, she was still angry at them. Still outraged that they would let her go her entire life without telling her the truth about her adoption. But Dawson was right.

They were still her parents.

A full day had passed since she called them, and even now as she wiped down tables at London Coffee, Maddie could hear the ache in her parents' voices. The sound had stayed with her and made her feel terrible about herself. But one thing among many Maddie had learned in her ordeal was this.

Forgiveness was hard.

Maddie ran the warm, soapy rag over the old wood table near the window, the one where she and Dawson had shared a dozen coffees in the last three weeks. None of this was fair. That was the problem. She had the right to know much earlier the truth about who she was, where she had come from.

That much would never change.

Forgiveness meant looking past the truth, letting it fade to the background. Choosing love because that's what God wanted for His people. Those were truths Dawson had talked with her about, and she could hardly wait till later today when they would talk again.

"Maddie." Louise was at the register. She smiled and motioned for Maddie to join her.

A rush of people had just arrived. Maddie dropped the rag into the bucket. "Coming." She hurried to the other register and after ten minutes the line was gone. "We definitely need another location." Maddie realized how easily she had included herself in the ownership. As if she'd worked here with her biological mother forever. Maddie grinned. "You've done such a great job with this one."

"Thanks." Louise smiled at her. "I'm glad you like it."

The two were getting closer every day. Maddie had no idea what that meant for the future, but it felt right for now. She returned to cleaning the next empty table. Her words stayed with her. *We need another location. We* . . . as if she were staying here forever with Louise, working at the coffee shop the way her sister had. As if a job—and her family—weren't waiting for her back home.

Wherever home was.

She collected the crumbs and spilled cream from the surface of the table and tried to imagine what the future held. Was she really staying here? Would she and Dawson ever talk about the attraction between them? Her mind was spinning.

Before she could move to the next dirty table, she felt someone walk up behind her. It took a single heartbeat to realize who it was. Maddie gasped and jumped back. "Connor."

"Hi." He wore familiar jeans and a sweater, but something was different about him. Where confidence once prevailed, Connor's eyes were full of fear. "I had to see you. So we could talk face-to-face." He shrugged. "I flew in an hour ago."

Maddie felt her heart melt. Her fiancé had come all the way here to talk? She dropped the wet rag in the bucket again. Connor deserved this conversation. It wasn't something Maddie wanted to have, but it was overdue. The way she'd been treating him wasn't fair. "Hold on."

She took the pail behind the counter and found Louise at the coffee bar. "I have to go. My . . . fiancé is here." Maddie hesitated. "The two of us . . . we need to talk."

Louise had listened to Maddie talk about her conflicted feelings for Connor every night for the past week. Ever since Maddie decided to open up to the woman. Louise put her hand on Maddie's shoulder. "Go, dear. Take your time."

Maddie took off her green London Coffee apron and hung it on a hook. Then she grabbed her purse and joined Connor by the door. "Okay." Their eyes met, but Maddie looked away. How had it come to this between them? She didn't smile. "Where are you parked?"

Connor held the door for her, like he always did. But today things felt more than a little off between them. Maddie had wondered how they would feel when they were in person again. Their phone calls had been so awkward, she could hardly wait to hang up.

Clearly he felt the same way.

"There's a park in Vancouver, just across the river." Connor kept his focus on the road. "I thought we could go there."

Neutral territory, Maddie thought to herself. "Sounds good."

They didn't talk again until they sat at a picnic table near the fountain at Esther Short Park. The sound of the water filled the painful silence between them. Connor straddled the table bench and she did the same, facing him.

Only then did he let loose a long sigh. He took her hands and ran his thumb over her engagement ring. "What's going on, Maddie?" He searched her eyes.

Maddie's heart pounded. She looked down at the place where their hands were connected. It was another warm day, the sun bright overhead. But Maddie's shoulders were shaking, like it was thirty degrees. She shook her head. "I'm not . . . I'm not sure."

"Please . . . will you look at me." He waited until she met his gaze. "I love you, Maddie. You're my fiancée. But on the phone"—he sounded beyond concerned—"it's like we just met."

Tears welled up and spilled onto her face. She couldn't speak, couldn't voice the truth. A truth she hadn't admitted even to herself.

"What is it?" Connor's voice was kind. Always. "I'm here, baby. Everything's okay. Just talk to me."

Dawson might not be someone she would ever date, but he had brought to light her feelings for Connor. The lack of feelings. And now . . . with her fiancé sitting across from her, she had no choice but to deal with that.

"I wonder . . ." Tears saturated her tone. "I wonder, Connor, if maybe we were only supposed to be friends. The two of us."

Connor looked like maybe he'd been expecting this. "You're confused. That's all." He studied her. "That's why I had to come. So you could remember who you are. Who we are."

"I know." Maddie gulped back a few quiet sobs. "That's what I want. Believe me." She pressed her hand to her heart. "But it's not what I feel." She told him everything she knew. That before finding out about being adopted, she had been completely sure about marrying him. "I never would've said yes, otherwise."

"Nothing has changed." The sun moved behind a lone cloud. Connor looked deep into her eyes, like he was trying to find the girl she used to be. "You're spinning out of control. I can see that. But I'm not only your past, Maddie. I'm your future."

The words sounded nice, but they didn't hit their mark. Here, with him sitting so close, she was even more sure of her heart. She shook her head. "I'm sorry, Connor." Fresh tears blurred her view of him. "I can't stay engaged to you. Nothing is the same." She covered her eyes with her hand and let the sobs come.

"Hey." Connor slid closer and took Maddie in his arms. For a long time they stayed that way. Clinging to what was left of their love. "It's okay, Maddie. We'll get through this."

When her tears finally let up, she used the sleeve of her sweatshirt to dry her face. "I don't know who I am, Connor. That's the problem."

He cradled her head against his shoulder for another few minutes. Then he faced her. "If you don't want to marry me, I can accept that." The anguish in his eyes was matched only by his determination. His voice rose a notch. "But you know who you are, Maddie."

Maddie wiped her face again. She could feel how swollen her eyelids were, but she didn't look away. "I don't know."

"Well, then . . . I do." His tone eased. He brushed a single tear from her cheek. "You are a beautiful girl who loves God and her family. A girl who loves me, even now.

No matter what the future holds." Each word was deliberate and healing, like balm to her soul. "You are intelligent and strong and you have the most amazing job waiting for you back home at the zoo."

Hot tears filled her eyes again, but she nodded. Every word he said was the truth.

"You are Maddie West." Connor leaned back and pulled out his phone. "I found this Bible verse the other day. Psalm 139. It says God knits us together in our mothers' wombs." He paused. "And He knit you together in the womb of Brooke Baxter West." Connor ran his thumb along her brow. "Which means you are forever a West. Forever a Baxter."

Maddie wanted to believe it. With everything in her she wanted Connor's words to be true. "But I'm not—"

"Shh." Connor's tone was even more tender than before. "Don't listen to a lie. You are Maddie West. You always will be." He paused. "Now talk to me, love. What's happening?"

The walls around Maddie's heart fell and she took a deep breath. He deserved to know. So much more had been happening than she'd ever told him on their short phone calls. She swung her one leg back over the bench and turned to lean against the table, and he did the same. They sat that way, side by side, arms touching. Connor Flanigan. Her childhood sweetheart.

Then for the next hour she told him. They talked about London and where she went to school and what she liked to do. Maddie shared about living with the Quinns and how London had looked so much like her, even as a baby. But there was no way to avoid the truth about how she'd been spending her time.

"Dawson's been talking a lot about forgiveness." Her mouth felt dry. "Sharing Bible verses, encouraging me to call my parents and work things out."

"Good." Connor looked long into her eyes. "What else, Maddie? You and Dawson . . . you've spent a lot of time together."

She nodded. "We have." The ache in her heart spread to her gut. "God put him in the right place at the right time."

Connor didn't respond to that. He just watched her, waiting. As if he knew there was more.

"Anyway . . . he knows what I've been going through and . . . he's helped. A lot." How could she tell Connor she was attracted to another guy? And what was the point? She wasn't staying in Portland forever, so Dawson couldn't really be the problem. He had merely helped her see that marrying Connor wasn't the right thing.

As painful as that was.

It took Connor a minute, but since Maddie didn't expound on the situation with Dawson, he had to ask. "Okay . . . so do you have feelings for him?" He seemed to hold his breath. "For Dawson?"

Maddie looked down for a few seconds. When she lifted her face, her eyes were dry. "Yes." *Help me, God. Give me the words that won't hurt Connor too badly.* "How could I not?" She wiped her face again. "I don't know what I feel. Dawson . . . he's in love with my sister. Even though she's gone." She fought to find her voice. "Anyway, he isn't the reason we're having this talk." She took his hand and he didn't pull away. "I think . . . you and I were only . . . only supposed to be friends." She drew a long breath. "Maybe I needed you to come here . . . to see that."

Time passed while they sat there, hand in hand. Not crying. Not saying anything. Finally Connor stood and helped her to her feet. He eased her into his arms and for a minute they stayed that way. Holding each other, grieving a future that would never be.

When he stepped back, he put his hands on her shoulders. His touch tender, acceptance in his eyes despite the hurt. "I will always love you, Maddie." He was such a good guy. Everything about him would forever remind her of her childhood.

"I'll always love you, too." She realized she might not have another chance to do the one thing she absolutely needed to take care of. She slipped the engagement ring from her finger and handed it to him. "One day, Connor, you will meet the right girl. And she will love you and adore you. And she'll be head over heels for you. So much better than I ever could."

It was the first time his eyes teared up. He looked like he didn't want to take the ring, but he must've realized that was the only thing to do. Because he slid it into his pocket. "I'll take you back."

They held hands the whole way there, and when he dropped her off, when he opened the door for her and stood on the curb waiting, his eyes grew damp. Even so, he found a way to smile. "I was afraid today might go like this."

She faced him, and he ran his hand along her hair. Then he moved a few feet from her. Maddie couldn't believe this was really happening. She had broken off her engagement to the guy she had always thought she'd marry. But a big part of her heart felt free and whole and new. Another confirmation.

Connor didn't break eye contact. "Either way . . . I had to come."

"I'm glad you did." Maddie hugged him and then she stepped back. "Tell your family . . . I never meant to hurt them. Or you, Connor." She fiddled with the place on her finger where the ring had been. "I'll always love you . . . all of you."

He nodded, and for a few seconds he just stood there, as if he was soaking in the sight of her. One last time. "Goodbye, Maddie."

Her tears came again. "Bye, Connor."

With a final look he climbed into his rented SUV and drove off. Maddie didn't move till he was out of sight. Then she walked into the empty house, headed for the room where she was staying and flopped on the bed.

The sobs overcame her and she didn't try to stop them. She needed this. Grieving all that would've been if only she could've kept her wayward heart in line. But then, that wasn't the truth. Just like she'd told Connor earlier, the problem wasn't her attraction to Dawson. She and Connor weren't right together, and when she looked back she could see the signs of that all along. Even so her heart felt shattered in a million pieces.

She could only imagine how painful the flight home would be for Connor.

• • •

THE TEARS DIDN'T fall the way Connor had expected. He ached and he was pretty sure there was a hole where his heart used to be. But he didn't cry. He kept his eyes on the road, and after a few minutes, he remembered his parents.

He had to call them. They were praying for him, after all. They deserved to know.

He called his dad first, and added his mom in before getting to the news. The conversation was brief. "Maddie and I broke up." Connor could hear the sadness in his tone. But his voice was strong. "She gave me back the ring."

"No!" His mom sounded heartsick. "I was praying that wouldn't happen, Connor."

His dad groaned. "I'm sorry, Son. Really."

"Better now than later." Connor meant the words. "I'll be home tonight." He told them he loved them and he thanked them for praying.

Then he focused his eyes on the distant road. His hurt would stay a long time, for sure. He would have to pray a lot . . . and spend hours talking it out with his family and friends. It might take a year or two, but time would heal. And the coming season would give him something else.

A way to let go of Maddie West.

The journey wouldn't be easy. But wherever it took him, there were better days ahead. Maddie was right. Somewhere out there was a girl who wouldn't have doubts about being his wife. She would be over the moon. And when he met her, he would look back on this time and smile. Because he and Maddie had done the right thing. Today was simply part of wherever he was headed.

Now it was just a matter of getting there.

22

Dawson could feel Maddie pulling away. He sat on his front porch waiting for her that Sunday afternoon, letting their time together play over again in his mind. Each moment, each conversation.

The air was cooler today, clouds thick across the Portland sky. The water would be cold, but Dawson didn't care. Maddie wouldn't care either. This might be their last time out on the river.

He looked to the overcast sky and he could see Maddie again, telling him about Connor and the broken engagement. Weeks had passed since Connor's visit to Portland, since he flew in for a few hours so Maddie could end things with him. At first Dawson had wondered if maybe that would free Maddie's heart for what was right in front of her.

The attraction and chemistry between them, that neither could deny.

Instead, she still hadn't talked about her feelings for him, and he hadn't said anything about his attraction to her. Rather, they had spent the days having the most beautiful time. They jet-skied on the weekends and hiked in the afternoons. She hadn't missed a Sunday attending church with him and his father.

But all that was coming to an end. The transplant was

tomorrow and then, after a few days in the hospital, Maddie would have to make a choice. If Dawson had his way, she would choose Indiana and the family waiting for her back home. Leaving would be the right thing.

Even if it killed him to see her go.

A breeze moved through the trees and brushed over Dawson. He stared down the riverfront road, looking for her. Maddie was using London's old car—something that had taken Dawson some getting used to. The pretty girl at the wheel of London's old car still had London's cheekbones and smile. But that wasn't a problem now.

He wasn't looking for similarities to London, anymore. He wanted to see Maddie. Only her.

A few minutes later she drove up. Dawson couldn't take his eyes off her, the swing of her hair, the way her face lit up when she saw him. Her eyes held his as she stepped out of the car. "Hi." She mouthed the word.

Again, he could see it in her face. She was leaving, going back home. Her choice was all but made and he had helped her make it.

He stood and waited for her to come to him. Then he slid his arms around her, and she did the same. "You're going home." He eased back and searched her face. "Right?"

"I'm still not sure." She sighed and rested her forehead on his chest. "I'm asking God to make it clear."

"Okay." If he didn't take her to the Jet Skis, he'd kiss her and beg her to stay. "Let's go for a ride. Maybe it'll be more clear in an hour."

A smile filled her face. "You're so good for me, Dawson."

She was so good for him, too, but he didn't say so. Any

hint or promise of a relationship between them was only going to make things more difficult. He had to think of Maddie, not himself. So today he would try to convince her again. Her life would only be complete if she went home and made peace with the people she loved.

They got into their wet suits and in no time they were flying up and down the river. But like their first time on the water, Dawson wanted to take her to the private island. One more time. Two Jet Skis would be better, because that would mean she wasn't holding on to him, her body up against his.

But since this might be their last time, Dawson couldn't help himself. He motioned for her to return to his dock, and this time Maddie didn't have to ask. She understood. And after she had tied up her Jet Ski, she slid into place on his. Then in a way that took his breath, she wrapped her arms around him and pressed her head against his back.

As they set out, Dawson fixed his eyes on the bridge in the distance. *She's everything I've ever dreamed about, Lord . . . I know she belongs back home, but what about this? What about us?*

There was no clear answer, no response. Just the feeling of her warmth mixing with his. She whispered near his ear. "Go slow."

And so he did. After ten minutes on the river he pulled the machine up onto the sand again. The sun had come through and it warmed the lonely island sand. There were no words as they both unzipped their wet suits halfway. Underneath, they wore T-shirts and shorts, Dawson's idea. Bathing suits wouldn't help anything.

Dawson didn't say a word as he found an area on the

beach. She took the spot right beside him and leaned her head against his chest.

"You are leaving." He leaned forward, his face alongside hers. "You have to go."

She tilted her head back, so their cheeks were together. She sighed. "I don't want to go."

The feeling of her face against his was heaven. Everything in him wanted to agree with her. Beg her to stay so she'd never go back. Instead, with a strength that wasn't his own, Dawson moved so he could see her face. She did the same. He took her hand and she eased her fingers between his. *Say it,* he told himself. *You have to say it.* He took his time. "You belong there."

Walls seemed to go up in her eyes. She stood and took a few steps toward the water. Dawson studied her. Was she angry with him, for doing the right thing and encouraging her to go?

Dawson was on his feet now, too. He put his hand on her shoulder and she turned to him. Her face was a mix of anger and sorrow. "You . . . you don't want me? Is that what you're saying?"

"Maddie." How could he explain himself? "You're getting this all—"

"Stop." She was clearly upset. "I've fallen for you, Dawson. Can't you see that?" She pointed to the spot where they had just been sitting on the beach. "And unless I'm clueless, it seems you feel the same." The fight left her and she locked eyes with him. "So why are you pushing me away? I sense that, more all the time, which is why I've tried to keep things simple between us." She shook her head. "But I can't. Not on days like this."

Every cell in his body wanted to pull her into his arms

and never let go. Instead he took the slightest step toward her. "Maddie . . . that's not it."

"So why?" She brought her fingertips to his face. "Why do you push me away?"

Whatever resolve Dawson had, it was gone. His own breathing was shallow now, faster. He worked his hands into her hair. "Maddie . . ." He didn't finish his thought.

Before he could stop himself his lips were on hers and he was kissing her the way he had longed to do since their first day together. She kissed him back and for the most breathless, beautiful minute they stayed that way. Hungry for all they'd avoided till this moment.

When he drew back, he studied her eyes, her face. "I love you, Maddie. I've . . . I've wanted to tell you for so long." He brought his lips to hers again. "When I'm around you . . . I can barely breathe."

She kissed him, pulling him close as if they were the only two people in the world. When their gazes met again, her eyes were alive, sparkling. "Why didn't you say so?"

"Because." Dawson needed time, needed to step back before he crossed lines he didn't want to cross. He steadied himself and eased his fingers between hers once more. "Because, Maddie. You really do belong . . . back home. In Bloomington."

The sparkle in her eyes faded, but she didn't deny the fact. Her cheeks were red and she was still out of breath. "Do you think . . . maybe you love me because. . . because of London?"

"No." Dawson had asked himself that question a hundred times. He fought the desire to pull Maddie close again. "With London . . . it was different. She was my best friend, so . . . I was in love with the idea of her."

Maddie nodded.

"But with you . . ." He slid one hand along her face and into her hair again. Gently he cupped the back of her head and drew her close once more. "I'm crazy for you, Maddie. You're . . . so different than she was."

Dawson could do nothing to stop the next kiss or the one after that. But finally he led them back to the sand. He sat beside her, closer this time. "I don't know . . . if there could ever be a way for us." He took her hand and their eyes met and held. "But I know for sure you need to go home."

She looked at the sand in front of her. "Maybe."

Their bodies were touching from their shoulders to their legs as they faced the water. "Definitely." He leaned over and kissed the top of her head. "You can't just start a new life, Maddie. You belong there."

Time passed and they stayed that way, connected as if they might never leave. But after a while, Dawson helped her to her feet. "You need to get home." He pulled her in again. "Big day tomorrow."

"Okay." She held his hand as they walked a few feet to the waiting Jet Ski. Then she clung to him all the way up the river.

When they were out of their wet suits and in their street clothes, he walked her out to the car and took her in his arms. He had planned to apologize for kissing her, for making her decision more confusing.

Instead, with her body against his, he did the only thing he wanted to do. The thing he wanted more than his next breath. He kissed her again and didn't let go. She was a dream, the girl he had always wanted and never known till these last few months. Their kiss was warm against the cool breeze.

But eventually Dawson forced himself to step away. Again he was breathing fast. "I'm sorry." He searched her eyes. "For kissing you. I promised myself I wouldn't."

She put her hand on the side of his face and shook her head. Her gaze never left his. "Don't be sorry." For the sweetest moment, she leaned up and kissed him one last time. A different kind of kiss. One rich with goodbye. Their eyes held. "I've wanted you to kiss me since the bridge at Multnomah Falls."

He smiled. "Me, too." For a few seconds, neither of them said anything. It was enough just being together, sharing the same air and heartbeat. "Can I pray with you? Before you go?"

The shine in her eyes was back. "Please."

Dawson took both her hands and lifted his voice to God. "Lord, Your precious daughter Maddie is going into surgery tomorrow. You led her to this decision, so You already know, of course. But I ask You by the power of Your Holy Spirit, to keep her safe." He held her hands a little more tightly. "Keep her in Your arms and at the end of the day let her and Louise both be healthy and well." He hesitated, his emotions strong. "In Jesus' name, amen."

"Amen." She gave him one final kiss, on his cheek this time. "See you when I wake up."

"Definitely." He paused. "Goodbye, Maddie. I won't forget this."

"Me, either." She clearly didn't want to leave him, but she had to go. She stepped into the driver's seat and he closed her door. Then he pressed his hand against her window and she did the same.

Finally he returned to the porch and watched her leave. Telling her she belonged in Indiana was the right thing. She needed to forgive her parents and make peace with her old life. Her real life. And if Dawson never saw her again, then he would leave this sad, wondrous season with no regrets. But one thing was certain.

He would remember today as long as he lived.

• • •

MADDIE COULD STILL feel his lips on hers as she drove back to Louise and Larry's house. Had she only been dreaming? Did they really kiss on their own little strip of paradise in the middle of the Columbia River? And had he really told her he'd wanted to do that from the beginning? Same as her?

She relived every minute, every kiss, everything she'd felt in his arms. Larry and Louise were at their friends' house with a group of people who wanted to pray for Louise before her surgery in the morning. After Maddie's day with Dawson, after the way he'd prayed over her at the end, Maddie didn't need a group of people tonight.

But she did need to make a few phone calls.

First was to Hayley. This wasn't the only time she'd called her sister, but if something went wrong tomorrow, it could be the last. Maddie didn't want to miss the chance.

Her sister sounded thrilled to hear her voice. "Maddie! I asked God for you to call me today."

"Yes." Maddie felt her throat tighten. "I wouldn't have missed it."

Hayley knew about the surgery, though she may not have understood all it entailed. Their conversation was sweet and simple and it ended with Hayley's brief prayer. "Help Maddie be safe, Jesus." She paused, and Maddie was reminded again how much she loved her sister. She could never leave her back in Bloomington, never stay here for a new life. Not now, anyway. Hayley finished the prayer. "And please bring her home soon. I miss her so much, Jesus. Amen."

Maddie's next call was to her papa. All this time she had thought about calling her grandpa John Baxter. But she'd let her anger and confusion keep her from reaching out. Now she couldn't find his number fast enough.

He answered on the first ring. Like he'd been expecting her call since the hour she left. "Maddie. Honey, how are you?"

Peace filled Maddie's soul. "Good, actually." It was the truth. "I have surgery tomorrow."

"I know." He exhaled. "I've been praying for you all day."

Of course he had. Happy tears sprang to Maddie's eyes, but she resisted them. She had too much to say. "Thank you."

"Are you sure? This is what you want to do?" Her papa's concern rang in his voice.

It had been the same with Louise earlier. Before church she pulled Maddie aside and asked her to reconsider. "I don't want you to do this, Maddie. I'd rather you go home safe and whole. With both your kidneys." They'd had the conversation several times, and always Maddie said the same thing. She wanted to do this. She wasn't worried, and the surgery wasn't too risky. If she and Dawson didn't have a chance, then the transplant was the reason she had come here. She was convinced.

Now Maddie needed to convince her grandfather. "I'm sure." She could hear the smile in her voice. "God brought me to Portland for this, Papa. To save Louise's life, which is only right because . . . a long time ago she and Larry saved mine."

He hesitated, but not for long. "I understand." Another pause. "If things go well—and I'm sure they will—you can travel in a week. I'd . . . I'd like to fly out and bring you home at that time. If you'll let me."

There was no stopping her tears. She let them come, embraced them. No matter how far or long she'd been away from home, this man was her grandfather, and he loved her. "Y-y-yes. Please, come get me."

She apologized for the pain and heartbreak she'd put him through. All of them. Then she told him she loved him, and he said the same. When the conversation ended, she collected herself. The most important call was next.

Maddie found her mother's name on her list of favorites, and when she answered, Maddie took a deep breath. "Is Dad there, too?"

"He is." Her mother paused. "He's walking over to me right now."

Again, Maddie squeezed her eyes closed. She should've done this a long time ago. If something would've happened to her parents before this moment, she couldn't have lived with herself.

"Okay, honey." Her mom sounded anxious. She was probably afraid of what Maddie was thinking or why she was calling. "We're both here."

"Hi, Dad . . . Mom." Tears filled her voice, but that was all right. This was the moment Dawson had been pushing for since the day they met. The moment God had been leading her toward. Maddie found her voice. "I'm sorry." *Give me the words, Father. Please.* It took a few seconds.

"I'm sorry for . . . for how I've been acting. I forgive you for not telling me." She brushed the tears from her cheeks. "I miss you all . . . so much."

"Oh, Maddie." Her mom never cried. She was an educated intellectual on so many levels. But here, in this moment, she broke down. "We miss you, too. You've been our daughter since . . . since the day you were placed inside me." She hesitated. "We've always loved you."

"I know . . . I love you both, too." Maddie grabbed a few quick breaths. "I have surgery tomorrow. Then in a week . . . Papa is coming here to get me." More tears filled her eyes. "I'm coming home."

And as the call ended, after her daddy prayed for her surgery in the morning, Maddie lay back on the bed and stared out the window. She had loved being here. But she was going back to Bloomington and one thing was certain, even with how she felt about Dawson.

Maddie could hardly wait.

23

Dawson was there when Maddie woke up. The surgery had been a success and now he moved to the side of her bed to tell her. "You did it."

Maddie blinked a few times and narrowed her eyes. "Dawson." Her throat must've been dry because it seemed hard for her to speak. "Louise . . . is she okay?"

"You should see her." He reached for Maddie's hand, careful not to disturb the IV line. "Her face is pink. Her new kidney is working fine." Dawson smiled. Everything about this moment was a victory, the answer they had prayed for.

"Mmm." Maddie closed her eyes for a brief moment. Then she found Dawson again. "I'm so glad. I want her to live . . . a long time."

You, too, Dawson almost said. But he stopped himself. The transplant had been a textbook operation, and now there was no reason to think Maddie wouldn't have a full, healthy recovery. With his other hand he soothed her hair from her forehead. "You saved your biological mother's life, Maddie. I can feel God smiling down at you."

The hint of a grin lifted her lips. "This is . . . why I was supposed to come here. I believe that." She stared at him, to the deepest places of his heart. "This . . . and you, Dawson."

Her words filled his soul. If only there was a way for

them. He wanted to promise to visit, beg her to try a long distance relationship. But that wouldn't work. His office was here . . . and her home was there. Instead he ran his thumb over her hand and sat beside her. "We still have today."

"Yes." Her voice was weak. "If only the sun wouldn't set."

He stayed with her until the nurse kicked him out. And he came back every day until they released her to go home with Louise and Larry. The doctor had given Maddie permission to fly home to Indiana tomorrow. Her grandfather was coming to take her back.

Dawson couldn't think about it.

On the morning of her departure, Dawson had important meetings with his father. Big changes ahead, his dad had told him yesterday. Changes that affected Dawson's future.

But he had to break away to see her, so he left the office. He wouldn't miss saying goodbye to her, wouldn't miss seeing Maddie West one more time.

Before she left Portland for good.

On the way to the Quinns' house, Dawson remembered the crazy circumstances that had led them all to this point. Embryo adoption? Embryos frozen for years without incident?

Dawson had done a little research, and what he learned was staggering. Back when Maddie and her fellow embryos were transferred to the fertility doctor in Bloomington, this sort of situation was unheard of. Only a handful of embryo adoptions had been done in Europe, and it was possible Maddie's was the first in the United States.

Now, though, there were more than a million babies on ice. One million. Tiny embryos from someone's leftover experience with in vitro fertilization. Souls on ice. To handle the need, a number of clinics had sprung up across the country. Turned out adopting an embryo was neither difficult nor overly expensive. It also wasn't technically adoption. Legally, embryos were passed from one person to another through a property transfer agreement.

But it definitely raised questions. Questions only God could answer.

Like with Maddie.

Dawson turned onto the Quinns' street. He didn't blame Maddie's Indiana parents anymore. Not after his research. At first it would've been easy to believe the pregnancy might have been a natural one. Who was to say whether the baby came from the implanted embryos?

Even after testing had told the story, even after Maddie's parents had known the truth, none of it would've been easy. Especially for a couple desperate for a baby. Telling Maddie at any point would've been difficult and complicated.

Anyway, all that was behind them. And Maddie was right. Maybe the whole thing had nothing to do with Maddie meeting him or her biological parents. But about saving Louise Quinn's life. They would never know this side of heaven.

Up ahead he could see a strange car parked outside the house. Dr. John Baxter, no doubt. Maddie's grandfather. He had flown in late last night and stayed at a hotel. Maddie had said he'd be there first thing in the morning. Dawson took a quick breath. He didn't have long. But the change of events at work had given him something he hadn't had before. Something he held on to as he climbed out of his truck and headed up the walk.

Hope.

• • •

AFTER AN HOUR at Louise and Larry Quinn's house, John was ready to leave. Maddie felt tired, and it was time to get her to the airport. She could sleep on the plane.

Louise was propped up on the couch and Larry sat in the chair beside her. For the past half hour they had talked about London, and Larry had showed John pictures of her life. The resemblance between Maddie and London was uncanny.

The two were most certainly sisters.

As they closed the photo album and put it away, John realized he had suffered a loss, too. He would've treasured the chance to meet Maddie's biological sister. To see for himself the similarities and know that Maddie had gotten the chance to know her.

John had missed out on that, the way they all had. It was something he hadn't expected to feel, but it was real. The loss would remain.

"Listen." John stood and shook Louise's hand, then her husband's. "Thank you. For housing Maddie, for being so kind to her." He glanced across the room. Maddie was sitting in an oversize chair. She looked too worn out to get up. John turned to Louise and Larry again. "I'm sure . . . she'll want to visit you again. From time to time."

"Yes." A weak smile flashed on Maddie's face. She had already told John she didn't think she'd be back often. The situation was too difficult. Too complicated. But sometime. Maybe.

John helped Maddie to her feet and she made her way to Larry first. "I think . . . we have the same eyes."

Larry put his hand on her shoulder. "We always will."

Next she went to Louise. The woman was smiling, despite her tears. "And I have your kidney."

Her smile faded. "Maddie . . . I'll never forget the day you told me you wanted to do that. And no matter how many times I've thanked you, words will never be enough. I'm alive . . . because of you." Her voice broke. "The truth is, I don't know when we'll see you again. "She paused. "But your kidney means I'll always carry you with me." She searched Maddie's eyes. "Thank you."

"It was God's plan." Maddie felt a deep sadness as she leaned down and hugged her. Louise was right. Despite what Maddie's grandpa had said, there was no telling when they might see each other again. "Louise, even though I won't be here, I have so much of you, too. In my heart."

"And you have, London, too."

Maddie nodded. "Yes. I always will."

Louise brushed away her tears, and managed to smile again. "You're doing the right thing, Maddie." She nodded. "And we'll always be here . . . whenever."

"Thanks." She looked to Larry and back to Louise. "Thank you for everything."

John felt his own eyes grow damp as he watched. Maddie hadn't grown up knowing these people, but they were her biological parents. Seeing them together now, there was no denying that.

Finally, it was time to go. John pulled Maddie's suitcases and followed after her. They were just out the door when a Chevy truck pulled up. Maddie froze in place and her voice dropped to a whisper. "Dawson."

They stayed there while a good-looking young man got out of the truck and hurried toward them. He held his hand out and the two shook. "I'm Dawson Gage."

"I've heard about you." He smiled. "John Baxter. Maddie's grandfather."

He took a step back so he wouldn't be in the way. As he did, Maddie set her purse down and went to the young man. The two embraced, but only for a few seconds. Their conversation was brief. Dawson told her he had to come see her off, and Maddie thanked him. It was what he said at the end that caught John's attention.

"Things . . . are changing at work." Dawson seemed to search Maddie's eyes. "I'll . . . I'll be in touch." Chances were the young man wanted to say more. But with John there, he seemed to keep his words sparse.

Confusion flashed on Maddie's face, but something else. A ray of light that hadn't been there before. Whatever these two had shared during Maddie's time here, the bond was special.

Anyone could see that.

Dawson and Maddie said their goodbyes and hugged once more. Then Dawson shook John's hand again and the guy was gone. In the car, John waited for a few minutes before turning to Maddie. "He seems . . . very special to you."

"He is." Maddie brushed a few tears off her cheeks. "He wanted me to stay, Papa." She reached for a tissue in her purse and pressed it beneath her eyes. "With all his heart . . . but he sent me back."

"Oh." John wasn't sure what that meant.

Before he could ask, Maddie finished her thought. "He sent me back because he knew . . . Indiana is where I belong. With you and . . . my family. He said that's what God would want."

A warmth spread over John's chest. No wonder he had seen something likable about Dawson. Too bad he wouldn't ever get to know him. He had a feeling he and Maddie might've been something special.

Either way, the young man had done the right thing by encouraging Maddie to make peace with her past. At least for now. John kept his eyes on the road. He could hardly wait for the flight.

Maddie was coming home.

• • •

HALFWAY THERE, MADDIE woke and looked out the plane window. Her papa was asleep in the seat beside her. She yawned and adjusted her position. Her body was still sore where her kidney had been removed. But she was feeling better every day. A few weeks of follow-up with her doctor in Bloomington and she'd be good as new.

The blue sky out the plane window made her think of Dawson. The way everything did these days. Already the pain of missing him hurt worse than any physical pain she was in. *God, I wish I didn't have to choose. Staying in Portland with Dawson . . . or going back to my family in Indiana.*

Maddie imagined the days ahead. Maybe in a few years she could apply to the Oregon Zoo and she and Dawson could give it a try. See if they might step back into what they had started these past few months. She tried to picture leaving Indiana forever, and it made her sad.

Dawson had said it once, and he was right.

Sometimes God brings people into your life for a short season. Even if the impact lasts till your final breath.

She couldn't imagine never seeing him again, but it was possible. After she healed, she'd start back up at the zoo and they would both return to living their separate lives. But she would never forget him, the man who took her breath and made her remember who she was. Whose she was and where she belonged.

Dawson Gage.

She closed her eyes and they were on his Jet Ski again, racing down the Columbia River. His back was warm against her and she didn't want to let go for anything. Halfway through the remembered ride, Maddie fell asleep.

This time when she woke up they were taxiing to the gate. She was home and beside her, Papa Baxter was grinning. "Everyone's at Ashley and Landon's house. They can't wait to see you."

"They . . . they're not mad?" Maddie had wondered. She'd talked to her parents and Hayley, but not to the others.

"Maddie, honey." He patted her knee. "They can't wait to see you. This is about to be the party of the year." He smiled. "A quick party. Everyone knows you need to rest."

The party of the year. Maddie smiled. Of course the Baxter family would gather together to celebrate her return. They loved her then and they loved her still. They weren't angry with her. An hour later when her papa drove up to the old Baxter house and pulled in the drive, he had barely parked when the door flew open.

First one out was Hayley.

Her sister.

She ran to the car as Maddie stepped out. "You're here! You came home!"

"I did." Maddie stretched out her arms and Hayley flung herself into them. "I missed you."

Then, from the door, Maddie saw her parents and her aunts and uncles, her cousins and Grandma Elaine streaming onto the front porch and down the steps. Her papa led her from the car and Maddie hugged each of them along the way.

Inside, her grandfather gathered everyone in the living room. "Family is not always by blood. Maddie has taught us that, but Jesus taught it first." He prayed then, thanking God for Maddie's safe return and inviting everyone to celebrate the fact for the next hour.

Maddie couldn't stop smiling. Her papa's words and prayer, the kindness of everyone in the house. Nearly all the people she loved were here, and the happiest thought occurred deep in her soul. She truly was home.

And if she had it her way, she'd never leave again.

24

Louise pressed her cold water glass to her face. Portland was in the middle of the hottest September in twenty years. She stared out the window. Two weeks had passed since Maddie flew back to Indiana, and now Louise had just heard the news from Dawson Gage.

He was moving. His father's company was expanding and Dawson was in charge of the new office. At least for now.

So many changes.

Louise walked to the kitchen and put another scoop of ice in her glass. A few days out of the year, often in September, Portland got real heat. Triple digits. This was that day, and the Quinn house didn't have air-conditioning.

The heat didn't bother Louise. She felt better than she had in years. Maddie's kidney was working perfectly, and every checkup since the surgery had held nothing but the best test results.

Larry was at work and the house was quiet. Too quiet. Louise used her phone to find a Ben Rector list and she hit play. The first song was one she knew well, one she'd found when she learned Maddie had made her decision to go home.

The song was called "Wherever You Are." And as it played Louise could see Maddie again, sitting at their kitchen table, asking about London. She could see London, too. Both her daughters were gone now, and Louise was learning to accept the fact.

God had something else for her in this season.

Music filled the kitchen and eased the emptiness in Louise's heart. For a moment she leaned against the counter and let the words wash over her. It was her anthem to Maddie. The girl she had never expected to meet. The daughter she hadn't known about.

Wherever you go, know that you're never alone. You're forever in my heart. And the moments you need me, no distance could keep me. I will be wherever you are.

Louise smiled through her tears. Larry was helping her stay strong. Her close friends, too. That, and she and Larry were attending church again, enjoying every Sunday more than the last. No telling why they had ever left. Every week was another message that spoke straight to her heart.

And something else. She was getting involved in a new movement sweeping the nation. The Seen Movement, it was called. She and Larry had already ordered business cards from the group's website. The two of them had stumbled upon the movement because of something one of their friends had said.

People want to be seen. It can change a person's life.

Louise and Larry agreed. After talking about it, they had gone to YouWereSeen.com and for a few dollars they had ordered twenty Seen cards. Cards that had the power to make a stranger feel special. A bit of paper that would direct them to God. The goal was to carry the cards in a purse or wallet, then hand them out to people who served. A waiter or waitress, a barista, or someone cleaning a public restroom.

The movement encouraged people to tip big. Generously. As if life were one exciting mission trip. Hand out the cards and thank a stranger. Tell them they were seen. Really seen. Then point them to the website, where they would be reminded that God sees them every day.

She could hardly wait for the cards to arrive.

Louise wiped at an errant tear. Crying was okay. Necessary even. She and Larry had lost much. But the Seen Movement was about to give them something to look forward to. A reason to leave the house.

"People save up for mission trips all the time," Louise's friend had told her. "What if you used that money right here. In your daily life."

She could already imagine the divine appointments just ahead.

In the meantime, she'd heard from Maddie. She was back safely where she belonged, with the parents who had raised her. She was home. And so was London, just in a different way.

"God . . . tell my precious girl I miss her." Louise's voice was barely a whisper as she looked out the window at the mountains behind her house. "I miss her so much."

Then as she'd done a thousand times since London's passing, Louise asked God if London might have a window. So she could see how Louise and Larry were doing and so she could pray for them. So that one day, when their time on earth was up, London would be there on that distant golden road.

The first one to greet them.

• • •

DAWSON WAS LEAVING in a few hours. His things were already on a moving van headed for storage until he could buy a house. But first he had one place to visit.

He drove north on the I-5 Freeway and thought about the past few weeks. The change had come quickly, but it was the right thing. The move had actually been his dad's idea. For a while he'd been looking for the next best city, the place where their development company might take off.

Now—for a number of reasons—Dawson and his father were both sure. This was the right thing. And sometime in the next year or so, his dad had even talked about selling the Portland office and moving across country to be with Dawson.

"After all," his dad had told him earlier today. "Life is short. Nothing's more important than Jesus and family." He patted Dawson on the shoulder. "I love you, Son."

"Love you, too, Dad."

The two had shared a long hug, and then Dawson had walked out the door. A new chapter ahead.

Dawson took the next exit and wound his way up the road and into the cemetery. Another hill and he was there. At London's grave. He left his truck and moved to the spot right in front of her tombstone. Last time he was here, Maddie had been with him.

But this was different. He couldn't leave Portland without stopping here first. It might be the last time he'd have the chance. A memory came to mind. The police officer, Jag, who had helped him in the minutes after London's accident. Dawson still had no idea how the man had known his name or London's. But he had been right about something else he had said.

She's okay. Jesus has her now.

Jesus definitely had London now. She was with Him. That's what the guy had said before he seemed to disappear from the area, and it was true. She was with Jesus. So she was really and truly okay.

For a while Dawson only stared at her grave. *Oh, London . . . I wish you were still here.* He pictured her, fun-loving, wild London, her dark hair flying behind her out on the water. Since meeting Maddie, Dawson was sure of something. London had never been the one for him. The girl he had been drawn to for so many years was right that night at Disneyland when she told him not to fall in love with her.

No matter their chemistry, the two of them had been wrong for each other.

Sure, maybe if she hadn't stepped in front of that pickup, their conversation might've led them to a changed relationship. He would never know. But the girl London was when she was alive was not a girl he would've dated. They were too different.

He had wanted her loyalty and faithfulness, her presence beside him at church on Sunday. That wasn't London, yet still he had been in love with her year after year. He loved her even now. He always would. But her death had started a spiral of events that had led him to a girl who was so much better for him. A girl who was everything he had ever hoped for.

Maddie West.

Dawson took a slow, deep breath. He stooped down and traced his finger over London's name. "I miss you, friend."

He couldn't talk to her. Death didn't work like that.

But Dawson knew the One who could. With his hand spread out on her tombstone, Dawson let the words come. "Lord . . . tell her how much I love her. How much we all love her."

Wind whistled through the far-off pines. Dawson felt the slightest sad smile inch up his face. He remembered then what London had said in her final minutes. She had a sister, she told them. She had somehow known.

A chill ran down Dawson's arms. How good was God to let London grasp that, even for only a brief moment.

He brushed a bit of dirt off her stone. "It happened, London." His smile didn't stop his tears. "Just like you said it would. I found her." Sorrow closed in around him and made it hard to breathe. He gave a slight cough and found his voice again. "Someone like you."

The afternoon was hot, and Dawson stood. He lifted his eyes to the clear blue sky. "Lord, you'll tell her, right? Please?"

Because even in heaven, where all things were whole and right and perfect, Dawson had a feeling London would want to know this one detail. And that in knowing, she would do something Dawson could still picture clear as day. London would smile. The way she would if she could've known where he was moving. To a city where his dad's company was expanding. A city where he would build his future.

Indianapolis, Indiana.

• • •

THE KANGAROOS SEEMED to remember her. And since Maddie was fully trained, her boss, Ms. Barber, had no problem leaving her alone in the exhibit. Especially on this uncrowded September Monday.

Every now and then, Maddie caught herself looking toward the bench near the lions. Or the one by the giraffes. Remembering how the events of this past summer first began. But Dawson wasn't there, of course. He was working in Portland, where he would probably stay forever.

Maddie gazed at the distant clouds. A part of her would always be in Portland, Oregon. Not just her kidney, but a piece of her heart. The piece that forever belonged to Dawson Gage.

Since Maddie had seen him on the way to the airport that day in front of Louise and Larry's house, Dawson had texted a few times. But he hadn't called. It was better that way. They each needed to get on with their lives.

She had seen Connor—just once. He had asked her to coffee, and she'd agreed. She owed him that much after all she'd put him through. Their time together had been pleasant. Connor admitted that he had doubted whether they were right for each other, too.

"It seemed like the right thing." His grin that day had been easy. "I just figured everything would work out."

Connor told her he'd had time to think about his life and hers in the time since their breakup. "You made the right choice." He had hugged her before they went their separate ways. "One day we'll both be glad. I believe that."

Maddie believed it, too.

A family entered the fenced-off area and made their way through the kangaroo enclosure. Maddie told them about the animals, their habits in the wild and their favorite foods. "Red kangaroos are herbivores." She smiled at the family's two little girls. "That means they like eating grass. Sort of like salad."

"Yuck." One of the kids made a face. "I like French fries."

Their mother laughed. "Looks like we have work to do."

When the family was gone, as he often did, the littlest kangaroo hopped onto the visitor path. "Joey . . . you're doing it again." Maddie approached him and scratched behind his ear. "This area is for the guests. Remember?"

She grabbed a handful of the kangaroo's favorite food and led him off the path. Maddie washed her hands and then, before she could stop herself, she looked at the bench in front of the kangaroo exhibit. One more time.

As she did she gasped. A man was sitting there drawing. From where she stood, he almost looked like . . .

The guy stood and . . . Maddie put her hand to her mouth. *How is this possible?* She had no answers, but it was him. Dawson had come to her.

And he was holding yellow roses.

He walked up, the flowers in his hand. He stood a ways from her and smiled. "Hi."

"Hi." Maddie wasn't sure if she was laughing or crying. "What . . . why are you here?" She wanted to run to him, but she couldn't. Not while she was on the clock.

Instead of answering, he came closer and handed her the bouquet. "Someone told me you like yellow roses."

"I do." She didn't look away, didn't blink. "But I like you better."

"Mmm." His voice soothed her soul. Gone was the sadness from the last time they saw each other. "When do you get off work?"

Maddie wasn't sure she could remember how to spell

her name. She put her hands to her head. "Umm . . . three o'clock." A shocked laugh spilled from her lips. "What time is it?"

"Two-thirty." Dawson was grinning now. "I'll meet you at the exit."

Then he left without looking back. As soon as he was gone, Maddie blinked a few times. Had that really just happened? Had Dawson really come to see her when he should've been in Portland? She looked at the flowers in her hands. Yes, he was really here.

The yellow roses were proof.

Thirty minutes seemed like so many hours as Maddie's shift wound down. Finally she clocked out, took her things from her locker and headed for the parking lot. The whole time she never let go of the flowers.

He was there, just like he'd told her. Waiting by the zoo exit.

Again, she wanted to run to him, but she controlled herself. Whatever his reason for coming to Indiana, she would accept it. Even if he was only here for a single day. When she reached him, they walked together to her car, and she set the roses down on the roof. Then like something from a dream, she stepped into his open arms. "You're here."

"Yes." He looked at her. His eyes felt so good on hers. "I had to come tell you my news."

Maddie searched his face. His news? What was this? "You came all the way here for that?"

He chuckled. "Not really." His hand came up alongside her face. "My things will be here in two days. I figured I should be here to meet the truck."

None of this made sense. "Your . . . your things?"

"Yes." He held her close again. "My dad's company is expanding to Indianapolis, Maddie." He chuckled. "I'm looking for a house."

"What?" Maddie let out the happiest scream. "Are you serious?"

"I am." He swung her around and then his smile faded. "I couldn't live without you. My dad knew that." And like he'd done on their own private island on the Columbia River, he kissed her. A kiss that took her breath and held promise for ten thousand tomorrows.

Maddie couldn't believe it. Dawson was here and he was looking for a house and he didn't want to live without her. The truth lifted her up and held her, filling her with a joy she had never known in all her life.

They kissed again, and Maddie remembered something that sent a shiver down her back. "Remember what London told you? One day you'd find someone like her."

His stare grew deeper, the moment as fully theirs as when they had stood on the shore of that island. "Someone"—he kissed her once more—"like you."

Her sister had known. And in that moment, Maddie was sure without a doubt who she was. She was a West and a Baxter. She had not one but two sets of parents. Her biological parents in Oregon, and her mom and dad here in Bloomington. And something else.

She would forever belong to Dawson Gage.

Maddie stayed in Dawson's arms. She had no idea if the love they shared would lead to a wedding one day. Her heart told her it would, but they had time. Whatever happened and however long it took, Maddie knew this. She was fully and completely in love with Dawson Gage. Her sister's best friend. The guy who had helped her know who she was. Who she really was. Even after she had forgotten.

And that was something Maddie would treasure forever.

The End

ACKNOWLEDGMENTS

I never could've put *Someone Like You* in your hands without a team of passionate, determined people working behind the scenes. On that note, I can't leave this novel and the deeply emotional journey it's been, without thanking the people who made it possible.

First, a special thanks to my amazing Simon & Schuster and Atria publishing team, including the keenly talented Libby McGuire, Trish Todd, Suzanne Donahue and of course the incomparable Carolyn Reidy. Also the rest of my gifted New York team who brings these books to you! I think often of our times together at the Simon & Schuster building in Manhattan, and the way your collective creative brilliance always becomes a game changer. You clearly desire to raise the bar at every turn. Thank you for that. It's an honor to work with you!

Also thanks to Rose Garden Creative, my design team. Kyle and Kelsey Kupecky, your unmatched talent in the industry is recognized from Los Angeles to New York. Very simply you are the best in the business! My website, social media, video trailers and newsletter—along with so many other aspects of my touring and writing—are at the top of the book business because of you. Thank you for working your own dreams around mine. I love you and I thank God for you every single day.

A huge thanks to my sisters Tricia and Susan, along with my mom, Anne. You give your whole hearts to help me love my readers. Tricia, as my executive assistant for twelve years; and Susan, as the president of my Facebook Online Book Club and Team KK. And Mom, thank you for being Queen of the Readers. Anyone who has ever sent me an email and received a response from "Karen's mom" is blessed indeed. The three of you are making a tremendous impact in changing this world for the better. I love you and I thank God for you!

Thanks also to Tyler for joining with me to write screenplays and books like *Best Family Ever* and *Finding Home*—the Baxter Family Children books. You are a gifted writer, Ty. I can't wait to see more of your work on the shelves and on the big screen. Maybe one day soon! Love you so much!

Also, thank you to my office assistant, Aurora Galvin. You create space for me to write! My storytelling wouldn't be possible without you.

I'm grateful to my Team KK members, who use social media to tell the world about my upcoming releases and who hang out on my Facebook page answering reader questions. I deeply appreciate each of you. May God bless you for your service to the work of Life-Changing Fiction™.

There is a final stage in writing a book. The galley pages come to me, and I send them to a team of several of my most dedicated reader friends. My nieces Shannon Fairley, Melissa Viernes and Kristen Kane. Also Hope Burke, Donna Keene, Renette Steele, Zac Weikal and Sheila Holman. You are my volunteer test team! It always amazes me, the things you catch at the final hour. Thank you for loving my work, and thanks for your availability to read my novels first and fast.

Also, my books only happen with the help of my family, especially my amazing husband, Donald. Honey, thank you for your spiritual wisdom and leadership in our home, and thanks for talking through books like this one from the outline to the editing. The countless ways you help me when I'm on deadline make all the difference. I love you!

And over all this, thanks to a man who has believed in my career for two decades, my amazing agent Rick Christian of Alive Literary Agency. From the beginning, Rick, you've told me to dream big, set my sights high. Movies, TV series, worldwide reach. All for God and through Him. You imagined this, believed it and prayed for it alongside me and my family. You saw it all playing out. You still do! While I write, you work behind the scenes on film projects and my future books, the Baxter family TV series and details regarding every word I've ever written. You are brilliant and driven, compassionate and dedicated. I used to dream of having you as my agent. Now Tyler and I are the only authors who do. God is amazing. Thank you, Rick, and thank you for praying for me and my family. That most of all.

Finally, my greatest thanks to God Almighty, who is First and Last and all things in between. I write for You, through You and because of You. Thank You with my whole being.

Dear Reader Friend,

I remember the day God gave me the story behind *Someone Like You*. I was speaking at an event and my hostess for the day pointed to a woman across the room. Running behind her were three children—all about the same age.

"See her?" My hostess smiled. "She had her triplets because of embryo adoption."

"What?" It took me a minute. "You mean . . . someone donated their embryos to her and now—"

"Right!" My new friend stopped me short. "She couldn't have children. She and her husband adopted the embryos and three were implanted in her." Again she grinned. "All three took!"

Embryo adoption. I did a little research and learned that more than a million embryos are on ice in adoption centers across the country. Google *embryo adoptions* and you'll see. The process of implantation is quick and painless, typically successful and less expensive than any other form of adoption.

But do people know about it, I wondered?

More than that, I began to think of the possibilities that could arise from embryo adoption. And certainly one of those is the story you just read. Fiction . . . but oh, so possible.

As you close the cover on this book, do me a favor. Think about who you can share it with. A friend or a sister. Your mother or coworker. The librarian at your child's school. Someone struggling to make sense of a loss or someone who needs encouragement, hope or simply a good love story. Maybe just a person who loves to read.

Remember, a story dies if it is left on the shelf. So please pass this one on.

Also, though these books are not part of a series, you will find out more about Dawson and Maddie and a number of the characters in my next book—*Truly Madly Deeply*. Look for that title to be released at the end of the year.

By now you may have heard about the TV series—*The Baxters*. This was something I only dreamed about back when God gave me these very special characters. The series has the material to go on for a very long time, and I know you'll love it like the rest of us do.

To find out more about *The Baxters* on TV or any of my other books or movies, visit my website, KarenKingsbury .com. There you can enter your email address to sign up for my free weekly newsletter. These emails come straight to you and offer my blogs and devotions, event updates and insights.

I release my biggest announcements to my newsletter first, so sign up today!

At my website, you can also find out how to stay encouraged with me on social media—Facebook, Instagram and Twitter.

Finally, if you are seeking a faith like that of the Baxter family, find a Bible-believing church and get connected. There is a reason you came across this book. Remember, the Baxters are not just my family. They are yours. And because of that, we are all connected. Until next time . . . I'm praying for you.

Thanks for being part of the family.

Love you all!

THE BAXTER FAMILY: YESTERDAY AND TODAY

For some of you, this is your first time with the Baxter family. Please know you don't have to read any other Baxter books to read this one. Like my other recent titles, *Someone Like You* stands alone! But if you read this and want to start at the beginning, the starting place is my book *Redemption*.

That's where the adventure of the Baxters begins.

Whether you've known the Baxters for years or are just meeting them now, here's a quick summary of the family, their kids and their ages. Also, because these characters are fictional, I've taken some liberty with their ages. Let's just assume these are their current ages.

Now, let me introduce you to—or remind you of—the Baxter family.

• • •

THE BAXTERS BEGAN in Bloomington, Indiana, and most of the family still lives there today.

The Baxter house is on ten acres outside of town, with a winding creek that runs through the backyard. It has a wraparound porch, a pretty view and memories of a lifetime of love and laughter. John and Elizabeth Baxter moved into this house when their children were young. They raised their family here. Today it is owned by one of their daughters—Ashley—and her husband, Landon Blake. It is still the place where the extended Baxter family gathers for special celebrations.

• • •

DR. JOHN BAXTER: John is the patriarch of the Baxter family. Formerly an emergency room doctor and professor of medicine at Indiana University, he's now retired. John's first wife, Elizabeth, died long ago from a recurrence of cancer. Years later, John married Elaine, and the two live in Bloomington.

• • •

DAYNE MATTHEWS: Dayne is the oldest son of John and Elizabeth. Dayne was born out of wedlock and given up for adoption at birth. His adoptive parents died in a small plane crash when he was 18. Years later, Dayne became a very visible and popular movie star. At age 30, he hired an attorney to find his biological parents—John and Elizabeth Baxter. He had a moment with Elizabeth in the hospital before she died, and years later he connected with the rest of his biological family. Dayne is married to Katy. The couple has three children: Sophie, 10; Egan, 8; and Blaise, 6. They are very much part of the Baxter family, and they split time between Los Angeles and Bloomington.

• • •

DR. BROOKE BAXTER WEST: Brooke is a pediatrician in Bloomington, married to Peter West, also a doctor. The couple has two daughters: Maddie, 22, and Hayley, 19. The family experienced a tragedy when Hayley suffered a near-drowning accident at age 3. She recovered miraculously, but still has disabilities caused by the incident.

• • •

KARI BAXTER TAYLOR: Kari is a designer, married to Ryan Taylor, football coach at Clear Creek High School. The couple has three children: Jessie, 19; RJ, 13 and Annie, 10. Kari had a crush on Ryan when the two were in middle school. They dated through college, and then broke up over a misunderstanding. Kari married a man she met in college, Tim Jacobs, but some years into their marriage he had an affair. The infidelity resulted in his murder at the hands of a stalker. The tragedy devastated Kari, who was pregnant at the time with their first child, Jessie. Ryan came back into her life around the same time, and years later he and Kari married. They live in Bloomington.

• • •

ASHLEY BAXTER BLAKE: Ashley is the former black sheep of the Baxter family, married to Landon Blake, who works for the Bloomington Fire Department. The couple has four children: Cole, 19; Amy, 14; Devin, 12; and Janessa, 8. As a young single mom, Ashley was jaded against God and her family until she reconnected with her firefighter friend Landon, who had secretly always loved her. Eventually Ashley and Landon married and Landon adopted Cole. Together, the couple had two children—Devin and Janessa. Between those children, they lost a baby girl, Sarah Marie, at birth to anencephaly. Amy, Ashley's niece, came to live with them a few years ago after Amy's parents, Erin Baxter Hogan and Sam Hogan, and Amy's three sisters were killed in a horrific car accident. Amy was the only survivor. Ashley and Landon and their family live in Bloomington, in the old Baxter house, where Ashley and her siblings were raised. Ashley still paints and is successful in selling her work in local boutiques.

• • •

LUKE BAXTER: Luke is a lawyer, married to Reagan Baxter, a blogger. The couple has three children: Tommy, 17; Malin, 12; and Johnny, 8. Luke met Reagan in college. They experienced a major separation early on, after getting pregnant with Tommy while they were dating. Eventually Luke and Reagan married, though they could not have more children. Malin and Johnny are both adopted. They live in Indianapolis, about forty minutes from Bloomington.

SOMEONE LIKE YOU

KAREN KINGSBURY

1 All her life, Maddie West was denied the truth about her background. How did she feel when she learned she had come from a frozen embryo? What do you think was the hardest part for Maddie?

2 How would you feel if you found out you had different biological parents? What makes someone family, in your opinion?

3 Were you sympathetic to Brooke and Peter West? What would you have done if you had been in their place?

4 London Quinn never knew she was conceived in a petri dish through IVF. Do you think her parents should've told her she was an in vitro baby? Why or why not?

5 London became interested in Dawson's faith the day of her accident. Coincidence? Miracle? Do you think

people have a knowing when their time on earth is through? Talk about that.

6 For her entire friendship with Dawson, London dismissed his faith—sometimes with sarcasm or humor. Why do you think faith in Jesus makes some people uncomfortable? Does faith matter to you? Why or why not? What is your faith story?

7 Louise and Larry Quinn stopped taking London to church when she was little. Over time their faith in God grew cold. How does this happen? Is it important for children to be exposed to faith? Share your thoughts.

8 Dawson Gage had an undying love for London. Still, sometimes a relationship simply isn't meant to be. Have you ever known a love like that or seen it in family or friends? Share that story. What was learned from it?

9 How do you think Jag, the police officer, knew about London and why was he able to comfort Dawson in his worst moment?

10 The Bible says in Hebrews 13:2: "Do not forget to show hospitality to strangers, for by so doing some people have shown hospitality to angels without knowing it." According to Scripture, angels are messengers sent from God. Do you believe in angels? Why or why not? Can you share a story about an incident where an angel may have been involved?

11 London had a dramatic and momentary return to consciousness in the minutes before her death. She was

able to see and speak and convey peace and love to Dawson and her parents. Have you ever seen something like this at someone's deathbed? What does this mean and why does it happen? Talk about that.

12 Maddie thought it was important to meet her biological parents. Do you know anyone adopted who thought this was important? Do you agree? Why or why not?

13 Many similarities existed between Maddie and her biological sister, London. Have you noticed uncanny common traits between you and your siblings, or pairs of siblings you know? How do you account for that?

14 Not all engagements last. That was the situation with Maddie and Connor. Could you see their breakup coming even before Maddie went to Portland? Share about that.

15 Have you ever wondered what happens to leftover embryos after the IVF process? What did you learn about this through *Someone Like You*?

16 What are other possible complications with embryo adoption? Would you consider adopting an embryo? Why or why not?

17 John Baxter prays for his family constantly, especially when things go wrong. Do you pray for the people you love? How have you seen prayer make a difference?

18 Several characters in *Someone Like You* had moments where they believed they heard the voice of God.

Has that ever happened to you or someone you know? Share that story.

19 In dealing with her loss of London, then Maddie, Louise Quinn and her husband got involved in the Seen Movement, a way of really seeing people who serve and appreciating them. Have you heard of this movement? How could something like this encourage people in any type of service industry?

20 Serving others is often the antidote for depression and discouragement. Share about someone selfless you know who serves others well. What is their life like? How about their faith? Do you think service makes a difference for them?

21 How will you share this book with someone else now that you've finished reading it?

THE SEEN MOVEMENT

Often people save money for an oversees mission trip.

But there are people in your own city who desperately need hope and encouragement, faith and recognition. They need to be seen. By leaving a Seen card and a better-than-average tip, you may change someone's life.

You may save it.

Always when you leave a Seen card, you will let a stranger know that their hard work was seen in that moment. They were noticed! What better way to spread love? The Seen card will then lead that person to the movement's website, where he or she will be encouraged and reminded that God sees them every day. Always. He knows what they are going through.

The Seen Movement was started by Karen Kingsbury and her family in 2019. "Too many people are overlooked in our day-to-day activities," Karen says. "We believers need to change that. Jesus said they would know we are Christians by our love. This movement gives us a chance to live that out."

Get involved in the Seen Movement by visiting the website www.YouWereSeen.com. Here you can get a pack of Seen cards and learn how to take part in an effort that is sweeping the nation.

Every day should be marked by a miraculous encounter.

Getting involved in the Seen Movement is one way to make that happen.

ONE CHANCE FOUNDATION

The Kingsbury Family is passionate about seeing orphans all over the world brought home to their forever families. As a result, they created the One Chance Foundation!

This foundation was inspired by the memory of Karen's father, Ted C. Kingsbury. Ted always said, "Life is not a dress rehearsal. We have one chance to love, one chance to truly live!" Karen often tells her reader friends that they have "one chance to write the story of their lives!"

Now, with Karen's One Chance Foundation, readers can join her in the belief that all of us have one chance to make a difference in the lives of orphans.

In the Bible, James 1:27 says that true Christians ought to care for orphans. The One Chance Foundation was created with that truth in mind.

If you are interested in giving to Karen's One Chance Foundation and having your dedication printed in one of Karen's upcoming novels, visit www.KarenKingsbury.com and click on the Foundation tab. The following dedications were made by some of Karen's readers, who forever are making a difference in the lives of orphans around the world.

- In honor of our 7 grandchildren. Love, Sara + Phil
- Mom and Ben, waiting—D.S.
- To my awesome, amazing husband, who always makes sure I have the latest KK novel! Love, Wifey Melissa
- Landon, you are the sunshine in my day. Remember to have courage and be kind. All my love sweet boy, Mama
- To our Mom and BFF—K & Z
- Tessa Serenity -Our Angel
- Keep reading KK, Little Girl, to help you manage life's challenges. Aunt Dawn
- JOHNNY, I MISS YOU, LINDA
- In honor of my daughter Mei Lin, whom I adopted from China, and in thanksgiving to God for her.
- My sister Renee, you're a blessing! Love, Susan
- Proud of you, Nicholas! c/o 2020 Love, Mama & Daddy
- Heather & Paul, your family is now complete! Adoption date 5/23/19. Lots of love! Sandra & Lionel
- In honor of Alejandra & Isaac, Love Granny
- Sue, Enjoy heaven! Love, Your Family
- Happy birthday, Kathy! Looking forward to many more years of good books and great times. Love you!—Steven Walker

- Mom, Love always!—Heather
- We love you Nancy Coffman!
- TR Brandon KJCE
- Jim, Loving & honoring you always! URmySome1. Love Jane
- Lora Wright, Love You! –Adam
- The Grace's in my life!—Judy
- To my loving sister Isha. Thank you for always having my back. I love you always, Elizabeth
- Rol, You are my world!—Tish
- RO & PAT, LOVE FOREVER NOW!—Mom
- Natalie, We Love You. Mom & Dad
- Vanessa Todd, Thank you for being my wife and best friend. Happy 41st birthday!!! Love Rodney
- God's Blessings to Cheryl
- Helene, Lots of Love!—Debra
- Danica Jade, We love you bunches. Gramma Becky & Papa John
- Mom: Love you!—Baby girl
- Billy, Loved you so much!—Judy
- Beloved son, Don Burnsed
- Jill, With love!—Your Kids
- Bishop the Honorable Dr. Carmen L. Stewart – An amazing woman of God; my mother & bestfriend – Forever in my heart! Carolyn

- Love my family!—Sharon Evers
- Debbie, everything we do, we can only imagine doing with you. Love always, Will and Noah
- Neva, You are amazing! Patty
- Bowman Family - I Love You!—Sherri
- Love you Madison, Grandma
- Adventure awaits Cheryl J
- Mom, I love you!—Morgan
- In memory of our angel embryo snowflake babies, can't wait to see you in Heaven! —Andy, Cecily & Theo
- To my sweet Sara Beth! You're in my heart forever but with your Savior! Miss you so much!
  Love, Mom
- To Mandy, my reading buddy. Love Kelli
- Emma Nelson & her dad-Cody-of Bloomington IN. Love you both so much! Hugs! Grammy/Mom—Dena Patrick
- Elizabeth, have strength & courage for the Lord your God is with you wherever you go,
  Love Mom & Dad
- We love U Carol!—Ann Marie
- To the One Chance Foundation –Gayle Collins
- Miss you Jeff ~Vandria Bower
- Kim, My best friend!—Karen
- Donna, My Sis & My Friend! Deb Z

- Marissa, Your light shines!
- Mom G, I love you!—Bill K
- Mom K, I love you!—Nancy
- I'm so proud of you Megan Marie, and I love that we read books together! Love, Aunt Suz
- I love you Sarah!—Jeff
- Chad, my son, I love you forever & then some more! Mom
- Love to my family!—Deb Mattson
- Love you Mom (Norma)—Nyle
- Carl & Marge Bostrom's LOVE inspires all!
- To: Jamie Rutherford
- To Alyssa, my sunshine!—AG
- In memory of Diana Bassett
- With love to Sandra—S&H
- We love you, Marilyn C
- Bobbie, You are my hero!—Bandy
- Thanks Mom & Dad—Love Mary
- My daughter Ashley Nicole Parsons—Love you with all my heart, Mom
- In honor of my mom, Elizabeth, and Jessica. My reading buddies. Rachel Kirk.
- To the One Chance Foundation –Jared Kirk
- Cliff - A gift from God, Love Sylvia
- Linda Eberly, I love you mom!! Love, Kelli Dart

- Mom, Your steadfast love & courage have made me the person I am today! Love you to the moon . . . Dava
- Love U Prayer Group –Pam E
- For my wife, Tami –Love, Jason
- We will never forget Emma Grace Rivera! —Lamentations 3:22–23
- Thank you Most Excellent Book Club ladies for sharing Phil 4:8 books with me!—Dell, Marge, Phyllis, Pam, Jane, Tracy, Karen & Eunice. Love you gals, Pam Sheldon
- To our friends in celebration of the love and support we've shared in our life's journey. —Dave & Jan Kukkola-Miller
- To Brenda Schruder, who is the most amazing mom, best friend, role model, & prayer partner. Love, Courtney
- Karen, God is with you!
- To my precious Bev ~ the most amazing twin sister & best friend ever! I am so thankful for you Wish we lived closer ~ I miss you so much! Love you always, Barb
- Patrick . . . Forever my hero!
- Karyn, Gerri's smile made you smile —Love, Melaney
- Nancy Rocha, Best Mom & Nuna - Love you more—Missy

- Bippe - best sis ever –Utte
- Mama Lynne and Mama Ruth, thanks for being the best moms/mothers-in-love! Much love, Linda & Jackson
- In loving memory of Lois Stone, dearest mother who taught me how to love & live for Jesus. Forever thankful God gave me to someone like you! Sheila Holman
- Debra- All My Love—Tom
- Sonia Matthews and Family
- To the One Chance Foundation –Jenny Price

KAREN'S TOP FANS

To my top fans and most loyal readers listed below: You were chosen out of countless thousands of my favorites, and so this dedication is yours! You are the readers who fall so in love with Life-Changing Fiction™ that you tell other people about my books. And for that reason, each of you are a gift to me from God. May He bless you and yours, and may you—my top fans—continue to share these books with the people you love. Jesus is still changing lives with the power of story. You are proof!

Abby Douglas
Adele Chang
Adele Musgrave
Adrianne Kincade
Adrienne Miller
Alexxis Rudich
Ali Cobrin
Alice Moore
Alicia Groenendyk
Alicia Havard Dunn
Aliseea Hooker
Alma Snowa
Amanda Beukes
Amanda Secor
Amber Blake
Amber Hawkins
Amber Stuckey
Amy Conner
Amy Daugherty
Amy Poisal
Andrea Chaney
Angela Gibbons
Angela P. Pope
Angela Phillips
Angelita Ali-Gonzalez
Angie Purgason
Angie Rarey
Anice Marie Bradley

Anita Sikes
Anita Wright
Ann Berg
Ann Black
Anne Kingsbury
Ariana Cru
Ashley Patterson
Ava Ramsey
Avery Ramage
Bailey Lorraine
Barb Cummings
Barb Fink
Barbara Wilcox
BeckiJo Disney
Becky Joslin
Becky Thompson
Belinda Fortunato
Belinda Hallman
Beth Farmer
Beth Johnston
Beth Magill
Beth Marshall
Beth Smith
Bethany Lyn Wolfe
Betty Medernach
Betty Monda
Betty Parrott
Beverly Beck
Beverly Bowers
Beverly Gray
Beverly Knudsen
Beverly Lilley
Beverly Potter
Bonnie McGowan
Brandi Edwards
Brandi Menzie
Brandi Staudt
Brenda Brandt
Brenda Brown
Brenda Kay Chema
Brenda Line
Brenda Pell
Brenda Provonsil
Brittany Phillips
Brittany Riley
Brooke Helsel
Bruce Swart
Caitlyn Council
Candi Miller
Candi Wooden
Candice Story
Carla Lowery
Carleen Davenport
Carol Baroch
Carol Fritz
Carol Hyzer
Carol Meinnert
Carol Reynolds
Caroline Holladay
Caroline Kyle
Carolyn Akins
Carolyn Antley
Carolyn Brush
Carolyn McCurry

Carolyn Salley
Carrie Rushing
Carrie Smart
Carrie Woodruff
Carrington Kingsley
Casey Darnold
Casey Robison
Catherine Andrus
Cathy Bowyer
Cathy DiBella
Cathy Schmidt Sims
Cathy White
Chantle Uthe
Charlotte Boudreaux
Charlotte Heck
Charlotte Hess
Cheryl Baker
Cheryl Rose
Cheryl Van Berkel
Chris McCoy
Chris Vroman
Christi Mendoza
Christie McFarland
Christin Bumgardner
Christina Wilson
Christine Evans
Christine Hall
Christine Johnson
Christine Shaw
Cindy Broker
Cindy Carver Bond
Cindy Gabbard
Cindy Myers
Cindy Power
Cindy Pritchard
Cindy Shively
Claudine Pruitt
Colleen Moses
Connie Salcido
Courtney Matis
Craig & Jill Morrow
Cris-Annette Nicholas
Crissy Nichols
Crystal Wynn
Cyndi Armstrong
Dacia Pitzer
Dana Bruce
Danielle Knowles
Daphne Gazdagh
Darlene Jarrett
Darlene Mitchell
Dawn Groves
Dawn Jenkins Foust
Dawn Kesterson
Dawn Smith
Deanna Whitehurst
Deanna Wickizer
Deb Zurawski
Debbie Beeler
Debbie Black
Debbie Dewhirst
Debbie Fox
Debbie Haakenson
Debbie Harmon

Debbie King Taylor
Debbie Marro
Debbie Pollock
Debbie Schniederjan
Debbie Troski
Debbie Wadsworth
Debbie Williams
Deborah Burgett
Deborah Raley
Deborah Shawver
Deborah Thompson
Debra Johnson
Debra Thompson
Deidra Kronstedt
Denise Gilreath
Denise Levesque
Denise Werstra
Diana Wilson
Diane Barnard
Diane Bassett
Diane Bickel
Diane Walsh
Dolores Bailey
Donna Clare
Donna Hadley
Donna Keene
Donna Perry
Donna Sue Jolliffe
Donna Toxey
Donna Tuttle
Dori Mitchell
Doris Beckman
Dorothy Powell
Earlene Edwards
Eileen Deelstra
Elaine Hons
Elizabeth Duff
Ellen Janney
Emily Gail Webster
Emily Jennings
Emily Kelley
Emily Potter
Emmalee Parnell
Erica Magilke
Esther Marmelo
Faith Hargett
Faye Bertelmann
Faye Stubblefield
Felicia Holmes
Flame Burns
Fontella Jamison
Francine Maffit
Gabrielle Hatley
Gail Brandt
Gail Erwin Hale
Gail Jenkins
Gary Snyder
Gay Case
Genevieve K. Lynch
Gennifer Winger
Georgiann Wilson
Gina Stephenson
Ginger King
Ginger Shriver

Glenda Jones
Glenda Spurlin
Glenn Winningham
Gloria G. Blakeney
Grace Cirillo-Fiore
Gwen Nelson
Hannah Miller
Harriette Brinkley
Heather Harris
Heather Hawkins
Heather Hoffmeyer
Heather Howell Harris
Helen Hayes
Holly McKnight
Hope Burke
Hope Grimball
Hunter Martin
Irene Ammacher
Jacki Holleman
Jackie Eades
Jacqueline Drumwright
Jacquelyn Brown
Jamalyn Norman
James and Donna Woods
Jamie Barnard
Jamie Smith
Jan Knecht
Jan Kukkola-Miller
Jane Daughdrill
Jane Houde
Jane Poplin
Janene Van Gorp
Janessa McNutt
Janet Decker
Janet Smith
Janet Stenger
Janet Tomes
Janet Wiggins
Janice Crow
Janice Grizzel
Janice M. Daley
Janice Roye
Janie Lynch
Janyse Heidy
Jayme Porter
Jayne Wiltshire
Jean Morgan
Jeanette Bigham
Jeanine Hodges
Jeanne Jacobs
Jeanne McAuliffe
Jeff Owens
Jen Barren
Jennifer Ann Miller
Jennifer Finch
Jennifer Moore
Jennifer Okano
Jennifer Stephenson
Jenny Davis
Jenny Foreman
Jeri Soll
Jerica McCracken
Jerri Dunn

Jess Morgan
Jessica Caroe
Jessica Forbes
Jessica Morgan
Jill Von Boeckman
Jo Ann Clark
Jo-Ann Mhishi
Joan Fessler
Joan Paris
Joanne May
Joanne Orris
Jodi Edwards
Jodi Jordan
Jody Brinks
Jody Meier
Joelle Mann
John Letourneau
Joy Armstrong
Joy Lee
Joyce Joblonski
Joyce Mcculley
Joyce Mullen
Joyce S. Ramsey
Joyce Spamer
Judi Hunt
Judith Hiler
Judith Strausser
Judy Church
Judy Garrett
Judy Mowry
Judy Roberts
Judy Swible
Judy Williams
Julie Clark
Julie Dykxhoorn
Julie Mills
Julie Petersen
Julie Wood
Kaeti Roberts
Karen Cossett Evans
Karen Davison
Karen Dingler
Karen Fitchett
Karen Green
Karen Hollenbeck
Karen Jones
Karen Kempf
Karen Mercadante
Karen Merklin
Karen Simpson
Kari Hyden
Kari Lostocco
Karma Bradley
Karma Smoke
Karyn Stoneberg
Kasy Long
Kate Kauffman
Kathleen Waffle
Kathy McCulloch
Kathy Tatsu
Kathy Tingle
Kathy Walters
Kathy Whitman
Katie Beavers

Katie Hickly
Kay Freeman
Kay Munson
Kay Murry
Kay Price
Kay Rhinebeck
Kay Wilson
Kaye Turner
Kaylie Olson
Kelly Brassington
Kelly Isenberg
Kelly Kendall
Kelly Osborne
Kelly Price
Kerri Naylor
Kerri Schnulle
Kerry Michael
Kimberly Frazier
Kingston Painter
Kirsten Jonora Renfroe
Kris Maurelli
Kristi Crook
Kristin Lee
Laura Eddy
Laura Herron
Laura Sunday
Laurie Barrett
Laurie Elizabeth Mercier
Laurie LeBlanc
Laurie McGowan
Lavinna Ashwell
Leandra Smith
Leanna Colonna
Leeta Stevens
Leigh Wallace
Lena Reimer
Leslie Hartzog
Leslie Rhyne
Leslie Ward
Lianna Burkovskaya
Linda Critcher
Linda Huddleston
Linda K Fenster
Linda Litton
Linda Rafferty
Linda Tom
Linda Vandivort
Linda Wagner Brown
Linda Welch
Linda Woodury
Lindsay Bryant
Lindsey Sentef
Lindy Anastis
Lisa Bean
Lisa Halvorson
Lisa Harris
Lisa Hobbs
Lisa Lovell Cromwell
Lisa Thompson
Lisa Wright
Liz Winship
Lora Chastain
Lori Heimbach

Louise Hicks
Lucille Watkins
Lynn Hunt
Lynn Robbins
Lynne Fowlkes
Lynne Kelley
Lynne Kratzer
Madelyn Mathias
Madison Chrestman
Madison Gannon
Maelyn Riley
Makayla Lee
Mallory Ellis
Marcia Casteel
Margaret Blankenbeckley
Margaret Harding
Margaret Henley
Margaret Rooney
Maria Heehn
Maria Zembrowski
Mariah Havens
Marian Houston
Marian S Ainsworth
Marianne Terpstra
Maribeth Griessel
Marie Crider
Marie Waters
Marilyn Coleman
Marit Joys Wigart.
Marley Mansfield
Marlo Jaques
Martha DeLong
Martha Farace
Marty Inman
Mary Beavers
Mary Ellen Yeager
Mary Evelyn Terry
Mary Hysell
Mary Jett
Mary Kay Delavan
Mary Kliora
Mary Marchand
Mary Milner
Mary Novinger
Mary Riggins
Maryann Quinn
Marylou Anderson
Maxine Garon
Megan Brown
Megan Hoyng
Melanie Cummings
Melessa Segal
Melissa Beasley
Melissa Craigen
Melissa Dodgen
Melissa Dykeman
Melissa Fryer
Melissa Lambrechts
Melissa Maples
Melissa Pierson
Melissa Sauter
Melissa Young
Melody Okke
Meri Long

Mette Mydland
Meza Lee
Michelle Cook
Michelle Flores
Michelle Hume
Michelle Watkins
Milisa Gardner
Mindy Snider
Miranda Chewning
Miranda Overholt
Missy Savage
Misty Westbrook
Mollie Halpin
Molly Hail
Molly Jaber
Myndi Downs
Nadia Tymciw
Nancy Gibson
Nancy McDonald
Nancy Miller
Nancy Peterson
Nancy Quiggle
Nancy Rader
Nancy Stein
Natalie R. Hudgens
Neshma Riggs
Nicola Reid
Nicole Blanchard
Nita Armstrong
Norma Pratt
Oakli Van Meter
Pamela Edmiston
Pat Inman
Pat Neal
Patrica Davis
Patricia Whitlock
Patsy Burnsed
Pattie Barton
Patty Kleck
Patty Miller
Patty Painter
Paula Miksa
Paula Myers
Paulette Wiens
Pauline Lottering
Peggy Kasaba
Peggy King
Penney Albright
Perlina Nelson
Peyton Mottern
Phyllis Fish
Phyllis Perry
Rachel Baker
Rachel Curtis
Rachel Midyette
Rae Johnson
Ramelle Collins
Ramona Chappell
Randy and Lisa Cox
Rebecca Burkhart
Rebekah G. Shipley
Rebekah Johansen
Renee Stalker
Renita Kelly

Rhonda Barnhouse
Rhonda Cordova
Rhonda McDaniel
Rhonda Robertson
Rita McClure
Rita Reitman
Robbie Temple
Robert Storrs
Roberta Hubbard
Robin Lewis
Roma Downey
Ron Hadley
Rosa Gross
Rose Pierce
Rosella Elifrits
Rosie L Perkins
Roxanne Ruble
Ruby Metcalf
Ruth Sharp
Ryan Senior
Sabrina Grobleben
Samantha Novak
Samuel Marsala
Sandi Nagel
Sandra Brown
Sandy Bloesch
Sandy Bowman
Sandy Heller
Sandy Morgan
Sandy Wood
Sara Beth
Sara Kiplinger
Sarah Bolduc
Sarah Carnes
Sarah Jane Fields
Sarah Nelson
Sarah Palmer
Sarah R. Kilbreth
Shannon Anderson
Shannon Castonguay
Shari Fox
Shari Jones
Sharon Dean
Sharon Kimberlin
Sharon Sloan
Sharon Turner
Sheila Holman
Sheila Hughes
Sheila Keeler
Shelly Satterfield
Sherri Hayes
Sherry Dennis
Sherry Sayers
Sherry Sutton
Sheryl Ewing
Shirley Delp
Shirley Hickman
Shirley Koestler
Shirley Mabry Thomas
ShirleyAnn Loomis
Stacey Swift
Stacie Campbell
Stephanie Bare
Stephanie Fidelak

Stephanie McCaslin
Stephenia Payne
Sue Barnes
Sue Collins
Sue Ellen Tucker
Sue Flowers
Sue Kennedy
Sue Taylor
Susan Birkins
Susan Edwards
Susan Glasgow
Susan Kane
Susan Reagan
Susan Thevenard
Suzanne Parrigan
Suzanne Stack
Tammie Hicks
Tammy Chidester
Tammy Williams
Tara B Calliham
Taunya Pittman
Teresa Fuqua
Teresa Yocham
Teri Scanlon
Terry Grimshaw Micks
Theresa Roderick
Tiffany Hulsey
Tiffany Stephens
Tina Campbell
Tina Loewen
Toni Lucky
Tracey Hagerman
Tracie Powell Duncan
Tracie Smith
Tracy McDaniel
Tricia Brann
Tricia Kingsbury
Trish Shinn
Trisha Ontiveros
Tyler Brady
Valerie Adcock
Valerie Lacroix
Vanda Human
Vangela Roeder
Velna Schilling
Venessa Crawford
Vicki Temple
Vickie Deal
Vickie Watts
Viola Dondo
Vivian Molisee
Wanda Buckley
Wendy Myers
Wilhemina Boyd
Yolande Kuystermans
Yvonne Hargreaves-Beatty